main

A KILLING WINTER

FORGE BOOKS BY WAYNE ARTHURSON

Fall from Grace

A Killing Winter

A KILLING WINTER

WAYNE ARTHURSON

A TOM DOHERTY ASSOCIATES BOOK

NEW YORK

A KILLING WINTER

Edited by James Frenkel

A Forge Book
Published by Tom Doherty Associates, LLC
175 Fifth Avenue
New York, NY 10010

www.tor-forge.com

Forge® is a registered trademark of Tom Doherty Associates, LLC.

Library of Congress Cataloging-in-Publication Data

Arthurson, Wayne, 1962–
    A killing winter / Wayne Arthurson.—1st ed.
        p. cm.
    "A Tom Doherty Associates book."
    ISBN 978-0-7653-2418-4 (hardcover)
    ISBN 978-1-4299-2460-3 (e-book)
    1. Journalists—Alberta—Fiction. 2. Murder—Investigation—
Fiction. 3. Compulsive gamblers—Fiction. 4. Edmonton (Alta.)—
Fiction. I. Title.
PR9199.4.A884K55 2012
813'.6—dc23

                                                              2011033167

First Edition: April 2012

Printed in the United States of America

0   9   8   7   6   5   4   3   2   1

To Auni and Vianne

ACKNOWLEDGMENTS

Thanks to the Alberta Foundation for the Arts and the Edmonton Arts Council for their assistance in the writing of this book. And to the Banff Centre for the Arts for having such a nice place to write. Also, thanks to Linn Prentis, my editor, Jim Frenkel, Forge publicist Alexis Nixon, Jim Whitelaw for pre-delivery copyediting and information on guns, and to my family, friends, and anyone else who supported me during the writing of this book and during the release of the previous one.

A KILLING WINTER

1

Marvin disappeared on the coldest day of the year. It was minus twenty-eight, but with the wind whipping through the canyon of buildings, it seemed like minus forty. There was no reason to be outside, but there I was, standing near the CBC station entrance of the City Centre Mall, my shoulders hunched over, hands shoved into my pockets, and my head stupidly exposed. Snow swirled around me, like white dust devils stinging my eyes, giving me no place to hide from the weather.

It was a good location to work. There were tons of people coming in and out from the bus stop or on their way to the main library branch. But on that frozen day, there was no one except me and a displaced office worker commuting between buildings. Even the diehard smokers and the usual gang of street kids that loitered around this entrance were smart enough to stay inside. I watched the lone commuter from across the street, and waited.

His head was tucked into his chin and he leaned forward to fight the wind. His hands were thrust into his pockets to keep them warm and to decrease wind resistance. He looked up only once, to see if traffic on 102nd Avenue would be a problem, and then dashed across, heading for the door of the City Centre Mall.

And, of course, me.

I knew he hadn't seen me because he didn't take the detour to the west side doors. As I waited, I planned my approach. Marvin liked to call my opening lines "The Warning." He appreciated the way I quickly told my story, that it wasn't that long ago when I was just like them.

"I had it all, you know; the wife, the two kids, the house, two cars in the garage, a mortgage with a happy banker, soccer practice and dance lessons for the kids. A TV in the bedroom and three weeks' vacation in the summer. I used to be like you but . . ." and I'd let it hang there.

Of course, something must have happened to fuck it all up, and of course, something did. There was no need to go into details with people, there was never enough time to explain it all, and everybody figured out their own reasons for my predicament. They usually thought drink or drugs, and they might have been right.

But it didn't take long, a year, maybe two, and next thing you know, you're hanging outside the City Centre Mall on the coldest day of the year, sizing up some office worker, wondering if that jingling sound in his pockets was just a set of keys.

The weather forced me to rethink my original strategy. At the speed the worker was walking, there was no time for a story. And with the wind making all that noise, he wasn't going to hear me anyway, even if he was listening. They usually aren't. Simplicity seemed to be the best strategy, so when he finally made it across the street, I hit him cleanly and quickly.

"Spare change, buddy?"

He yelped and jumped back. He looked at me, his eyes squinting through the wind. If I looked like Mom instead of Dad, I'd be just another drunk Indian on the street, dismissed without a thought. But I was fortunate that way. There was a second or two of disbelief on his face, as if I was a strange creature from a parallel universe, but then he recognized my genotype. I was no alien, I was human just like him, related by evolution, but from his point of view, we lived in parallel universes.

I expected a brush-off and started to move away. But he surprised me. He reached into his pocket and tossed me a toonie, a two-dollar coin. "I don't care what you buy, paint thinner, heroin, coffee, whatever," he said, his voice barely audible over the wind, "just get the fuck out of the cold."

I caught the toonie in my cupped gloves and before I could thank him, he dashed through the mall doors. I stuffed the toonie into a jacket pocket, took the Suit's advice and followed him into the building.

The air in the mall was warm and welcoming, but the people weren't. I barely made it past the entrance to the CBC studios when security was on me. Sure, they tried to be casual about it, but two dudes hanging around like they were about to ship out to Afghanistan—camo pants, pseudo flak vest with the word SECURITY written in bold block letters on the back, and a utility belt that would make Batman envious—stood out like yellow stains in the snow.

I walked past them, intent on ignoring their presence, but they split up to flank me, like watching me was some kind of military exercise. I was followed as I walked past the soft black leather couches that I wasn't allowed to sit on. Past the flickering of the glassed-in natural gas fireplace that I was not allowed to stand next to, to warm up. Past all the retail outlets that I was not allowed to enter, lest I annoy the paying customers with my presence, which was a reminder of what could occur if they suffered a couple of difficult moments that derailed their lives. And in these times with the U.S. economy tanking and the price of oil dipping below $40 a barrel, oil-rich Alberta was suffering one of its signature bust events. A life on the street was much closer to some of these people now that it was just a year or so ago.

Edmontonians may have had a vision of their city as a liberal-leaning island of good people in a land of mean-spirited penny-pinching conservatives, but their personal reactions to those living on the street was no less harsh.

Especially when a second question, "You sure you don't have any spare change?," could have brought on a charge of aggressive pan-handling.

So instead of making my way to the Light Rail Transit like a good street person not looking to cause trouble, I decided to have a bit of fun. I headed to the lower level, as the two security dudes a few people behind me on the escalator tried to look casual by chatting about the Oilers' last home game.

A few steps before I got to the bottom, I gave them a quick, suspicious look and ran the rest of the way down. I took a quick right and started to jog through the mall toward the underground pedway that connected the City Centre Mall with the Churchill LRT station.

I heard one of them grunt "Shit!" and then panicked footsteps rushed after me. For kicks, I stopped at the end of a cell phone kiosk and grabbed a pamphlet with my left hand, feigning interest in the low monthly rates. I kept my right hand in my jacket pocket.

They whirled around the corner, keen on a chase, but almost ran over each other when they saw that I was waiting for them. They stumbled over each other, but feigned laughter and clumsy palsy-walsyness so they could keep up the charade. I kept reading the pamphlet, but out of the corner of my eye, I watched the two secu-rity dudes get into character by hitching up their belts and stepping toward me with a sense of law-enforcement purpose. One of them even reached across his chest to activate the radio clipped to his shoulder, tilting his head to alert headquarters of their actions.

I knew that somewhere in this mall there was a bank of video monitors. A number of security officers were now watching those connected to the cameras that covered the area underneath the escalators near a cell phone kiosk.

When I was a kid, my friends and I had this scheme when we wanted to get chips, pop, and whatever from the corner store but didn't have enough money. We used to walk in en masse, but the owner of the store, a middle-aged Chinese merchant who also ran a bookie business in the back, knew exactly what we were after. So he yelled at us to get out.

As part of our scheme one of us, usually me 'cause I had the more innocent face, went in and would actually buy something, usually small pieces of penny candy. I would slowly count my change, making many mistakes as I did. While I did this, another friend would come in and loudly demand to know where a certain item was. After getting the directions, he would walk through the store, every few seconds demanding to know if he was in the right location. And then our other friends would come in, and while the store merchant was distracted by the idiot counting change and the other one shouting for directions, the others would fill their pockets.

I imagined some of my old friends quietly committing petty theft while the bulk of the City Centre Mall security staff was focused on my harmless presence.

But I wasn't that harmless. In my right pocket, I gripped an item that would turn what looked to be a typical security rousting of a street person into something more interesting.

I waited until they got closer. I waited until the shorter of the two guards approached me while the other stood a couple steps behind. His right hand was still across his chest with the radio, the left hovering near the can of pepper spray on his belt.

I waited until the approaching guard asked, "Can we help you?," when in truth the only help he wanted to give me was to leave the confines of the City Centre Mall with as little fuss as possible.

In the old days when I did this, I was trying to score a day or two at the Remand Centre, with hot showers, clean sheets, new clothes, and three square meals a day while I waited to be arraigned on a public mischief or nuisance or whatever kind of charge these guys could come up with. For guys like me and other petty criminals, the Remand Centre was pretty safe. Hardened criminals were on another floor entirely, so there was nothing like what they portray in the movies. In the remand lockup you could watch TV, read some books, and play a little chess. Compared to begging for spare change, it was a cakewalk. Of course, once you were in the remand lockup, there were ways to stretch out the time: a little fight between friends, some laxative to create an abdominal problem, or Imodium if you wanted to go the other way.

And there was another route entirely, a chance to spend the expected two-week cold snap inside, warm and tight. Suicide could always be faked with some superficial slashes on the wrist just before the lights-out count. It was an easy way to score twenty-one days under the Mental Health Act and maybe some extra money every month for disability.

But this wasn't the old days and I wasn't going to give these security morons the satisfaction. I looked up at the security guard, smiled without showing my teeth, and then whipped my right hand out of my pocket, flicking the switch as I did. The two guards flinched; the larger one wrestled with the clip on his belt to remove the can of pepper spray.

"Yeah, my name is Leo Desroches and I'm a reporter with the *Edmonton Journal*," I said quickly. "I'm working on a story about the life of Edmonton's street people and I was wondering if it's the policy of the City Centre Mall to follow and question someone who, in truth, has committed no crime nor done anything to warrant attention from security except to be dressed in a certain way?"

The first guard stepped back, hands raised and palms out in a defensive gesture, as I stuck my recorder in his face. I leaned forward and gestured at the other guard. "Also, is it City Centre Mall policy that its security personnel carry a weapon prohibited in Canada?"

The two of them stepped back again, looking left and right, eyes either scanning the area for any TV news cameras that would be rolling or for any witnesses who might be filming the scene for future YouTube use.

I stepped forward. "Have you used that illegal weapon before? And if so, could you please tell me the circumstances?"

Instead of answering and making themselves look even more foolish, the two security guards turned without a word and walked away. "I'll take that as a 'no comment,' okay?" I shouted at them.

I set the cell phone pamphlet back on the kiosk, ignoring the stunned stares from the kiosk employee and all the rest of the downtown worker bees. I turned off my recorder and put it back into my pocket. I looked up, searched for a security camera. When I found one underneath the up escalator across the mall, I waved at it.

Then I turned and headed to the Churchill LRT station. I grabbed the next available southbound train and for the next four hours I remained underground, out of the cold, riding the LRT back and forth along the free-fare zone between the Churchill and the Government stations. It was annoying to change trains every ten minutes or so, but at least it was warm.

I could have headed back to the newsroom and chronicled the

events of my day. But I had only been on this story for a short while. Larry said it was important that I immerse myself in the street culture before writing anything substantial.

I also had to figure out what the heck had happened with Marvin.

2

The casino on 101st was an ugly building. It looked like someone had stuck an old brick brownstone into a strip mall. They tried to hide the ugliness with garish neon but that only made things worse. The neon was supposed to excite people, to suggest a touch of Vegas, but in the cold night at the edge of a deserted downtown, the neon gave the casino a spooky, dangerous glow. Of course, those of us who wish to gamble don't really care what the building looks like on the outside. It's what's inside that calls to us.

The inside of the casino was so bright, I felt assaulted by the glare. I stood at the front door, blinking quickly, a deer caught in the headlights. It was quieter than usual but there was still a buzz of excitement. My heart beat a faster rhythm and my breathing became labored because of the highly oxygenated atmosphere they pumped into the place. I felt my adrenaline starting to kick in and my head clearing itself.

Outside in the real world, there was nothing for me, but inside the casino, the real world didn't exist. It was like moving into a new home, the sights and smells of a fresh beginning obliterating my past life and its sins.

The rent-a-cop at the door looked me over with suspicion, but offered a forced smile. "Good evening, sir," he said. But at the same time he gestured to a couple other rent-a-cops circulating nearby. They quietly moved closer, a little more subtly than security at the

City Centre Mall, but these guys were paid better. They also knew that looks were deceiving; I might be some street guy stepping in just to get warm, but then again I might be some eccentric rich freak out to lose a few thousand bucks.

When my breathing returned to normal, I gave the doorman a nod and slowly made my way toward the ATMs. The machines were strategically located just to the right of the door, set so when you came in, you could quickly access your money. And when you decided to leave after blowing your wad, you could change your mind before you stepped out the door. Instinct forced me to look about before I bent down and pulled my bank card from my left sock. The card was old and faded, the numbers rubbed so low that even a blind person couldn't make them out.

But somehow, even after all these years, it still worked. There was $64.57 left in that account; the money was supposed to last until the end of the month, a week or so, but I figured if I just took out forty and left the rest, I'd be okay. I knew I was supposed to gamble only the money people gave me from the street, but because of the cold, I only had the toonie from the office worker. Besides, I figured, with the extra money I'd make tonight, I wouldn't have to worry too much about surviving till the end of the month.

When the machine spat out the bills and my card, I turned to face the tables. My escorts had moved away and forgotten me. For a brief moment, my two twenty-dollar bills made me an accepted member of this society. Who I was, what I did, or whether I had a regular place to sleep made no difference; the money in my hand was my membership card in this club.

I made my way to the blackjack tables and sat down at one of the five-dollar spots. Only a couple of people were playing the game: a Chinese man in a white shirt and black tie, and a woman, probably in her thirties but looking closer to my age, late forties.

The Chinese guy's face was sullen and exhausted behind his horn-rimmed glasses, his suit jacket, like his dignity, lay at the foot of his stool. The woman was wearing a loose sweatshirt and elastic pants that clung to her plump figure. Her drink glass bore the red marks of her lipstick. Unlike the Chinese guy, her eyes were alive and she even managed to greet me with a slight rise of her eyebrows as I sat down.

I gave her a quick smile and looked over at the other player, but he ignored me. Even though the dealer announced my arrival— "New player, ladies and gentlemen, new player!"—I wasn't ac-knowledged. He was my kind of guy. Who cared who you were playing with? It was the cards and the game that counted.

The dealer was the brightest of this bunch, a semienthusiastic guy about twenty-five years old, sporting a goatee. His eyes were clear and alert, and his manner was efficient and helpful as he broke my first bill into ten two-dollar chips. The other two had already placed their bets on the table. Once I dropped my chip in the spot, the dealer began the hand.

His dealing, like his demeanor, was efficient and crisp; he dealt each card out of the box with a quick snap and distributed it to a player at the same speed as every other card. Even though nobody said a word, there was no discomfort in the silence. The cards were the important things at this moment, in my case probably the most important things in the world. More important than the missing Marvin, and I have no doubt, more important than my job and my children.

After six rings, nobody was answering. My mother's voice spoke in my head, with her good advice on phone etiquette. "You should never let the phone ring more than six times. You should be able to reach any phone in your home, no matter how big, within that time. If you take longer than six rings to answer a phone, and it's still ringing, it would be impolite for you to answer. It shows the person on the other line that you don't think they are important enough to answer the phone quickly. If it's an important call, they'll call back within two hours. If they don't, then it wasn't important and you weren't missing anything. Of course anybody who calls and lets the line ring longer than six times is being very rude. If you pick it up after the sixth ring, they'll think you're at their beck and call and will let the phone ring for as long as they want."

Mom had always been full of that kind of advice. Being a teacher, she had continued to teach even out of the classroom. Maybe that was why I married a teacher, who knows?

I was about to hang up after the sixth ring, when the call was connected.

"Hello," I heard my ex-wife say. Joan's voice sounded tired and nasal, like she was fighting a cold.

"Hey," I said, and then added when she didn't immediately respond, "It's me."

There was a two-second pause on the line and I knew she was trying to decide if she should continue and deal with me or just hang up. But just like at the blackjack table where I was up two hundred dollars, luck was with me and she decided to stay on the line.

"What do you want, Leo?" she whispered.

"Can I speak to Peter?"

She sighed deeply. "It's nine-thirty, Leo, he's in bed already. You should know that."

"He's probably not asleep yet."

"No, he's probably not, but I'm not going to get him out of bed to talk to you on the phone. I'm sick as it is and this is the first moment I've had to myself all day."

"Oh, come on; just let me speak to him. I'll only talk for a couple of minutes and then you can put him back to bed."

"If I let you talk to him, he'll be up all night and I'm not in the mood for going through that."

"Got a cold?"

"Yes, I've got a cold. It's probably going to turn into the flu."

"I don't know what's worse, a cold in the dead of winter or a cold in the heat of summer."

"I don't care when I get a cold, it just sucks."

"Are you drinking plenty of fluids, taking vitamins, and getting plenty of rest?"

"Yes on the fluids and vitamins, but rest, no."

"You should get some rest."

"I'd love to get some rest, Leo," she said sarcastically. "But it's tough being a single mother."

"You're not a single mother."

"Yes I am. Just because you call after Peter's bedtime doesn't qualify you as being a father."

"You don't have to be nasty."

"I have every right to be nasty. It's freezing outside and I have a cold that will probably turn into the flu and then when I decide to get my first rest of the day, Leo manages to call, demands to talk to Peter after his bedtime, and then has the gall to tell me to get some rest when there's no one else here to take care of the kids while I get that rest."

"I could come over and help."

"No. You can't. I won't let you."

"I'm back on my feet again."

"I know, Leo, but it's not a good time, okay?" she said, resigned. "Where are you anyway? It sounds loud."

"I'm at work."

"How come the call display shows a pay phone."

"I'm in a mall," I lied. "Doing research on a story."

Joan laughed, cold and harsh like the weather. "Geez, Leo, I hope you're not gambling again."

"Why would you automatically think I was gambling?"

"You said you were doing research on a story. When we were married, that's the lie you used when you were gambling."

"I'm not gambling. I'm working on a story about street people and I'm in the mall and it's closing time so I'm watching security roust the homeless."

"Remind you of old times?" Her voice was bitter, angry.

"There's no talking to you when you're sick."

"Then hang up. No, wait, let me."

"WAIT, WAIT! At least give Peter a message from me."

There was another pause but no dial tone so I knew she was still there. "Okay, what should I tell Peter for you?"

"Tell him I love him and I miss him. Eileen, too."

She sighed deeply. "I'll tell Peter but not Eileen. She'll never believe that." She hung up and left me alone with the lights and sounds of the casino.

3

When I returned to the table, something changed. The cards stopped going right for me. They were the same cards and they fell in the same way as they did when I was winning, but something wasn't quite right. I also noticed that the rhythm the four of us had established had gone out of sync.

Everybody paused when my cards were dealt; they seemed to be waiting and watching for my response. I tried to regain my focus and establish a new rhythm, but when I doubled down on nine to make up for the bit of loss since my return, there was an audible gasp from the sweatshirt woman. The dealer said nothing, but I could tell by the way he dealt my next card he was thinking, "Are you sure you want to do this?"

Soon, we were all losing, and after a couple of hands, the woman quickly gathered up her belongings, gave me a dirty look, and left the table. I watched her walk around, checking out the other tables. Every few seconds she looked over to me like I was some kind of criminal. Finally, when she saw there were no empty spots, she shrugged and headed toward the lounge.

A few hands later, the Chinese guy let out a big sigh like he was deflating, picked his jacket up off the floor and left the table. Unlike the sweatshirt woman, he never looked back; he walked directly out of the casino.

I should have followed him, should have gathered up all my

money, should have stayed when I hit, should have stayed away from the phone. But for a gambler like me, should-haves are a way a life. There are a lot of things we should have or should not have done, but those thoughts always came later. When I'm playing, the only words I listen to are *only a few*. Only a few more hands and I'll call it quits. Only a few more dollars and I'll have enough to quit. Only a few more lucky breaks and I'll be back on my feet; and only a few more tries, I'll see my kids again.

Two hours later, I was outside again, fighting the wind, the cold, and my thoughts. My brain was buzzing, my thoughts stuck in an endless loop replaying my losing hands over and over again, chastising myself for hitting when I should have stood pat, doubling down when I should have sat back. And why did I ever think I could win on a split? It was like some psychotic meditation that was sucking me deep into my mind to review every mistake I made that night. I scrutinized every hand, every decision, every gesture, and bashed myself on the head with each of them. I began to talk to mentally beat myself over and over again.

My old sponsor Phil used to call these moments, moments when you realize how stupid you've been, your little times in hell. There was almost a wistful look on Phil's face when he talked about it.

"Sometimes I still miss those visits to hell," he had said, and before anybody could ask him why, he continued. "I know it was hot and nasty and I never really wanted to go back. Nobody really wants to go back there. It's a terrible place to be. Beating yourself about the head like that. But at the time, it was one of the few places where I felt really safe, like I belonged. It's those times that are the hardest, because many of us just slip into a trance and do what we've always done. When you get out of your trance you'll realize that the world can be a scary place, but at least you're awake."

I thought about calling Phil. To confess it all, let him know where I was, what I had been doing. But then I realized that Phil had found religion. That in itself wasn't a bad thing, but Phil had taken it many steps further by immersing himself completely in his religion, living every aspect of his life based on the tenets of his chosen god.

He was no different than most people like me; we don't really quit being addicts, because it was wired into our system. Instead we switched addictions, trading socially unacceptable and harmful ones for those more palatable to the general public. Religion was one of the most popular choices.

So I banished Phil and my own voice out of my head, and woke from my trance to find myself heading west on Jasper Avenue, shivering with ice crystals forming on my fledgling beard. It was late, I could tell, because all the shops and restaurants were closed and there was minimal traffic on the street.

I needed to find someplace warm; I realized that walking west toward the richer neighborhoods past 109th Street would be a waste of time. Sure I lived there, but there was no way I would make it in this weather. I quickly headed in the opposite direction, toward the part of town I was supposed to be part of as a street person.

I walked past Canada Place and crossed 97th Street, traversing a demarcation line of sorts that separates the good parts of downtown from the bad. The city changed almost instantly in that one block.

Gone were the tall towers of bureaucracy and corporate culture. Gone were the funky shops, the trendy cafés, the newly built condos and delightful restaurants. East of 97th Street, between Jasper and the old railway tracks and then several blocks farther on, it was a whole different universe. The buildings and houses were old; many of them were condemned, but still standing because no one thought it worth the time and effort to knock them down. Nobody made plans to rebuild, because if they did, the street people would have to move somewhere else and nobody wanted those kinds of folks in their backyards. Any plans for downtown revitalization always seemed to stay on the west side of 97th Street.

Average citizens, those who had regular jobs and relatively decent places to live, ignored this part of town, this dead zone in the middle of the city. They stayed away in droves, except for those who tooled around in cars and trucks looking for hookers.

My first thought was to head toward the Herb, the closest shelter, but it would be full by now. No doubt, they'd let me hang around the main foyer with the drinkers who didn't want to give up their bottles and the smokers who didn't want to give up their smokes. Still, I didn't think I could take a whole night standing up, breathing in that haze.

It would be the same situation at all the other shelters; my only choice left was the Churchill LRT station. The city kept it open and provided blankets and hot drinks on cold nights like tonight. And even though they couldn't stop people from drinking and smoking, the station was big enough that I could find some place by myself.

Three and a half blocks.

That's how far the Churchill station was.

Not far.

But in this weather, it would be pretty tough. There might be some minor frostbite on the toes but at least I'd be somewhere warm.

It was what my French-Canadian grandfather had called *un hiver de meurtre*, loosely translated to a killing winter. He had visited us once when I was a kid. It was the middle of winter and the weather was just like it was now, howling wind, temperatures in the minus mid-thirties and about to get colder. And that was when he used that term.

It was the kind of winter that would kill, if you gave it the chance. It had already killed one, a teenaged girl who had walked home after a party. She only had a two-block walk, but she was a bit drunk. Halfway home, she decided to rest for a second. A neighbor found her body on his lawn the next morning.

I jiggled storefront doorknobs as I walked; maybe a place would be open so I could stop for a few seconds to get warm.

About two-thirds down the block, one knob turned so I opened the door and stepped in. I walked into a long, dark hallway; the plaster was peeling from the walls, the floor creaking with every step. There were no other doors in the hallway, and although it wasn't heated, the lack of wind made it warmer. Halfway down the hall, there was light coming from a small TV sitting on a little table.

An old Chinese man sat behind the table; when I walked toward him, he started to stand. It took him forever to get up; he pushed heavily on the table with his palms, and I could hear joints cracking and his voice moaning with effort. By the time I walked those few steps to the table, he was still pushing himself up. When he finally made it to a standing position, he looked at me with a pained expression.

"You want to watch movie?" he shouted.

"What? A movie?" I replied.

"Yeah, you want to watch movie, it's five bucks!"

"Five bucks?"

"Yeah, five bucks to watch movie. Triple X."

I point toward his little TV. "Five bucks to watch a movie on that?"

The old man shook his head and muttered something in Chinese. He pointed toward a door farther down the hall. "Big screen in room. Triple X movies. You want to watch, it's five bucks!"

I rummaged through my pockets and discovered five bucks I still had left over. I looked at the cash, wondered how much money I had left from my last paycheck and whether I should blow this last bill. I must have been working on my decision for a long time because the old Chinese man started shouting again.

"If you want to see movie, it's five bucks! If you don't, get out!"

"How long is the movie?"

"You pay for one movie, you can stay for all."

I shrugged, and because it was kind of warm, I handed over my five bucks and walked through the door to see my movie.

Even with the big-screen TV shoved against the side of one wall, the room was so black, it felt like being slugged by darkness. A musky smell drifted over and placed an arm around my shoulders. I waited at the door for my eyes to adjust, watching the action on the screen. It was your typical XXX movie, two unbelievably thin women, both with that late-eighties heavy-metal hair and breasts so round, so symmetrical . . . too large to be real. The soundtrack featured pseudo guitar rock and plenty of moans, groans, and yeses. Penises would go in and out of several places, sometimes more than one at a time and then they'd be replaced by another one from the line. The camera angles seemed gynecologically designed and never showed a male face.

When my eyes adjusted, I could see about fifteen ragged rows of metal folding chairs. There were five or six men scattered throughout the room. But in the two back rows, in the darkest part of the room, there was something else going on. Two, maybe three guys were entwined somehow and they moaned out of sync with the action on the screen. Surrounding them was a semicircle of men, their backs to the big screen, their bodies jerking and twitching.

I decided the best place for me would be at the front. I grabbed a chair in the second row, several seats away from anybody else. The closest person was slumped asleep in his chair, his jacket pulled over him like a blanket. He snored softly, a little whistle with each breath. I settled in my seat, stuffed my hands in my pocket, and tried to let the cold filter out.

The movie continued on to its predictable ending. The actresses seemed like baby birds waiting to be fed, mouths open wide in expectation, as the group of penises crowded around them for the climactic end of the XXX experience.

After the movie ended, there was a brief moment of darkness. Someone tapped me on the shoulder.

"Jesus Christ!" I erupted out of my chair, fumbling in my pocket. I whirled around, brandishing a pen like some sort of *West Side Story* thug. "What the fuck do you want?" I growled.

The guy fell back, his chair clattering to the floor, stopping all the action in the back rows. But only for a second or two. My "attacker" curled up in a ball, his palms raised to the ceiling. "Oh Jesus, I'm sorry. I didn't mean to scare you. Don't hurt me, don't hurt me."

"What the fuck do you want?"

"I just wanted to see if you needed some help getting warm. Please don't hurt me."

I sighed and relaxed my pen hand. "No, thanks." I laughed. "I'll be fine by myself." I shook my head and sat down, heart dancing, skin tingling. I tried to settle myself by breathing deeply. I heard my friend skitter away but I didn't watch him leave. I started to shiver, but not from the cold. I was no longer cold. I let the shivers do their business; if I held them back then I wouldn't be able to relax.

Fortunately, another movie started. Instead of being arousing, it was hypnotic. And even before the first penetration, the weight of my day pulled me down and I drifted off.

4

❋

I met Marvin a couple years ago, when I was really living on the street. He was fifteen, sixteen, tops. I'd see him around various shelters and drop-in centers. At first I thought he was just one of those suburban kids who liked to play poverty, to pretend they were some kind of street kid for a couple of days a month, only to be picked up by their parents in their soccer-mom SUV when they got bored, wanted a hot meal or to sleep in their own bed.

I thought this because Marvin dressed differently than the other street kids. His clothes were relatively clean and in decent shape. His face was alive, his eyes were bright, always looking around, checking things out. He seemed healthy.

Most street kids are also sullen types, wary of others, even of their own kind. Which is understandable because there are a lot of people out there who have no problem taking advantage of some fucked-up, inhalant-sniffing teenager who is looking for something to eat, a warm place to stay, or another hit. Street kids don't look anyone directly in the eye. They are like beta dogs, always looking down, making only brief eye contact with side glances or quick peeks. Street kids also consistently show symptoms of being sick: a runny nose, watery red eyes, a hacking cough, mostly due to sniffing inhalants, gas, glue, Lysol, whatever they can get their hands on.

Of course, a lot of them are into harder things like meth, crack, or heroin, but those kinds of drugs are expensive. The only way they can get their hands on those on a regular basis is to sell the only thing they have of value: their bodies.

Marvin was different. When he walked, he walked with his back straight, like he had someplace to go, people to see. He liked to talk to people, and not just kids his own age. When he talked, it wasn't about something outrageous he or someone he knew had done; he liked to get to know people and ask them questions.

One day, he came up to me in the main branch library. When I lived on the street, I always made an effort to visit that library. They always had the current edition of most newspapers in the country. Also, it was relatively welcoming to street folks. As long as they didn't fall asleep or bother any of the patrons, they were welcome to stay as long as they wanted.

"Leo, right?" he said, standing over me, but not in a threatening way. "I've seen you around at some of the shelters."

I looked up but said nothing. I had seen him around but had never talked to him. I wasn't much of a talker when I lived on the street; I was focused mostly on gambling and trying to find something to eat.

After several seconds of silence, he stuck out his hand. "My name's Marvin."

I looked at his hand but didn't shake it. When you're homeless, the only reason someone offers to shake your hand is to try to get something from you or convert you.

"Mind if I sit?" he asked.

I replied with a shrug so he sat down on the chair next to mine. "You read a lot of newspapers, don't you?"

"Is there a reason why you're bothering me?" Even though I had been a journalist for more than twenty years, I didn't like people asking me questions.

"I'm just curious, man," he said, holding his hands up. "Most street folks come to the library to rest, they pretend to read because they have to. But you actually read. Not only that, I've seen you mark it up and then put it back."

I slapped the paper closed, so hard that the noise it made drew a "Shhhhh" from a nearby librarian. "You going to turn me in?"

"No, man. Like I said, I'm just curious. I've seen you do it and I know most folks would just ignore it, put you down as a crazy man, but you don't seem the type. So I figured the only way I'm going to find out why you do it is to ask."

I looked at this teenaged kid, wondering where he got the balls to come up to one of his street elders and disturb him in such a way. Most kids his age, even those who lived on the street, wouldn't talk to someone like me. But Marvin was a curious kid. He wanted to know something so instead of making an assumption, like I might be crazy, he decided to ask me.

At that moment, I didn't tell him why I would always mark up the paper. I didn't tell him that I was a former journalist who had a gambling problem and had screwed up my entire life. And that marking up the paper was my way of not letting my old skills deteriorate.

But the fact that Marvin asked me that question, that he wanted to find out something and went looking for the answer, reminded me of my old self. He reminded me that even though I was living on the streets, part of me was still staying connected to that other life. And that if I really wanted to, I could get back to that old life.

It wasn't long afterward that we became friends.

5

Somebody was banging on the bottoms of my feet, telling me to go home. I first thought it was Dad coming out of the bar and hitting me as I slept on the curb waiting for him, but Dad had been dead for a couple of years. I opened my eyes and saw the old Chinese man standing beside me, hitting my feet with a broom handle. "Wake up. We're closed."

I slowly sat upright, rubbing the sleep out of my eyes. A few fluorescents threw some light on the room. The TV screen was blank and I looked about and saw that all the spectators had left. "What time is it?"

"Closing time. You have to leave now."

"No, I mean what time is it really!"

"Closing time," he shouted, threatening me with the broom. "Get out!"

I jumped to my feet, waving my arms over my head. "Okay, okay, I'm leaving. Jesus Christ."

I shuffled out of the room and down the dark hallway toward the exit. I heard the wind howling outside in the street and felt a freezing draft coming through the door. Bits of snow drifted underneath the door. I stood there, clutching my coat, reluctant to step out. I slowly put on my thin gloves, taking as much time as possible. I figured if I kept quiet and still, I could trick the old man into thinking that I'd left. That might give me an hour or two.

But the old guy was probably used to people like me, and after a couple of minutes he stepped into the hallway, one hand on his hip and the other brandishing the broom handle. He waved it at me. "Closing time! Get out."

I was beaten, so there was nothing to do but offer a friendly wave and step outside.

"Have a nice day," I said.

The wind assaulted me, pelting me with pinpricks of snow and driving cold. I leaned into it, painfully shuffling down Jasper, trying to find an open door so I could get out of the freezing wind. My ears started to sting and my cheeks went numb. My fingertips tingled, even with my hands shoved into my pockets, and the wind just tore through my ripped jacket. I could feel burning in my thighs and hard stabs of cold in my toes. When I walked past Canada Place the clock tower told me it was 3:30 A.M.

The middle of the night.

The coldest time of the night on the coldest day of the year.

Half a block later, I found a little alcove, some kind of delivery entrance, which got me out of the wind. I collapsed against the glass door, catching my breath. Instinctively, my hand reached for the handle but the door was locked. Getting out of the wind was a brief respite but it was still cold. I touched my hands to my face but I couldn't feel any sensation in my cheeks or nose. My fingers barely functioned and the pain in my toes had disappeared.

I knew I couldn't stay here for very much longer because I felt a strong desire to sleep. I craved sitting down in that quiet corner, shutting my eyes and letting myself drift away like I had in the XXX movie theater.

Man, that would be nice, I thought, and shut my eyes. Almost immediately, I felt the cold slipping out of me. A deep warmth that seemed to come from the depths of the universe slid over me, enveloping me in its embrace. *Oh, yeah, this is the life,* I thought.

I jerked awake, screaming, "Holy crap! What the fuck are you doing, Leo? Snap out of it!" I jumped to my feet, slapped my face a couple times, feeling nothing, but it was enough to keep from dropping off again. I stepped out of that little space, back into the world and the wind, staggering down the street, yanking on doors, battling fatigue. Every step was a struggle; the wind beat down on me like a hammer, but I forced myself forward. I had no choice.

If I stopped, I'd want to rest. If I rested, I'd want to sleep. If I slept, I'd never wake up. And then Peter would have to deal with the trauma of his old man dying. My daughter Eileen would say she didn't care, but it would still be tough on her if I died. Part of me hoped it would be tough on them but another part realized that they might not really care.

I moved forward, one block, half a block. Pulling on doors, trying knobs. I kept my head down to fight the wind, but I stumbled on a piece of ice. I caught myself in time, using a window for support, and then I saw the glow.

It was small and red, but it was enough. I fumbled about, lifting up my pant leg, pulling down my left sock to reach my ancient bank card. After my visit to the casino I knew it still worked!

The numbness in my fingers and the material of my gloves made fine motor movements difficult. I could barely pull the sock away from my leg, and once I did, I had a hell of a time pinching my fingers together to pull out the bank card. When I finally got it out, a gush of relief came over me, but my fingers gave out and the card fell to the ground.

"Fuck! Son of a bitch!" I shouted and dropped to my knees, digging through the snow. The wind blew the snow around me, obscuring my vision. My fingers were numb with cold so it was difficult to distinguish the difference between the ice on the sidewalk and my little plastic card.

I had to find it.

If I didn't, I'd never get into the bank and I'd be dead, my body frozen on this spot. My children would hear that their dad was dead but probably not told why. They would learn sometime later that their father had died, frozen, on the streets of Edmonton. Not a good story to discover later on in life.

I pushed those thoughts aside and kept digging through the snow. Something underneath moved so I traced the edges of it and discovered my card. It was flush with the ice and I couldn't get a fingernail underneath it. I pushed the card along the ice until it hit some kind of bump or ledge, giving me enough leverage to pick it up. Before I could drop it again, I reached up and jammed the card into the slot. I pulled on the door but nothing happened. The red light by the slot still shone brightly. I yanked on the door again and again, rattling the glass. "Fucking bastard! Open up! Open!"

I realized then that I had to pull the card out first to release the lock. I did, and a bright green light replaced the red one. I pulled the door open and crawled through, collapsing onto the floor, landing on my side and banging my head on the inside window. I saw a bit of a flash and felt a sharp pain in my ribs, but the elation of finding someplace warm made it seem minor.

My body felt like it was melting in the warmth; there were bits of water dripping from my face and within a few more seconds sharp pains stabbed my ears, nose, cheeks, hands, and feet. I laughed out loud and rejoiced in that pain because it meant I was safe for tonight. The floor was hard, wet, and sticky, and the hum of the fluorescents was incessant, but I didn't care if I fell asleep. For tonight, I was safe and warm.

I wondered if Marvin was as lucky as me.

6

Marvin was one of the first people I wanted to interview for my story. He was young and, like many homeless people, he had some kind of work, just nothing that paid him enough so he could establish himself or rent a decent place to live. He was also native and statistics showed that there were more homeless natives in Canada than any other ethnic group.

I found him at the Kids in the Hall, a downtown restaurant that employed street kids like Marvin, offering that all-important work experience, and their wage as a means of moving up in the world or a source of funds to start an education or to get their own place.

Marvin was happy to see me yet disappointed at the same time. I had shown up there around two thirty, after the lunch rush, so he had time to sit across the table from me, stretching his arm across the back of another chair, the tattoos on his wrist and forearm peeking through his long sleeves. He flicked his head back, draping the ponytail that held his native braid behind him. A hairnet valiantly covered the huge knot of the ponytail. Marvin's face was gaunt and drawn, the bone structure clearly defined, like a male model. He was the idealized image of the young native male, the person that Europeans feared, mythologized, and persecuted from when they first arrived in North America until the present day. In reality, Marvin was a harmless sweetheart.

"Jesus Christ, Leo. Haven't seen you in a while," he said, smiling.

His smile reminded me of my son, innocent and cheerful, like I held all the answers in the world. The difference was that Marvin wasn't that innocent; you can't be when you've been a street kid for a number of years, but he always seemed upbeat.

"I've been around," I said quietly.

"Yeah, I heard you got yourself a respectable job. Even moved out of Charlie's old room in the basement." His smile faded as he looked me over. There was disappointment in his tone, like I had let him down. "But maybe people were lying to me, because you don't look like a civilian. You look pretty down and out to me. You need anything?"

I couldn't help but smile because the question was pure Marvin. He was a street kid, but he was a particular kind of street kid. He was a provider—some may have called him an enabler or codependent— who looked out for others. Unlike many street kids, he actually had a place to live.

His tiny apartment was in a dilapidated high-rise in the lower downtown, the area just south of 102nd Avenue sandwiched between the legislature building and the flood plain of the river valley. And it wasn't just a place for him to live, it was a place to crash for countless others of his age: runaways, addicts, thieves, prostitutes, losers, and wannabes.

Only one person paid rent in that apartment and that was Marvin. He only worked part-time at the Kids in the Hall. The rest of the time he was flying flags like "Will work for food," or "Spare change for a hot meal," or working the windows with his squeegee and bucket.

If you needed a meal, he'd get it for you, either through the restaurant and its coupons or he would give you his last five bucks. If you needed medication, a bottle, some pot, a bag of chips, beef jerky, information about government services, a piece of clothing, a bit of cash, someone to talk to, or just a witness to watch you fall apart, he'd do everything he could to help. If you wanted a connection for hard drugs, or help finding johns, he'd refuse, but he would take you to a place for treatment or somewhere safe, away from your pimp.

Doing all of that, giving kids of his ilk a safe place to shoot up, bring clients, or just to crash, was his way of saving the world. Everybody who knew Marvin or heard about his work thought of him as some kind of hero, a saint of the street.

Unfortunately, Marvin's helpfulness was just another addiction like mine; it would ultimately destroy him unless he found the strength to take care of himself.

"This? This is only a front," I said, pointing down at my clothes. I told him about my job at the paper, what I was working on and why I wanted to talk to him.

He looked skeptical and I wasn't sure if that was because he didn't believe my story or he didn't want to talk to me. "I don't know, man. Sounds pretty sketchy to me."

"No, no, it's on the up-and-up," I said, pulling out a card from my pocket and handing it to him.

He looked it over for about thirty seconds and he still didn't look convinced. He tried to hand it back to me but I waved him away. "Keep it. I've got plenty."

He shrugged. "Okay, so what do you need from me?"

"A couple hours of your time?"

"Now?"

"If you can."

He shook his head. "Can't do now. It's a busy weekend. Gotta head back to the reserve."

That was a bit of a surprise because in all the time I had known Marvin, he had never been back to the reserve. A lot of native street kids didn't like going back because in many cases there was nothing back there for them.

"What? Is there a big powwow you gotta dance in?" I jokingly asked, and immediately regretted it because it probably seemed insensitive.

But Marvin took it as a joke. "There are no fucking powwows in the winter, white man. I just gotta head back to the reserve and take care of a few things."

"Like what?"

"Business stuff," he said with a frustrated tone. "If you're native and you're turning eighteen, that always involves a lot of paperwork. Guardianships, trustee forms, bank stuff, band stuff, a whole shitload of paperwork."

"Really? You're turning eighteen," I said with enthusiasm. "Happy birthday. Is there going to be a party at the reserve?"

He sighed and rolled his eyes, just like the teenager he was. "I wish. But it's just going to be me and my uncle Norman hanging out, him hassling me to come back to the reserve and do what's right, whatever that is."

"Pain in the butt, huh?"

"Tell me about it. He's always on about it. Ever since my parents died, he's been on my case. 'Do something right with your life, don't hang out with those guys. Remember your people and the land that you came from.'"

"He's just trying to look out for you," I said. "That's what families do."

"Naw, there's more to it than that. He's really into that tribal band stuff, be true to the land, fight for your people, all that shit they try to put on you while at the same time they're only building houses for their friends and sucking up to the oil companies and government dicks for more money," he said, bitterness creeping into his voice.

"He also used to be chief for a long time so he's really pissed I left the rez and moved to the city."

I knew nothing about Marvin's situation, but as a father, I knew that his uncle probably only had good intentions despite being a big pain in the ass. So I nodded to acknowledge his comments and again wished him a happy birthday.

"Thanks," he said, smiling. "I'll be back on Monday, and if you still want to meet, we could do it here, same time."

"Sounds good," I said, pulling out my notebook to note the date. But he didn't show.

When I asked the folks at the restaurant if he was in the back, they told me he hadn't showed up for his shift. But for them, that was nothing really new; a lot of kids missed their shifts. But Marvin was known to be pretty reliable so I went to his apartment. No one answered the door. I tried at the restaurant the next couple of days but he still hadn't showed up.

I let it slide for a couple of days but when I was on that cold street begging for change, I realized that, street kid or not, it wasn't like Marvin to miss an appointment. Or to not show up for work. So I decided that I would try to find him.

7

Someone stepped over me and there were little mechanical blips from the ATM. I opened my eyes to see a guy, all bundled up in winter wear, parka, toque, snowmobile pants, stuffing a couple of twenties into his wallet.

I pushed myself to a sitting position and the guy turned around, a look of fear in his face. I stood up as he warily moved to leave my temporary bedroom. But I slipped on the wet floor and he jumped toward me and grabbed my arm. His grip was firm, just enough to hold me up but not strong enough to be threatening. And he only hung on long enough to steady me; once I was balanced, he let go and stepped back.

"You okay?" he asked.

Our eyes met and I saw that there was an actual look of concern on his face. There was pity, of course, but he truly wanted to know if I was okay. I know Canadians get a lot of flak for our politeness, for the way we say *please, thank you*, or *sorry* like some kind of fixed action pattern. But what comes with that is acts like this. A stranger instinctively reaching out to help someone he feared just a second ago.

"Yeah, thanks," I said. "Cold night," I said, rubbing my arms.

"I'll bet. They say it hit minus forty-two last night," he replied, as if we were regular folks talking in the coffee room. Nothing brought Edmontonians together like talk of the weather. From the richest person in town to the most destitute, we loved talking about it. The weather affected all of us.

"First time in more than five years it's gone lower than minus forty," he added.

"Yeah, I can't remember it being so cold, and I've seen a lot of cold." I thought about asking him for some change but held back, knowing that it would ruin our moment of connection.

"Yeah, I'll bet," he said with a smile. "Well, you have a good day. Try to stay warm." And with that, he left the bank and walked out into the cold. He would probably forget me in a few minutes as he got caught up in the events of the day, and I thought I would, too. But then I realized that there was a way to remember this connection and to make it known to a bunch of people.

My mind was in the midst of a strange sort of dichotomy. On one side I was out on the streets again, living the life I thought I would never live again. But this time I was dong it by choice. What I'd told my ex-wife Joan from the casino wasn't a lie: I actually was doing research for a story. It was one of those this-is-what-it's-really-like-to-live-this-experience stories told from the point of view of a reporter. They were popular a decade or so ago and were still somewhat popular in the magazine trade and for nonfiction books.

So Managing Editor Larry Maurizio thought it would be a good idea to include more of that kind of journalism in the paper in an effort to bolster declining readership. Circulation had been going down for years now, due to the blogs and news sites on the Internet.

The homeless always struck a chord with journalists because it was a way to highlight the failure of governments, corporations, and consumerism, while at the same time not twigging too much guilt from our readers. It was also very easy for a newspaper reporter to go undercover as a homeless person.

Though many print journalists are solid, contributing members of society, more of them are on the cusp of becoming homeless when compared to more upscale professionals like lawyers, engineers, doctors, or businessmen. I was the perfect example of that, and no doubt my past experience of living on the street for a couple of years made me the perfect choice to write these stories.

Since it was only a block and a half away, it was now time for me to check back in at the paper. Again, once I stepped through the main door of the paper, security was on me. This time, there was only one of them. He was dressed in a uniform but it was an old-style rent-a-cop uniform: black pants, blue shirt with shoulder patches showing the name of the security company, a black clip-on tie, and only a ring of keys hanging from the belt. There was no effort to look like a member of the local SWAT team.

He was cautious but not threatening. His name was Amid Sengupta and in another life he had been a doctor in the Indian state of West Bengal. He was thorough in his duties yet also very friendly at all times. And despite the fact that he had to work as a security guard instead of practicing medicine, he wasn't bitter. In fact, he understood why people like him weren't allowed to practice medicine, despite the fact that his education and experience were not only equal to that of our home-grown doctors but probably surpassed it.

"Can you imagine what would happen if you Canadians let anyone who called themselves an M.D. practice medicine in this country?" he had asked me one day when I complained about the unfairness of his situation.

"Yeah, guys like you could be doctors instead of security guards and we wouldn't have a shortage of doctors," I had replied.

"Yes. But soon you would have a major surplus because every doctor in India would immediately move here, and to be honest, you really don't want that to happen. Take it from me, Mr. Leo. It's better this way."

I didn't really understand what he meant, but I wasn't an expert on immigration issues or on medical practices in India, so I didn't disagree with him. I still felt it was unfair.

To show Amid I was harmless after coming in from the cold, I slowly took off my toque, brushed back my hair, and stood tall. I also held my employee ID card in front of me. But he recognized me without needing to look at the card.

"Mr. Leo?" he asked, peering at me. I had asked him many times not to call me Mr. Leo—he had trouble pronouncing my last name— but he told me it was his way of showing respect to others he served.

"Yes, it's me, Dr. Sen," I replied. In return, I insisted on calling him "doctor." "Sorry if I frightened you."

"No, no, you didn't frighten me. I've been watching you for the last few minutes on the security cameras and I was worried that you were some poor soul trapped outside in the cold. I was going to invite you in to let you warm up for a bit."

He came closer to me, and placed a hand on my shoulder. He looked into my eyes, examining my face. I knew that he was not acting as a security guard at that moment. His face turned pensive after a few seconds. "Are you okay? You seem out of sorts."

He was right. I was out of sorts. There were a number of reasons for it. I had been pretending to be a street person for the last couple of days, and a couple of times I had felt like I was back in that life again, even though I knew I wasn't. Also, the city was going through one of the worst cold snaps it had seen in years.

And then there was the fact that barely two weeks before I was assigned this story, I had moved into a real apartment, one with more than one room, regular furniture, and what were once luxuries to me like a fridge, a stove, and my own bathroom.

My old place had been a small room underneath the basement stairs of an inner-city rooming house—a place that used to belong to a friend. Moving out of it and getting an apartment that befitted an unmarried reporter for a major metro daily was a major step in my efforts to become a regular member of society.

Being assigned to experience life as a street person again while all this forward movement was going on was disconcerting and confusing. My old and new lives were crisscrossing and there were times when I was having trouble remembering which one was real. And spending two days in and out of character seemed to be affecting my health. I was probably coming down with a cold, and that wouldn't help things.

I didn't tell Amid that whole story; I only told him I thought I was coming down with a cold. He examined me again, this time feeling my pulse and my forehead. He nodded.

"Yes, I think you are, possibly the flu, if you don't take care of yourself," he said. He let go of my shoulder and stepped aside to let me pass. "Plenty of fluids for you, take some vitamin C. And get some rest. As much as you can."

I thanked him for his advice, wished him a good day, and took the elevator to the fifth floor, home of Editorial, the newsroom.

It was a big open room, the size of a small warehouse, a seemingly chaotic collection of desks covered with the detritus of the news: papers, books, and other printed material strewn over every single desk. Along the outside walls were a series of offices; the workplaces of various editors or more senior reporters or columnists, separated from the main room by glass partitions. The place would normally be packed with reporters and editors working on the stories that filled the paper on a daily basis. But it was early in the morning, so there were only five or so people scattered around the space. Everyone else was at home or on their way to work.

It felt odd coming into the newsroom without the buzz of everyone working, but at the same time, it was reassuring. I had been in newsrooms for more than twenty years; some at weeklies that were smaller than a living room of the average-sized home, and some that were just as big as this one. So I felt comfortable here, even though it was eerily quiet. As I weaved my way to my desk and sat down, I deflated; the pressure of trying to find someplace warm and the worry that I might have died went rushing out of me like water from a high-pressure hose.

I knew everyone in the newsroom was watching. Most knew that I was on this story but most were probably not prepared for my physical appearance.

I ignored the looks. For the next half hour or so I chronicled the events of my day into the computer, from the mall securi-goons to the XXX flophouse to the ATM guy. I didn't set out to write in story form but I couldn't help it; the journalism instinct was too deeply ingrained in me. When I got to the end, I didn't wrap it up into a tidy package, I just let it be, which was the way I was taught to write a news story. I leaned back in my chair and sighed.

I probably could have fallen asleep, but I felt a hand on my shoulder. "Man, when you immerse yourself in a story, you go all out, don't you, Leo?" said a woman's voice.

I turned. Smiling at me was Mandy Whittaker, the assistant city editor, and officially my boss. She was a tall, thin woman in her mid-thirties. She normally wore her long hair with a ponytail but today she wore it loose. The bright smile on her face gave her an attractiveness that I hadn't seen before. It could have been due to the fact that I had been hanging around the most destitute in our society where blackened teeth, blighted skin, and scraggly hair were typical features among the regulars.

It also could have been because I was warming to Mandy. Our

relationship had been rocky when I first started at the paper. She didn't like that I had been hired on during a now-ended strike: a scab.

And though I thought she was a decent editor, I didn't like the fact that she always seemed to have a chip on her shoulder when dealing with me. But our brittle relationship had softened a couple months ago when I was working on a series of stories about a murdered prostitute and she realized that I had the chops to be in this newsroom. I was also in a very bad place at the time, dealing with the story I was writing, transitioning from being a street person to working as a regular citizen, and getting back in touch with my family.

We discovered that both of us had problems with addictions, her with alcohol and me with gambling. So. while we weren't the best of friends, we did respect each other and worked well as colleagues. I still didn't like that fact that she could be hard-nosed at times but accepted it because she had a tough job. Even though her title was assistant city editor, there was no city editor. The former one had refused to come back to work after the strike and management had not yet replaced him.

I answered Mandy's smile with one of my own and held my arms out to show off my attire, a stained old army jacket that used to belong to my dad and a pair of jeans that showed my long underwear through several holes. I had draped the lady's winter coat that I got at the Goodwill over the chair. "I'm just setting a trend. Soon all crime reporters will be wearing this ensemble for the spring season."

"Well, I hate to say it, Leo, but it kind of suits you," she said, sitting back on the desk behind her. "If you don't mind, I'd like to get a shooter up here and get some shots so we can run it along with your story. That is, if you have one?"

"Have I ever let you down, Mandy? Have I ever missed a deadline?"

"Nope. But you've been out of touch for a few days and we got worried you weren't coming back."

"When you say *we,* you're actually talking about Larry, aren't ya?" Larry Maurizio was the managing editor. He was Mandy's boss, a tough, obnoxious editor who thought he was the second coming of television's Lou Grant. He had broken the back of the newspaper's unions during the strike by hiring scabs like me so he could continue to put out the paper and get advertising money. There was talk he would soon be moving to use the uncompromising tactics he employed here to whip one of the bigger eastern papers into shape.

Despite all that, I liked him and would miss him if he left. We had known each other for a long time—I had given him his first job in journalism almost fifteen years ago—and while he could be a dick sometimes, especially when someone screwed up, he would always acknowledge staffers whenever they did good work.

"Mostly. But I was also wondering when you were going to be done with this story," Mandy continued. "Things are getting tight around here and it looks like they're getting tighter."

"What happened? Franke get picked up again?" Franke was a crime reporter with a history of drunk driving. I had meant my comment as a joke but the way the smile disappeared on Mandy's face told me that I had made a mistake.

"Oh, man, did he actually get picked up?" I said, a worried tone in my voice.

Mandy shook her head. "No, he's fine. But he took a package."

"Damn. That's the sixth in the last month." Because of the worldwide recession, the corporation that owned the paper was bleeding money, so they were making cuts anywhere they could. And since part of the agreement to end the strike was that the paper couldn't lay off any editorial staffers for a couple of years, the company was offering early retirement packages to some of the long-serving employees. Even though the packages were quite generous, almost too generous to refuse, these folks were at the top of the wage scale so it was a winning strategy for the company.

The only problem was that none of these retired folks were being replaced, so it was up to those of us remaining to pick up the slack.

"Yeah, so with Franke gone, I need you back into the assignment rotation as soon as possible," Mandy said.

"I bet."

"I know you really want to do a good job on this story but could you give me an idea when you'll be done?" Her voice sounded tired.

I pointed at my computer. "I actually wrote a bunch just this moment. I don't think it's really finished but take a look and let me know what you think."

She nodded but said nothing. I looked at her more closely and could see that there was something else she wanted to say. So I asked her.

"Nobody knows who's going to be next to get a package. Could be anybody. Even me. And it's driving everyone a bit crazy."

"Don't be silly, Mandy. Larry couldn't get rid of you."

She laughed. "Of course he could. I haven't been here as long as Franke or others that got a package, but I've been here long enough."

"But you're the city editor."

"Unofficially, yes. Officially, no. I'm assistant city editor, which is a big difference. It's easier to lay off the assistant city editor."

"Yeah, but who'd edit the city section?"

"Who knows? Maybe he'll just hand my duties to one of the desk editors or make one of the reporters a half-time editor. That's what he did to the entertainment section."

"Maybe he'll lay me off instead. Since I'm not part of the collective-bargaining agreement, he can let me go without a package."

"He wouldn't do that. He likes you too much," she said with a smile. "And besides, with you, he gets the skill of an experienced reporter with the salary of a newbie. Chances are, he'd give you my job once he let me go."

I shook my head. "No, he wouldn't. I'm a lousy editor and he knows it. And he knows you're a good editor. He'll keep you until your scheduled breakdown, which based on my calculations should occur in about eighteen months." Because of the pressure of the job, the tenure of a city editor of a major metro daily was about two to three years, sometimes a bit longer depending on the personality and stamina of the particular editor. And their term of office usually ended with some type of breakdown or outburst of emotion. Of course, there were always plenty of breakdowns and emotional outbursts in a newsroom. But the breakdown that ended tenure of a city editor was always much more substantial. And after the breakdown, the former city editor would be moved to another spot in the paper, something quieter like Lifestyle, or Wheels, or Style. And they rarely became city editor again. Those who did were legends.

Female city editors usually lasted longer than male ones. And based on what I knew about Mandy, and what I saw of how she worked, I figured she would last longer than most. And I told her so.

"Thanks, Leo. But it all means nothing if I'm just the assistant CE for those three years. Nobody's going to be impressed when that word *assistant* appears on my résumé. If I could get that part removed, I'd be happier."

"You want me to talk to Larry?"

"Thanks, Leo. That's really nice. But I've tried many times. I don't know what you could accomplish."

"Well, as you said, Larry likes me. And we do go way back. So if I put it to him in a way that I know he'll understand, it might work."

"If you can pull it off, I'll owe you big-time."

"No worries. Just give me some time to finish working on this and I'll talk to Larry for you." I slowly turned my chair to signal I wanted to get back to work on my story, but she stuck out her foot and stopped me.

Mandy paused, looked up at the ceiling and sighed. "I know I was joking when I said you were really immersing yourself in this story but there was more to it. You look like you've immersed yourself too much in this story, and since we didn't hear from you for a few days, everybody was worried about you. We really didn't think you were coming back."

"When you say *we,* you are talking about . . . ?"

"*We* means *us* here at the paper. Me, Anderson, Larry, even Franke, who said you were never coming back. We were all worried about you."

"Because you're short-staffed and need me back on the rotation."

She sighed and gave me a look that told me I was the dumbest guy in the room. "Yes, that, but . . . I'm sorry to say, Leo, we're also your friends. And some of your friends understand what it's like to live with what you live with. And we don't want to see you fall back into that again. It's a dark place. I know it 'cause I've been there. And so has Franke."

I didn't know what to say. I was surprised to hear that these people were worried about me and not just because they needed more help. But I shouldn't have been surprised. Even though we were different in many ways, we were all journalists and we all loved our jobs and putting out the paper on a daily basis. And when you get that many passionate people in the same room together day after day, you can't help but make connections. I didn't know what Mandy did after she left the office. I didn't know what Larry did when he left, and he was probably my oldest friend in the world. But that really didn't matter because we had the paper in common, and for many of us, that was enough.

I stood up and put my hand on Mandy's shoulder. "I'm sorry. I guess I got a bit caught up in the story. But if you take a look, you'll see that it's worth it. And even though I'm a bit tired, I could probably take on an assignment right now if you want."

And I probably could, as long as I stuck with phoners instead of face-to-face interviews.

Mandy smiled her bright smile again. And I felt warm when she did. "Sorry, Leo. I hate to say it, but you look like shit. To paraphrase Larry, our fearless leader, 'get the fuck out of here.' You look like you need a bit of a rest, so go home, clean yourself up, get some sleep, and come back tomorrow. In the meantime, I'll look at your story so far and if it needs anything else, I'll let you know."

So I sent her the story, put on my old lady's winter jacket, and went back into the cold.

8

I should have taken her advice and gone home. I had a real bed in a real bedroom. And just down the hall, I had my own bathroom with a shower and a bathtub with massaging jets. There was actual food in the kitchen, some leftover French-Canadian pea soup that I had made, using my mother's own recipe. I had heat and a real TV, albeit small, but with digital cable.

Going home, taking a bath, grabbing a bowl of mom's pea soup, and then crashing for the next day or so would have been the smart thing to do.

But Marvin's disappearance nagged at me. It wasn't like him not to be where he was supposed to be. Sure, he had all the looks of a street kid, but he was reliable and loyal.

So instead of grabbing a westbound bus at the corner of Jasper and 101st, I went down to the LRT station. I had only one stop to go and in any other weather I could have walked. But the nasty turns that Edmonton's winters could take was one reason why they built the downtown section of LRT underground. Even so, I still had to walk. Once I got off at the Churchill station, I headed north, past the courthouse exit, into the easternmost branch of the city's underground pedway system.

This section was relatively new. The smell of glue or paint or some oily chemical hung in the air, and the walls were white, lacking the years of accumulated dust and dirt of older sections. A long length of hallway stretched from the southwest corner of 97th Street and 104th Avenue to the underground parkade of City Hall, more than three city blocks. It was empty except for me and a large orange bucket that caught water dripping from the ceiling. A cool breeze wafted from the west.

I came up to street level at the Brownlee Building, a government administration building, and stepped outside to walk half a block east to police HQ.

It was pretty quiet at the main downtown cop shop, only a few people were slumped in the seats and on the benches, so I took a number and waited. When my number was called, about fifteen minutes later, I walked up to the desk, where a thick sheet of Plexiglas separated me from the frontline cop. Her right hand was busy writing on some kind of form. She didn't look at me as she asked, "What can we do for you today, sir?" There was a bit of a sigh in her voice, a tone that sounded helpful and resigned at the same time. I didn't take offense from her seemingly indifferent attitude because I knew that in her position, as the first public contact at the downtown cop shop, it was no cliché to say that she had seen it all.

I leaned against the front counter. "I'd like to report a missing person."

The cop stopped writing for a second and looked up. She was about thirty or so, dark circles under her eyes. Her hair was pulled into a bun at the back of her head but a few straggling strands had broken loose. The silver badge over her right breast gave me her badge number and name: Const. E. Harris. She assessed me in a second, filing me into the proper category, and then returned to her paperwork.

"How long they been missing?"

"A week, I guess."

"You sure it's been a week?"

"Yeah, I'm pretty sure."

"They've got to be missing at least seventy-two hours before we can officially call someone a missing person, unless there are extenuating circumstances. It's very busy at this time so are you only pretty sure they've been missing a week or really sure they've been missing a week?"

"I'm really sure."

"Okay, when was the last time they were seen?"

"I haven't seen Marvin in about a week."

"No, I mean when was the last time they were seen by anybody? Just because you haven't seen them in a week doesn't mean they're a missing person. You sure he's not just laying low somewhere warm with someone you don't know?"

"Marvin's pretty sociable and reliable. We were supposed to meet for coffee a few days ago but he never showed. I went to his job and they said they haven't seen him in a week," I said. "He hasn't answered his phone or returned any of my calls. He's pretty reliable."

She looked up at me again, staring directly at my eyes for several seconds. I knew she was looking for a lie, or anything else. I had to make her believe me. I had to make her understand that Marvin was missing, that it was bitterly cold out and he was missing, that I was desperately searching for him, that I needed her help to officially sanction my search because if I didn't convince her, then maybe Marvin wasn't really missing. Maybe he was, as she said, just laying low with someone I didn't know. Then my plan was a total waste of time and I would be better off in . . .

No! I shouted in my head. Marvin *was* missing. He *had* to be missing. There was no other answer for me. Marvin was missing and I was the one who had to find him. Because if I didn't keep the focus on that, I'd lose the key to the story. And I didn't know what Larry would say to that. Maybe he'd just shrug it off and assign me another one. Or maybe he'd invite me into his office for a chat, the same way he chatted with Franke. And if I lost this job, I'd be lost in a whirl of cards I really didn't want to play, lost in a plethora of horses racing on TVs in warm, faraway cities, lost in double downs and daily doubles, cold hands and quenelles, dead draws and trifectas.

My desperation must have convinced Const. E. Harris that I was telling the truth. She nodded once and reached into one of the countless cubbyholes behind her desk and pulled out a blue form. She slid it to me through a slot at the bottom of the Plexiglas.

"Fill out this form in as much detail as you can, including the stuff you just told me, and a complete description of the missing person and what they may be wearing," she said. "It's vitally important that you be as detailed as possible to make it easier to find your friend. When you're finished, bring it back and we'll send it up to Missing Persons. They'll probably have a few questions for you after that, so you'll have to wait. There are bathrooms around the corner and vending machines to the right."

I took the form and nodded. I opened my mouth to speak, but she read my mind and slid a pen through the slot.

After two decades of reading crime reports to find stories for various newspapers, I'm pretty adept at writing in a police style. At or before such a time, in and around such a place, a native male, around a hundred eighty pounds, between five feet eight and five ten, last seen wearing something or other, et cetera.

I took my time writing the report. I had to think about each word, each phrase, each sentence in advance, because making a mistake would only make it more difficult for the police. They don't like reports with a lot of cross-outs and scribbles; it distracts them from the main message of the report. As soon as a cop sees something crossed out, instinct and training make him wonder what was crossed out and why it was crossed out. I didn't rush as if there was a deadline looming, I wrote carefully, as though I was working on a feature for the Sunday Reader section and had a whole day to get the story just right.

I was also unused to thinking through a pen, so I had to make sure my handwriting was clear and readable. After I finished my report, I went through it several more times, rounding out *a*'s so they didn't look like *u*'s, making *b*'s, *d*'s, *t*'s, *l*'s and other similar letters stand up straight, adjusting the feet of *g*'s, *j*'s and *p*'s so they dropped below the line, and dotting all the *i*'s. I did this carefully, making sure my repairs would look as natural as possible so they wouldn't distract the judicious and suspicious eyes of a city cop.

When I felt it was complete, I returned to Const. E. Harris and slid the report into the slot. She looked up, blinked for a second while she searched her short-term memory for my category and then nodded. She took the report and slid it into one of the many plastic baskets surrounding her desk.

"Missing Persons will be made aware of your report as soon as possible and then they'll go over it," she said. "The members will probably want to interview you as well, since you filed the report, so it would be best if you sat and waited. Unfortunately, it could take a while, maybe a couple of hours, but if you're serious about your friend being missing, it's best if you take a seat and wait. There are bathrooms around the corner—"

"And vending machines to the right," I finished for her.

She nodded, gave me a quick upturn of her lips, and then went back to her reports. For several seconds, I watched her write and then sat down and waited.

9

Several cops came to the desk; some of them just grabbed reports from the baskets without saying anything, some exchanged a few words with Const. E. Harris. Others lingered, chatting and laughing about something or another, but no one stayed more than five minutes. On-duty cops are busy folks with a lot of things to accomplish in a short period of time, and most have to put in overtime to get all their duties completed. Const. E. Harris probably spent a few days of the week on the street, so while she answered questions from the general public and offered missing persons forms to folks like me, she had her own reports to complete and file.

After trips to the bathrooms around the corner and one reluctant use of the vending machines to the right when my blood sugar seemed to be running low, someone in plainclothes came into Const. E. Harris's area and grabbed a report from one of the piles. He started to walk away, reading the report as he did. But then he stopped and turned. He looked around the room; his eyes stopped on me for a second but then went on to the next person.

He walked up to Const. E. Harris, whispered something to her and showed her the report. A second later she looked directly at me, her tired eyes connecting with mine, and pointed with her pen. I looked at the new cop just in time to connect with his eyes.

He was older than Const. E. Harris, not quite middle-aged but close. He was chubby but not fat, had a military haircut, and wore wire-rimmed reading glasses that perched on a boxer's nose. He wore a dark blue sport jacket that hung loosely on his body, wrinkled dress pants, and his eyes had the resigned, tired look that Const. E. Harris sported. But there was a bit of edge to his look, a predatory stare.

He stepped up to the door next to the desk and waited for Const. E. Harris to push the button to release the lock. I sat up in anticipation, and after a buzz, the new cop pushed the door open.

"Leo Desroches?" It was a question and a command to come.

I stood and went to the door. "I'm Leo Desroches."

"Detective McKinley," he said, offering a hand. I shook it. "You filed this missing persons report?" He looked down at the sheet. "For Marvin Threefingers?"

"Yeah. Is there a problem?"

"Is it legitimate? Is he really missing?"

"Haven't seen him in a week," I said, and then added a lie to make it more emphatic. "Neither has anyone else. And it's pretty cold out so I was worried."

"Right. Okay. Come with me," he said, holding the door for me. He turned to Const. E. Harris. "Ellen. Could you give me a visitor's pass for Mr. Desroches here."

Const. Ellen Harris pulled a laminated necklace from under her desk and slid it, and a clipboard, across the desk. "Sign in please."

I filled in the blanks completely, putting down my old address instead of my present one. A few months ago, I had had a bit of a run-in with some of the less fine members of our local police service and I was a bit paranoid about it. So that's why I did that. The only space I left blank asked for the "Department Visited." Ellen took the clipboard from me, turned it around, and filled in the blank. "*Homicide,*" she wrote.

"Holy crap," I exclaimed, my head exploding with surprise and dread. "What the hell is going on?"

The two cops showed no emotion. Detective McKinley placed a hand on my shoulder. "Come on," he said softly, yet gave a strong squeeze on my shoulder that told me not to make a fuss. "We should talk, but not here."

And he steered me away from Const. E. Harris's desk and down the hallway that led into the bowels of police headquarters.

After a few steps, he pulled his hand off my shoulder. "Please follow me," he said. I nodded and he set off down the hallway, him in front, glancing down at my report every few seconds. We pushed through a door and into a white, nondescript hallway lined with more doors. McKinley walked quickly, his department-issue shoes clomping against the white-tiled floors. He led me through a maze of hallways filled with doors and bulletin boards peppered with a hodgepodge of notices: missing children, wanted criminals, departmental memos, items for sale, unfunny jokes, and the ubiquitous notice not to post notices unless approved by so-and-so. I heard voices chattering through the doors, disembodied murmurs drifting like secondhand smoke, the words jumbled and garbled, sounding like English but making no sense. Phones rang, lights droned, and the plumbing system gurgled, but always through a wall or another door.

There was evidence of life all around us, but McKinley and I met no one as we marched from hallway to hallway. I was completely lost in this maze, my sense of direction distorted by all the doors and hallways that we turned into and traveled through. If McKinley disappeared through one of these doors, or asked me to find my own way back, I would be forever trapped.

My heart beat against my chest, trying to force its way out of my rib cage. My skin turned clammy and cold because of the forced-air heating system and my hands trembled. I stared at McKinley's back, my mind a whirlwind of thoughts. I wondered why Homicide was interested in Marvin. He wasn't dead, he was only missing. But maybe he was dead. Maybe he hadn't found a warm place and had frozen somewhere on the street. Maybe he got hit by a car or decided to partake of some of the drugs he always told the other street kids to avoid. But Homicide wouldn't be interested in an accidental death like that. There had to be other reasons.

I couldn't take it anymore and stopped following McKinley. I watched his back pulling away. He punched the code for another door and was almost through when he must have suspected something was missing. He turned around.

"Mr. Desroches," he said, gesturing for me to come through the door. "This way, please."

I didn't move. My eyes began to tear. "Why is Homicide interested in my report?" I blurted out. "Marvin's missing, he's not dead."

Detective McKinley let the door close and stepped up to me. He placed his right hand on my shoulder and gave me a squeeze, just enough to feel pressure but not pain.

"I know it's hard, Mr. Desroches, but I'd rather we talk somewhere else. There are several questions I need you to answer, but this is not the place. Please, just a few more steps."

"But Homicide means Marvin's dead," I said. "Or presumed dead, am I right?"

McKinley nodded and lifted his hand off my shoulder. "That's true. *Presumed dead* is the proper term for our situation here. Your report matches one of our files in Homicide, but we, you and I, can't be jumping to conclusions at this time. I need to ask you to help clear things up and I promise, if possible, to answer any or all the questions you may have," he said. "I know this all sounds very difficult and surprising, but then again, you can't be too surprised or you wouldn't have filed this report. Please, if you follow me, we'll try to clear this matter up for both of us."

I sighed and nodded. "Lead the way," I said.

McKinley nodded back and we resumed our trip through the maze. The detective was right. Death was always a possibility, I knew that. I had hoped to find Marvin alive, or at least to hear that someone else had seen him and he was alive somewhere. If not here, then maybe in another city or back on his home reserve an hour or so outside the city. But I knew there was always the possibility that he was dead. Christ, I almost froze to death a couple of nights ago. Death was always a possibility for folks who are on the streets, even decent guys like Marvin. It was a fact of life, but I had kept pushing those kinds of thoughts down, burying them under veils of hope and expectation, and the snap of playing cards.

We walked into an open office area divided into quarters by a cross-shaped path. There were four cubicles in each quarter, some occupied and some vacant. The folks in the room were evenly divided into those in uniform and those not. Some may have been plain-clothes detectives or higher ranks, I couldn't tell. Despite their presence, the sound level remained consistent with the sound level in the hallway. People talked softly on phones, rustled quickly through files, or patiently read sheets of paper.

It seemed like an average office, conducting average business, save for a grisly crime scene photo I spotted on one of the desks. It was a shot of a torso, a faded bloodstain, paled skin, gender indistinguishable, washed out in the glare of the flash.

And there was a whiteboard of names that dominated the left wall of the room. Some names were written in red, some in black, some in green and the odd one in blue. Each name was also written in a different hand, so each had its own characteristics of size, shape, and angle, the uniqueness of each serving as a reminder of the individuality of each victim.

No one looked up, save for one or two of the uniforms. They only looked for a second to confirm that we were permitted to be here, and then they went back to their work. McKinley strode through the room, turned left at the intersection, and went through another door. I followed on his heels.

On the other side of the door, a flight of stairs led down and our footsteps echoed heavily against the concrete. At the bottom of the stairs was another unmarked door, but McKinley stopped and pressed a button near the handle. I heard a buzzer from what seemed to be miles away.

A few seconds later, a voice crackled through the speaker. "Yeah?"

"It's McKinley from upstairs. I came to see about the John Doe you've got back there."

"Right, come on in." There was another distant buzz and we stepped into what looked like a reception area for a doctor's or a dentist's office. There was a long, chest-high counter across from the door and several chairs arranged around the outer walls. A few of the chairs had magazines sitting on them. The atmosphere was heavy and antiseptic.

McKinley pointed to one of the chairs—"Have a seat, Mr. Desroches"—and walked up to the counter. I sat down, picking up a magazine and tossing it aside a second later. I was in no mood for reading. I tried to relax into the back of the chair, placing a foot on the opposite knee, but something in the leather dug into my lower back.

Somewhere in a room behind the counter was Marvin or, because of my report, someone that the police now thought was Marvin. I leaned forward, elbows on the arms of the chair, my hands gripped together at my stomach. But the wooden arms chafed at my skin. I took off my old lady's coat and used it as a cushion as I leaned on one elbow, but my hipbone started to throb. I fidgeted for about thirty seconds, searching for the right position to settle into, but the only one that seemed right at the time was to perch at the end of the chair, bouncing on my toes.

It was a mistake to come here. I should have taken Mandy's suggestion and gone home to bed. I knew it was stupid to think it, but I told myself that if I hadn't filed that report and gotten the attention of Homicide, then Marvin would still be alive. At least officially. His body might have been back there in some kind of refrigeration unit, but to me he still would have been alive. Missing but alive. Gamblers, even those like me who are officially on the wagon, think thoughts like this all the time.

McKinley leaned against the counter. After a few minutes of waiting, a middle-aged man in a white lab coat came from the back. His head was round and large, his hair was shockingly white, but neatly permed into three distinct waves.

Like most of the people I had seen so far in this building, his eyes looked tired and distant. He quickly glanced at me and then looked back to McKinley. There was no politeness or small talk between them; it was all business.

"You said you have information on one of our John Does," the lab coat said, gesturing with the clipboard that he carried. "I've got a list of about twelve, so which one are you looking at?"

"Number eight. From the suburbs, a couple of nights ago," McKinley said. "Remember him?"

Lab Coat nodded and tapped his clipboard. "How could I

forget," he said, turning the clipboard around. "Just to be official, take a look and see if we're talking about the same guy."

McKinley looked at the list and nodded. "Right. That's him. Can you get him ready for us?"

"Next of kin?" Lab Coat said, gesturing at me with his chin.

"Friend. Reported a Missing Persons," McKinley said. "Number eight might be a match."

Lab Coat exhaled sharply through his nose. "Right. Give us a few minutes to get things ready. Have a seat, explain the procedure, get him prepared, and I'll come get you." And then he left.

McKinley turned, took a deep breath, and sat down next to me.

I blurted out the question I had been holding in since I saw Const. E. Harris write the word *Homicide* on the sign-in sheet. "Is Marvin dead?"

I scrutinized McKinley, trying to interpret his body language for an answer in the affirmative. McKinley was passive. He didn't nod or shake his head, raise his shoulders or stiffen at the prospect of giving bad news. He looked directly at me, but there was no sympathy in his eyes, none of that "I'm sorry that I have to tell some bad news" expression, a look that I've seen before and one that I've also used when trying to get a comment about a recent newsworthy death.

There was only a touch of empathy. His face softened into a slight frown and he blinked a couple of times, but he didn't look away. I couldn't read him; he was blank to my question. And when he spoke, he spoke quietly, not reverently, and without a deep breath in the beginning.

"Were you once a member?" he asked, as if we were simple strangers on the street and he needed to know the time.

"A member?" I sputtered for a second before I understood the question. Police are members of a force, or in the case of municipal police, a service. In official capacities, such as in reports or during testimony, they referred to one another as "members." It was also an unofficial code to determine if you belong to the same club. Like the mob and its "friend of ours, friend of yours" introductions.

"No," I said. "Is that important?"

"It's just the language in your report." McKinley rattled the sheet of paper. "It's not the kind of language a civilian would use."

"I used to be in the news business," I lied. If he knew I was a working reporter, he would stop talking and I would be shown the door. I would never find out if John Doe Number Eight was Marvin.

"Ahhh. That explains it," he said, nodding to himself. "But not anymore, right?"

I thought about lying again, but instead of responding, I said nothing. McKinley took my silence as confirmation to his last question and nodded again, changing my category in his head, albeit slightly.

"Okay, as for your friend Marvin, I can't confirm or deny anything right now about his situation. All I can say to you is that we have a John Doe fitting Mr. Threefingers's description and the only way we can confirm whether it's him or not is through a positive identification from someone who knows him. Of course, we'd prefer a next of kin, but for now, we need you. And if you positively identify John Doe Number Eight as Marvin Threefingers and we do discover that he does have family in or around the Edmonton area, we'd use them for the official identification. Yours would be only the preliminary identification, but still very important in this case at this time. Did Marvin have a criminal record? Or serve in the armed forces?"

"He was only a kid so he was never in the armed forces," I said. "But he might have been arrested, I don't know. It's not really something people talk about."

"Good, good," he said with a nod. "If he was, then that means Marvin's prints could be on file, so we can try to match them to John Doe Number Eight."

I brightened. That was good news. "I guess you don't need me then, to ID the body. You just have to run his prints through the system."

McKinley offered a sad smile. "Fingerprinting is an inexact and painstaking science. Despite what you see on TV, it's still mostly done by humans. Getting a match would take at least a week, probably more because we're very busy. I'm sorry, but we still need your help on the ID, to determine if John Doe Number Eight is your friend Marvin or not."

"Has he been murdered . . . ?" I had started to say "Marvin," but stopped myself. I couldn't wrap my mind around Marvin lying on a gurney in the room next door. Best thing was to act like Detective McKinley and depersonalize the person. I switched to journalist mode, trying to fool myself into thinking I was just trying to get the facts for a story.

"Was he murdered, this John Doe Number Eight?" I asked in a much stronger voice. I felt my hand instinctively rise, as if I was holding a tape recorder.

McKinley must have registered the movement and the change in my voice because a wall came up and displaced the look of empathy.

"I can't really say at this time. All I can do is explain the procedure and help guide you through it," he said. "It's pretty simple, the procedure, I mean. The subject will be in a room and we'll be in another, separated by a pane of glass. There'll be a venetian blind covering the glass, and when the technician is ready, he'll ask if we're ready. Just nod and I'll signal him to open the blind and then you'll see the body."

Marvin, I thought. *I'll see Marvin.* I swallowed quickly. I felt my stomach drop and my sphincter tighten. *I don't want to do this. I really don't want to do this. Why did I—*

The technician came into the room, disrupting my train of thought. "Ready to go," he said.

10

When the technician disappeared into the back to operate the blinds, McKinley stood up. I didn't stand with him. I couldn't. I knew I had to, and my brain was suggesting the move, but my body rejected the idea. It was quite content to remain in this uncomfortable chair for hours, even days, especially since the alternative was to discover Marvin was dead.

McKinley placed his gentle hand on my shoulder. "It's difficult, I know, but you've obviously seen dead bodies before, am I right?"

I nodded.

"Then you know what it's like," he said. "This isn't anything new to you. So use that."

The images of notable car accident victims, found bodies, victims of violence, flashed before me like a slide show on fast-forward. A blur of images, like the crime-scene photo in the Homicide room, with blazing streaks of red, human flesh, twisted metal, or domestic tableaus acting as the background. Strange as it seemed, the reminders of my past, the victims whose names I had written in stories in the same Canadian Press style—so-and-so, thirty-four, of someplace—established a small barrier between the storm of emotions and the real world. The professional journalist part of me offered the protection I needed at this time. I could do this, it wouldn't be the greatest experience of my life and I would probably have nightmares, especially if it was Marvin, but I had enough strength to get through this.

I stood up. McKinley nodded and led me past the counter and to the back.

It was just as he described. We stood in a medium-sized room with a wide window in one wall. Off-white venetian blinds covered the glass from the other side. He led me up to the glass and stepped to the side, taking a position about five feet away and slightly behind, far enough to give me space, but close enough to offer support.

"When you're ready, say so or just nod and as I explained earlier I'll get the technician to open the blind. You'll be given as much time as you need to make a positive or negative identification. You'll have to make a verbal comment like 'that's not him' or 'no' or 'yes.' Do you understand?"

I nodded, and a second later realized that his question was a dry run for the real thing. "Yes," I said.

"That's good, Mr. Desroches. Whenever you're ready, you just let me know and I'll notify the technician. He won't raise the blind until he knows that you're ready."

I took a deep breath, opening my mouth to form the words *I'm ready,* but I couldn't speak yet. I stared at the glass and the blinds. I took all of my will and forced it through those two substances to change the body. It was something gamblers did; we believed that we had the ability to change a card into what we needed before it was flipped. We believed that we could manipulate a photo finish, that we could make the right bingo numbers be chosen. We believed in our hearts that we could change the immediate future, and if you asked any gambler, he would tell stories of how he changed a card into an ace or dropped the ball into black 34 or whatever.

Some called it prayer and some called it divine intervention.

Some called it telekinesis and some called it manipulating the threads of fate. It didn't matter. Every gambler, serious or not, had at least one of those stories. And if efforts didn't pay off and the wrong card fell, then we truly believed that larger forces were working against us or we hadn't tried hard enough and thus deserved to lose.

So that was what I was doing to the body. Even if it was Marvin behind those blinds, I would change it into someone else, someone I didn't know or wasn't looking for. Someone without a family, without friends, with a terminal disease or an evil disposition, so their death would be a welcomed event, or at the very least wouldn't cause anyone pain.

McKinley must have thought my delay was apprehension or fear. His voice came across the room like a gentle summer breeze. "Try not to look for a person but for features. The silhouette of the face, the length of the nose, the outline of the lips, the cut of the cheeks. If the features match or if they don't, then say so. Look for familiar features, not the person. Do you understand?"

"Yes," I replied for the second dry run. I sucked in a breath. "I'm ready."

This will only be a body, I told myself as I waited. *You've seen many bodies in your life.*

Many bodies. Car accident victims, crushed and mangled by the metal and plastic of their cars. Found bodies—missing children, lost hunters, Alzheimer patients—curled underneath a tree or in the sweeping high grain of a farmer's field. Heart attack victims or drug overdoses found blocking the doorways of cheap apartments, stumbling to escape or to get help but never making it in time. Victims of domestic violence slumped in an Ikea-style dining room chair, or left on the floral pattern of a linoleum floor, remnants of a meal clinging to the dirty dishes, murder victims looking like sleeping campers underneath the orange tint of a crime-scene tent.

My first body was the victim of a motorcycle accident. A young man, still a teenager, nineteen, in the proper CP style, took a corner too fast on his much too powerful motorcycle and hit the curb before flying through the air and striking a wooden telephone pole. I arrived five minutes after the accident, so the body was still in the road, covered by a large tarp while the police investigated.

I remembered the shoes, the only part not covered by the tarp. They stuck out as if he had fallen asleep with them on and someone had affectionately covered him up. They were relatively new shoes but the left one had a few scuffs near the toe. Scuffs that probably annoyed him, because his new shoes were no longer new, but also gave him pleasure, because they came from shifting gears on his new bike. I stared at those shoes for what seemed like a long time but realized I couldn't focus my attention on the dead youth and the senseless waste. I had a job to do, a paper to fill, and this was a story.

Since I was a reporter/photographer, I needed a photo to go with the story I would later write. I pulled out my camera and started shooting, keeping the shoes a key part of the shot because that made the scene more human. I won an award for that photo.

McKinley pushed a button on the wall, and a second later, the blinds opened. The journalist put up his wall of detachment and I stared through the glass, remembering to look for features, not for a body or a person.

"Jesus Christ!" I gasped, jumping back from the glass. My stomach lurched and bile jerked into my mouth, the acid burning my throat as I swallowed a half second later. I pulled my right hand in front of my face to cover my eyes, but couldn't erase the horrible image in front of me.

There was a body on a gurney behind the glass, covered by a

white sheet with only the head exposed. But the face . . . half of it was unrecognizable. There was a streak of black, the color of burned steak, all the way across the right side, stretching over the top of the head and down to the neck, and presumably down the rest of the body under the white sheet.

The right eye was gone, the blackness reaching even into the open socket. Most of the hair on the right side had been burned away, leaving only charred wisps to cover the scorched skin. The lips were gone, the exposed teeth and gums giving John Doe Number Eight a grisly grin. The rest of the face still had identifiable features, but the skin was mottled and blistered with grisly patches of black, brown and red. The left ear, the one that faced the window, dangled from the head like a loose thread.

This wasn't a basic John Doe, a victim of the elements or natural causes. This was a burn victim. Whether it was accidental or not, I had no idea. I really didn't care at that moment because I started to shake and stumbled backward. McKinley jumped across and held me up, his strong hands gripping my shoulders.

"It's okay. It's okay," he said in his calm professional voice.

I settled into his grip, using his authority and control to calm me, but the anger rose up and I pushed him away.

"What the fuck is that?" I gasped, pointing at the glass, but refusing to look. "You could have warned me."

McKinley raised his right hand, like a traffic cop. "I wanted to warn you but I had to confirm whether or not you knew about the condition of the body. Obviously you didn't, based on your reaction."

"What? Was I a suspect or something?"

"Or something," McKinley said with a nod.

"But obviously this guy, whoever he is, died in some kind of fire. Even I can see that. He wasn't murdered."

"Well, that's not entirely true, although I can't get into the details of what killed John Doe Number Eight. But when I discovered your Missing Persons report, I had to make sure that you were honestly filing a Missing Persons report and not looking for someone who was involved in this death. And the way to do that was—"

"Not to warn me about the condition of the body," I said, finishing his sentence.

He nodded. "Right. I'm glad you understand."

I nodded but I didn't really understand. Surprising me with the state of John Doe Number Eight was unnecessary and cruel. It showed me that McKinley was a conflicted cop, that he wanted to be seen as a decent member of society and a sympathetic police officer. A good cop. But that he also liked the power his career gave him, and relished wielding that power. He may not have consciously realized that about himself, but a few of his actions—not telling me about John Doe Number Eight, dragging me through the corridors of the EPS headquarters to disorient me and taking me into and through the Homicide Department so I could see the photos and feel the weight of the place—were signs for me.

He also wasn't a creative thinker. The way he showed me the body in order to glean whether I was involved in this death or not was amateurish, something he probably saw on a cop show and had been waiting years to use.

I caught my breath, leaned against the back wall, and put aside my anger as much as I could. My heart still hammered in my chest, and my throat burned because of the acidic bile, but I was calming down. I knew the best thing for me was to get away from here as quickly as possible.

"So do I still have to ID the body, or have I passed the test and am now allowed to go home?"

McKinley smiled slightly, but there was no empathy in his face.

"It would be very helpful if you could look at the body and try to see if it is your friend Mr. Threefingers."

McKinley gestured at the glass as if we were on some game show looking at the grand prize. "It would make things easier."

Easier for you, motherfucker, I said in my mind and reluctantly stepped forward to the glass. I stared at the ceiling for several seconds, the image of the body and its injuries in my peripheral vision, and then looked down.

I shut my eyes at the sight but forced them open, calling up all my resources. I imagined I was working on a story and the glass I was looking through was a lens of the camera. I pretended I was checking the light and the focus as I scrutinized the details that I could see. I focused on the identifiable features on the left side of the face and tried to ignore the horrors on the right.

Based on the features I could make out—the coloring of undamaged skin, the remnant of black, straight hair, the broadness of his nose, and the shape of his eye sockets—I assumed John Doe Number Eight was native. I wasn't completely sure; he could have been Latino or someone from northern China or Mongolia. But I had listed Marvin as aboriginal in my report. And if you're in Canada and you are talking about a street person with this type of features, odds are he's native rather than Asian or Latino.

And even with the burn injuries, I could tell that that body behind the glass was the same age as my motorcycle accident victim from so many years ago. This guy was late teens, the same age as Marvin— *No. Don't think of Marvin, this is only a body! Look for the features.*

I leaned forward, intent on doing a good job at identifying or not identifying the body. The features looked familiar, yet different. I couldn't tell if this was Marvin or not. Even without the injuries, I would have found the task difficult.

That's the problem with viewing a dead body in this kind of clinical setting; it looks human but the humanity is gone.

I moved my gaze away, using the white sheet to distract me from the actual face, to see if I could recall someone familiar and connect it to what was in front of me. But I froze as soon as I saw the left hand peeking out from underneath the sheet. It was mostly undamaged, which told me that John Doe Number Eight was probably unconscious when the fire started.

When you're on fire, your initial reaction is to bat at the flames with your hands, just as you do when someone attacks you. John Doe Number Eight didn't bat at the flames as he was burning so he was either already dead or deeply unconscious. That made me feel a bit better, knowing that he hadn't suffered too much. He probably died of smoke inhalation or shock, which isn't a great way to go but it's better than being burned to death while still conscious.

The sight of those four fingers and the thumb and palm caused my force field to dissipate. I stumbled for a second, but caught myself with my palms on the glass.

You can learn little about someone from their death face, except maybe the color of their skin and what they died of. Even then, it was a blank slate, because everything that made that face human was long gone. But the hands . . . nothing was more human than hands. That was why when you saw a photo of a dead person in the newspaper, you rarely saw the hands. The hands of the dead were more powerful than the faces of the dead. They spoke volumes. They revealed snippets of a person's story, fragments of his or her life.

The nails of John Doe Number Eight were frayed and bitten. There was a long scar along the inside of the thumb, scrapes on two of the knuckles, and a string of calluses where the fingers met the palm.

I tried to decipher the marks, tried to fill in the story, tried to recall if I remembered Marvin's hands like that. I could have stared for hours, lost in this one hand, but thankfully McKinley snapped me out of it.

"Is this your friend?" he asked.

I broke out of my trance by shaking my head. McKinley must have taken that for a sign.

"I know it's difficult," he said, trying to sound sympathetic but not really succeeding, "but you have to give me a verbal answer. Were you saying no?"

I shook my head again, and returned to examine the face.

"Is this your friend?" McKinley asked again.

I wanted to yell "I don't know! Leave me alone!" but I didn't have the strength. I just stared at the body, looking for my friend, but not looking for my friend.

"Is this your friend?" McKinley asked again, his voice somewhat agitated. "Is this Marvin Threefingers?"

Marvin? Is that you? I asked myself. I searched the face once more, but it told me nothing. The mask of fire hid its secrets. But I glanced back at the hand and found what I was looking for. Since the fire hadn't damaged this side of the body, there was a mark on the back of the hand, a tattoo.

It was red, a stylized version of the letters *R* and *N*. They were joined together, the letters drawn with sharp angles with a flag hanging on the front of *R* and a spear or an arrow as the final line of the *N*. Marvin had that tattoo; every time we'd run into each other, I'd see it. And every time he saw me look at it, he would casually cover it up. But he never mentioned what it meant and I never asked.

I stepped away from the glass, a great weight coming down on me. It pushed me to the floor.

11

When I came to my senses I was sitting in a small white room. McKinley was sitting opposite me, a table between us.

He pushed a small glass of water toward me, a line of condensation trailing behind it.

As I took a sip, McKinley cleared his throat. "So I'm guessing from your reaction that this is your friend on the table back there."

My hand that held the glass of water was shaking so I decided to put it down on the table before I spilled it all over myself. *Damn you, Marvin*, I thought. *Why'd you have to be so stupid that you got yourself killed?* I tried my best to remove the image of his charred body from my mind but it kept coming back over and over. My throat tightened and I gagged a couple of times. To stop myself from throwing up, I grabbed the glass of water, downed it in one gulp, and then slammed it back on the table.

McKinley barely reacted to my violent movements; a brief raise of an eyebrow and a short scribble in his black, police-issue notebook. He cleared his throat again. "But just to be sure, I need a verbal confirmation from you that the body you saw a few minutes ago is in fact Marvin Threefingers, is that right?"

I nodded, a shiver running through my body. *Jesus, Marvin, how the hell did you end up there, unidentified and burned almost beyond recognition?*

"I'm sorry, Mr. Desroches," he said, pronouncing my name incorrectly. "As I told you before, I need a verbal confirmation. So again, was that body you saw a few minutes ago your friend Mr. Marvin Threefingers?"

I didn't like McKinley's tone. He was only doing his job, trying to find out who John Doe Number Eight actually was, and I seemed to be his only lead in the case, but the way he kept asking me the question, with a sarcastic edge and forcing me to continue picturing Marvin's charred body lying underneath that sheet, backed up all my defenses. It seemed as if he was getting a bit of a kick out of it. I had to change the power structure of our relationship.

"Actually, it's Desroches," I said. "There isn't an extra syllable at the end."

"Excuse me?" McKinley blinked a couple of times and he started to smile but then stopped himself.

"You've been pronouncing my name wrong all this time," I said, trying to sound indignant but not really succeeding. "I'm letting you know and asking that you say it correctly from now on."

McKinley stared at me for several seconds. It was a cop stare, one that said "Do you really want to go down this road?" The one they give when they're called to defuse a situation and someone, be it a bystander or a participant, decides to push things further. The one they give you as a warning before they pull out the Taser and the cuffs and the next thing you know you're facedown on the ground, your pants soiled with your own piss, and there's a boot pushing your face into the cement. Based on McKinley's age and body shape, it had probably been a while since he'd pushed someone into the concrete, but that sense of power never leaves a cop. But after a second he smiled and leaned back.

"Of course, Mr. Desroches," he said, pronouncing my name correctly. "I apologize for the error." But there was no contrition in his voice, he just didn't feel like getting into a power struggle with me, because, despite my efforts, we both knew that it didn't matter what I did, he would always have the power in this room.

"But back to the identification, if you don't mind. I really need a verbal confirmation."

I waited for a second but knew that no matter what I did to stall, I had to accept that Marvin was dead and that he'd died a painful and fiery death. So again I nodded but this time I spoke. "Yes," I said quietly. "That was Marvin."

McKinley scribbled in his notebook. "And if you don't mind"— which meant "I don't care if you mind, I'm going to ask this question regardless"—"how were you able to identify the body considering the considerable burn injuries your friend suffered?"

"There is a mark on his left hand. A tattoo, red with the letters *R* and *A*."

"Right, the gang sign," he said, again with a scribble.

His tone was nonchalant, matter-of-fact, but my reaction wasn't. I jerked up, shocked at the notion that Marvin could even be in any sort of gang. "What gang sign?"

"The tattoo. It's a gang sign."

I shook my head. "No, no. Marvin wasn't a gang member. He liked taking care of people. If you were a street kid and needed help, Marvin was the one you went to."

"That's all well and good, but the only people who get a Redd Alert gang sign tattooed on their bodies are gang members."

"Red Alert. What the hell is that?"

"Redd Alert, spelled R-e-d-d, is probably the biggest native gang in the country. Affiliated with the Hell's Angels, they control much of the criminal activity on most Canadian reserves, and they're also active in cities that have reserves nearby and that means al- most every city in the country. That little red tattoo on your friend's hand is their sign, their way of knowing who's a member, which is pretty useful in places like prison."

My mind was reeling. Not only was Marvin dead but he was a member of the biggest native gang in the country? "No, that can't be right. Marvin was just a kid. He was barely eighteen."

"Makes no difference," McKinley said with a shrug. "The gangs on the reserves get the kids early. Most of them have no parental oversight because Mom and Dad are usually drinking or on drugs. And life on a reserve is pretty dull so to make things interesting, many of the kids follow their parents or turn to gangs."

There was an institutional attitude that aboriginal parents are bad parents and McKinley's comment only reinforced that racism. But I didn't feel like getting into a discussion about the causes of problems on reserves. McKinley had his prejudices and would never change.

But Marvin a gang member? It didn't make sense and I told McKinley so.

He smiled at my naïveté. "If he has that tattoo on his hand, he's a gang member. No one else is allowed to have one. In fact, if you aren't a gang member and you put that particular sign on your body as a tattoo, someone will come over and scrape it off of you. A cheese grater is usually the weapon of choice."

"You can't be serious?"

"Dead serious." He leaned forward, and though he was speaking softly, I could clearly hear his words. "These native gangs are the real deal. They aren't social groups hanging out at the sweat lodge, these are serious, dangerous criminals, no different than the Hell's Angels or any of the Asian gangs in our city. They deal in drugs, prostitution, protection, anything and everything they can to make money. They rob, they steal, they hurt, and they kill. Even their own people. In fact, the ones they harm the most are their own people because native gangs such as Redd Alert control much of the illegal drug traffic in reserves. And even if you don't want to think about it, your nice, yet dead, friend Marvin was a member of that gang; you can't argue that away. The tattoo is confirmation.

"And the other thing is that because of that tattoo and the way your friend was killed it's obvious that your friend angered someone in the gang and they took action."

"Angered them? How?"

He laughed. It was cruel but it was understandable considering my stupid question. "Who knows? Maybe he looked at someone the wrong way, maybe he said the wrong words, maybe he stole some money or drugs. Maybe he was a traitor, was considering joining another gang or turning someone in to the police. Or maybe . . ." He stopped speaking and looked up at me.

"Maybe? Maybe what?"

"You said your friend was a nice guy. Someone who helped others. And I see you, intelligent, older, with a background as a community member but obviously someone with problems of your own. And you have no gang affiliation or even awareness of what these gangs are. So I'm thinking that maybe your friend wasn't a traitor or a thief. Maybe he was trying to quit."

"Quit the gang?"

McKinley nodded. "It's a possibility."

"They would kill him for that? They would set him on fire for that?"

"Joining a criminal gang isn't a temporary act. It's a lifetime membership. So the answer is yes, they would."

"But fire? That's pretty cruel."

"If it's any consolation, he was probably unconscious and close to death when the fire hit him."

"But why would they do that?"

"It's just like the tattoo. It's a sign. They are telling everyone, including their own members, 'Don't fuck with us. Because if you do, this is what happens to you.'"

I realized that I was slowly slipping into journalist mode. I was no longer a regular citizen helping a police officer but a representative of the paper working on a story. Although I wasn't recording this interview, I was getting information for a story. I would quote McKinley a couple of times, especially concerning that bit about the way Marvin was killed being a sign to other gang members.

"They've done this before?" I asked, trying to be as casual as possible. I didn't want to tip McKinley off.

"Your friend Marvin isn't the first gang member to be killed in this city, you know." McKinley looked at me as if I was as naïve as a kindergartener, a look I've seen many police officers adopt when dealing with the public. I hated it because it told me that McKinley was one of those cops who thought he was tougher and better than regular civilians like me. And to him that meant I had to be judged by a different standard than regular folks. It also meant that McKinley was one of those cops who was always expecting and looking for the worst from people, even in benign situations.

It was cops like this who caused other cops, good cops, not to turn in their fellow members when they know they've committed a crime. And this attitude also created situations in which four burly cops could Taser and then kill a hapless and confused foreign traveler, like what happened to Polish national Robert Dziekanski at the Vancouver airport a couple years ago.

McKinley's attitude also assuaged any guilt I was feeling about not letting him know his information and words would be used in a story in the local paper. Of course, he would argue that I hadn't identified myself as a member of the media. But I would argue that I did. That prior to showing me Marvin's body, he had asked if I had been a member of a police department in the past, and I replied that I had been a member of the media, and thus was covered.

There was also the fact that I was "undercover" for a story on what it was like to live on the streets, a fact that the paper had been promoting for the last week to garner attention for my upcoming story. So I was covered there, as well.

It would come down to an argument about semantics. And sure, I knew I was stretching the boundaries of journalism ethics but I didn't care. I didn't like McKinley. I didn't like his attitude and I didn't like how he had blindsided me with the condition of Marvin's body. What he did was like a hockey player taking out an opposing player who's head is down. My story about this incident would be my open-ice hit in return.

"But when gang members are killed," I said, continuing with my stealth interview, "it's usually members from another gang killing each other, like what happened in that gang war a few years ago, when those Asian gangs kept shooting each other in their cars."

"Not all of the killings in that gang war were between opposing gangs," he said, still in this superior I've-seen-it-all-and-you-haven't mode, so he had not noticed that I was now interviewing him rather than the other way around. "A few of those killings were members being killed by their own gangs because either they had been co-opted by the rival gang or they were sick of the war and trying to quit."

"So that's what you think happened to Marvin? He was trying to quit?"

"Possibly. He still had his tattoo. And normally when a gang kills one of its own for being a traitor, they remove the gang tattoo prior to the killing. It's a way of telling other gang members that this is what happens to traitors. Like I said, for Redd Alert, a cheese grater is the typical weapon of choice."

"But Marvin still had his tattoo."

"Which tells me they didn't consider him a traitor, someone who was joining another gang or working for the police. So they didn't remove it. It's that, or they hoped that the fire would remove it."

I realized that if I didn't stop this interview, I would fall apart. I had to get away.

But he continued. "It's just like the tattoo. It's a sign. They are telling everyone, including their own members, 'Don't fuck with us. Because if you do, this is what happens to you.'"

12

When I left, I got out of that building so fast. I had to get as far away from that place and the image of Marvin dead on that gurney as I could. My breath came in gasps and I thought I was having a heart attack.

At times of great stress and discomfort, my first instinct was to head to a casino, a track, or any other place where bets can be placed. Gambling wasn't the best place in the world for me, but it was a place where I was welcome, a place where at least I knew what my role was, what I was supposed to do, and how I was supposed to act. Gambling was a place where I stepped into a trance, a state of unconnected being, of suspended animation, parallel universe where I could escape the reality of the universe the rest of the world lived in.

That real world was difficult, dangerous, and full of human interaction—love, decisions, and people who rely on you or let you down. And even though my body was suffering through some kind of attack, my brain ran through an extremely detailed map of where I could gamble without a break for hours. I imagined the brightly lit halls with rows upon rows of video lottery terminals, the dank basement rooms with only a couple of round tables and endless decks of cards, and the few Internet cafés, where, for an extra couple of bucks or a percentage of your bets, they'd adjust their server to access offshore Internet casinos. They would even open a temporary credit card account for you with a limit that you paid for in advance, either with your own credit card, a debit card, or with something they would take in trade at the pawnshop next door.

That imagining, and adding myself to those images, actually helped me regain my equilibrium so I could continue on my way.

I thought about the downtown casino again, but I didn't really want all the noise and bright lights. And to get there, I would have to walk a couple of blocks outside, and I was still trying to recover from the other night.

I decided that my next destination would be the Cecil Hotel, a decaying and neglected piece of real estate on Jasper and 104th Street. For years, owners of the hotel had come and gone, every one of them declaring that they would demolish the dump and replace it with something more suitable and respectable, like a loft-condo development, a high-end restaurant, or a ritzy retail strip. But for some reason or another, those plans never panned out and the Cecil remained the perfect hangout for street people of various strata, their friends and hangers-on, their suppliers and clients.

My hope was to find solace there, in the dark, with a friendly VLT. With the pedway system, I could walk all the way there, the only time I would have to step outside would be to climb out of the pedway system to get to the door of the Cecil.

Walking kept my head focused on what lay ahead, and not think about what had happened just a few minutes ago. Marvin was dead but that was old news. I had stuff on how he died and my "interview" with McKinley, but I really couldn't think about that at the moment. I needed to create some space between me and Marvin, and working on a story about him was the worst thing I could do. It would be good for my career, at least in the short term, especially since I had been able to finagle information from McKinley about a couple other killings related to Redd Alert. But it would not be good for my psyche.

Even with the medication I took, my mental state was a fragile thing. And it had taken a pretty tough beating in the last couple of days, especially in the last couple of hours. I needed to find someplace where I could lose myself for a few hours. I had to gamble.

By the time I got to the Cecil, it was already dark. The days were getting longer but only slightly. It would likely be March before we realized that the sun was staying longer in the sky. Clouds of snow blew straight south down 104th Street. Jasper Avenue was full of traffic, each vehicle belching a miasma of exhaust, like a dinosaur trapped in the nuclear winter of a meteor strike, but 104th had just a short line of three cars, the drivers impatiently waiting to turn right and join the procession down Jasper.

I tucked my head into my chest, my hands deep into my pockets, and tightened my shoulders for the quick run across the street.

The pinpricks of snow struck like a blaze of biting insects and the wind sliced through me and my layers of clothing. My face felt like it was being scraped with sandpaper and my ears sizzled with a sharp biting pain. I did my best to ignore the cold and pain, but it's difficult when the weather's trying to kill you.

My trip across the street took only a moment, but in those brief seconds outside, my core temperature dropped. I stood in the foyer of the Cecil Hotel tavern, gasping for breath, my shoulders aching with the effort of keeping them tense, and I knew it would be hours before I got truly warm again.

The Cecil tavern was a dark and gloomy place, with no windows and a small foyer between the outer and inner doors, so the last time daylight penetrated the place was the day before they built the roof. Booths ringed the two outer walls and a series of round tables and chairs covered the main area. A dusty bar with a few taps took up another wall, with glasses hanging like bats above it.

A fourth wall was covered with VLTs, but I made it my business not to look at that side of the bar. To a guy like me, VLTs are like crack, with the promise of the quick game, the quick high from the fast deal of the hand—no matter how fast a dealer is, he can never beat the speed of a machine—and so there is no need to wait to see if your decisions paid off, no need to linger and lament your loss, just press a button and your mistakes are gone, and in an instant, you're in the running again, the flash of a new game in front of you. And if you've won, then it's the same, no need to delay the pursuit for the next rush of winning; maybe pile on two in a row, double the sensation, double the endorphins, double your winnings so you can continue playing, because there's nothing better than the game, even though you know it's not right and that it's probably the worst thing that you can do to yourself.

There's nothing more comfortable because the game is simple: win or lose, black or white, no shades of gray, no mixed messages, no relating to the variety of other people and the reality of the world, just the simplicity of the game and the bet, nothing more, nothing less, the empty time of the gambler's soul.

A voice called out—"Have a beer, Leo?"—pulling me from my meditation on the VLTs. Jake the bartender stood across the bar from me. I flushed, feeling like a boy being caught jerking off, but Jake showed no shock or judgment. We had known each other when I had actually lived on the streets and he knew about my problem gambling. He knew about almost all of our problems, but he didn't seem to care. His job was just to pour drinks, not to judge. "Have a beer, Leo," he said, this time not really a question.

I nodded back, relief sighing through my body as I pulled myself away from the VLTs. "Hey, Jake. Yeah, give me a glass of cheap draft. Can't afford that trendy dark stuff."

"Who can?" Jake said, with a slight laugh. "That's why we don't serve it."

It was our regular joke, our greeting to each other, a sign that now I was just content to drink beer. He pulled out an old Liquor Control Board glass, the kind shaped like a nuclear power plant cooling tower, and filled it with beer the color of piss.

My eyes were now adjusted to the gloom and I noticed that there was someone else in the bar, sitting in a booth, intently staring at something in his hand. His name was Video Mike, an old street regular. He was the spitting image of Grizzly Adams, the old TV character, except Video Mike's bush of a beard was white, and instead of a cowboy hat, a black trucker cap covered his long gray hair.

He was muttering to himself, surrounded by a collection of empty beer glasses. Like the rest of us, Video Mike wore the same outfit he always wore; inside, outside, in winter, in summer: a pair of faded black jeans, his blue long underwear visible through a couple of holes, steel-toed work boots, and a checkered flannel jacket, red and black, that probably covered several layers of work shirts of a similar pattern.

Everything else he owned, he carried in an olive brown canvas backpack that probably had seen action in World War II, the buckles made of real steel and the straps, actual leather.

Video Mike was the stereotypical old-school street person, a fading alcoholic whose age could be anywhere from forty to seventy, who talked only to others of his kind, but mostly liked to be left alone with whatever thoughts, memories, and regrets he had in his head.

Video Mike's only divergence from the stereotype was the handheld video game he had been playing since forever. Every time I saw Video Mike he had that video game in his hands, his fingers and thumbs pushing the buttons with more dexterity than any preadolescent.

Nobody knew where he had found the game or what game he was playing. Or, more important, where he found the batteries that continually powered it. It was one of those questions that you always thought about when you saw something intriguing, but knew you'd never ask and forgot about until you saw that same intriguing thing again.

Jake set down a coaster in front of me and placed the glass on top. "Ninety cents," he said.

I tossed him a five. "Add another one when I'm done with this and then keep the change."

"Big tip," he said, and he wasn't joking.

I smiled, but said nothing. I sipped my beer, the bitter taste biting into my tongue. I kept telling myself that if I sat here and drank my beer, I would forget about the VLTs. But if I forgot about the VLTs then I would have to remember that image of Marvin. And the fact that he was dead. I looked toward the VLTs, grabbed my glass of beer and started to move.

But Jake stopped me. "Damn cold, ain't it," he said. It wasn't an unexpected statement. It was the middle of winter, we're Canadians, what the hell else are we going to talk about? But it was his way of helping, of trying to stop me from making the move that I shouldn't be making.

"No shit," I said while sipping. "I was out working the sidewalks a couple of days ago, looking for change, but there was no action on the street. Everybody stays in when it's like this."

Jake gestured at the mostly empty bar. "No action in here, either. Cold makes everybody stay at home and watch TV or sleep."

I turned in my stool to check out the room again. Still only Mike, muttering to his game. "How long has Mike been here?"

Jake shrugged. "Dropped in a few days ago, just when it was

getting cold. Spends the days here but I think he's been crashing in the Bay station at night."

"Transit cops not moving him out to Churchill?"

"Doubt it. If they were, he wouldn't be coming back here every day when it's like this outside. Those guys don't force the issue, as long as you don't cause any trouble. Mike's pretty quiet, plays his game all the time and won't bother you unless you bother him."

I nodded. "Yeah, and the security cameras are probably keeping watch on him all night, to make sure he's all right."

"That's probably true," he said. After a pause, he asked, "You see the Oilers game last night?"

"Nope. Don't watch a lot of hockey," I said, shaking my head, hoping Jake would get the message. He didn't. Like most diehard sports fans, Jake thought so much about hockey, football, or whatever, that he figured everyone else must do the same. So he didn't really register my response. He wanted to talk about the Oilers game last night and he was going to talk about the Oilers game last night. Or maybe he was just working to stall me.

I let Jake go on for a few minutes, to be polite and to get to my second beer, which he poured exactly like the first, but when he took a break after asking me a question that he already had an answer for, I jumped in.

"Sorry, Jake, I don't mean to be rude, but I didn't come in here for the beer."

He looked at me, a sadness in his eyes. "I know that, Leo. But I heard you were getting your life back."

"I am, but I've had a tough couple of days."

"Yeah, I hear ya. You wanna talk about it?"

I thought about it, but only for a second. I really didn't want to rehash my last couple of days at the moment, especially since I had just rehashed my night for the paper, and barely a half hour ago, I discovered that the guy I was looking for was not only dead, he had been killed in a terrible way as some sort of gang vendetta. No, I didn't want to talk about it, I wanted to forget about it. And there was only one way that I knew how.

Only a few games, I thought. *Once the change in my pocket is gone, that's it, I'll walk away, only a few minutes, at the most ten, and that'll be it, I'll get my fix.*

But thoughts like that are lies, rationalizations; it was never going to be only a few minutes, just enough to get a fix, because time spent gambling was empty time, the time that doesn't really pass, it just happens, an instant and eternity at the same moment. And it can never be filled, like a glass chock-full of holes; you can add as much water as you want but it will never fill.

Empty time was where all addicts live when in the midst of a fix; it was the time we all lived for, even died for, but it was a void, always and endlessly empty.

In a few minutes, my change was gone, so I stepped out of empty time, only for a second or two to break one of my twenties, and then later to get more money using my bank card in Jake's debit machine.

In these first few moments, Jake tried to distract me with more talk of the Oilers and the weather, but I was too far gone, so he gave up. It was only when the debit machine system went down on some sort of daily maintenance, or at least that was what Jake said, that I was able to escape. But not completely.

"You sure it's down?" I asked when Jake told me he couldn't access the system so there would be no money for the VLTs.

He shrugged. "Happens. Nothing we can do about it. Could be ten minutes, could be an hour, never know."

I sucked in a breath, eager to get back to the VLT, keen to get lost again, because if I couldn't, facing all that I would have to face would be a difficult task.

"Think the bar could spot me another forty bucks or so until the system comes back online? You know I'm good for it. The card works. You saw it."

He shook his head, and even though he quickly covered up his look of disappointment, it was alive long enough for me to see it. But it didn't bother me, because in my time I had seen countless such looks from people more important than him.

"You sure nothing can be done, Jake?"

He shook his head again. "Just following policy, you know, Leo. If it was just me, I'd help you out, but my hands are tied." I knew it was a lie, because Jake was smart enough not to trust an addict like me, but I appreciated the thought. It made me realize that maybe it was time to go. That happens. You step far and long enough away from the empty time, and you begin to feel less of an urge to go back. It was still there, the ever-present and powerful urge to gamble, and though I was not strong enough to fight it, I was too weak to keep pushing Jake.

Gambling took money, and once the money was gone, there was nothing you could do but walk away.

So I did. Without a word to Jake or a look back, I stepped out of the Cecil and back into the cold.

My mind was still in that postrush daze, so the cold, although present, wasn't as powerful as it would have been if I was in a more solid frame of mind. And it was too early for the regrets and re-criminations of getting lost in gambling once again.

That would come, but I was in hierarchy-of-needs mode; I needed to get home, maybe get something to eat then sleep. Fortunately home wasn't too far, about seven blocks.

It took me only about twenty minutes of hard walking to make it. And all that time, I thought of Marvin, saw his burned body underneath the sheet, the only way to identify him a jagged red tattoo on his left hand. And I realized that if I wanted to help Marvin somehow, doing what I was doing wasn't working. I had to push back at my old life and find some other way in the new one.

13

The next morning, I was back at the paper, shaved and clean. The reaction from the staff was muted. A few people looked up when I walked into the newsroom or glanced my way while talking on the phone, but for the most part, everyone was focused on the stories they were working.

Even the guy who had the desk next to me, another crime beat reporter named Brent Anderson, was focused. Brent was decent, hardworking, a few years younger than me. He had worked at the paper for about seven years, so like me, he probably wasn't going to be offered a package any time soon. He didn't cost the paper much money, and though he probably wouldn't get a raise, he'd get more work piled on.

He was multitasking, writing a piece and doing a phoner at the same time, probably something about a fatal car accident based on the tone of his conversation. Even so, he managed to acknowledge me by giving a slight lift of his head when we made eye contact.

I gave him a wave, slid my toque and gloves into the sleeves of my coat, which I then draped on the desk behind me, the one that used to belong to Franke, who had just been let go.

It was just then that I realized I had forgotten Franke's first name. Sure, it must have been on the byline of the stories he wrote, but I couldn't recall it. And now that he was gone, it would only be a few months before I probably forgot even his last name. And the only thing I would remember about him was that he was a mumbling, sullen kind of guy whose only praise about his own or anyone else's stories was that they "didn't suck."

I began to write my next piece, my computer monitor coming out of sleep mode. I wondered if I would adopt that comment as my own. I hoped I didn't, but it was true that after several years in the business, most journalists had a tendency to become like Franke, sullen and cynical, unwilling to praise anyone's work, even their own, except in a way that was also a backhanded insult.

But I put those thoughts behind me because today I had a mission. I was back at the paper, not only to return to the crime-beat rotation but to write a story about Marvin's death. I knew the story had legs, especially with the type of death he had suffered and the connection to native gangs, but I hoped to accomplish more. I wanted to tell a bit about Marvin's life, to show that even though the tattoo confirmed he was, or had been, a member of Canada's largest native gang, he was trying to turn himself around.

Maybe it could turn into a larger feature on native gangs and their impact.

So I started writing and had gotten a few paragraphs into the story when I heard someone shouting my name. I, and the entire newsroom, turned at the sound. The voice belonged to Larry Maurizio, the managing editor. Larry and I had known each other for almost twenty years; I had given him his first job in journalism at a small Alberta weekly back in the days when computers were first starting to make their presence known in the business.

Back then, Larry was an obnoxious journalism school grad who thought his first job was beneath him because he was convinced he knew everything about the business and the rest of the people at the weekly were out-of-touch hicks. He quickly realized that he was wrong and in the end turned out to be a decent journalist, even though he was still obnoxious.

But as the managing editor of a major metro daily that not only had suffered through a major labor disruption less than a year ago, but was also enduring the worst recession since the Great Depression, he had every right to be obnoxious. Even though Canada hadn't been hit as hard as the United States and other countries, ad sales had shrunk by almost fifty percent, while circulation had plummeted. Regardless, our paper was still doing pretty well compared to many newspapers in the U.S. We were pulling our own weight, and while we weren't as profitable as we had been in the past, we were at least close to breaking even. In fact, many newspapers in our chain were in the same situation. But the media corporation that owned the paper was a step or two away from bankruptcy. That's because fifteen years ago, they decided to open a flagship paper out of Toronto and push it as Canada's national newspaper. And that paper was bleeding money before its first issue was ever printed. So the head office was actively seeking someone to buy many of its assets, which included our paper and almost every other major metro daily in the country. And the way to do that was to cut costs.

So while people like Mandy, Brent, and every other reporter were worried about losing their job, I knew that Larry could also be on the chopping block. Especially if the paper changed hands. During major changes like that, it was always the key management types like Larry who were sent packing. I wasn't worried, because unlike many people on staff, losing my job wouldn't be the worst thing in the world for me.

My three weeks of pretending to live on the streets reminded me what it had been like to hit rock bottom. Being laid off from this job was miles away from there. My life was, for the moment, relatively stable, and if it came to it, I could probably find work at some small-town weekly.

For some at this paper, such a move would be seen as a step back, but I knew better. The pay at a weekly might be lower, but if you could fit into the community, it could turn into a long-term position, possibly even a lifetime one.

So while others in the newsroom thought that my summons to Larry's office meant that I was being let go, I wasn't worried. Much worse things had happened to me, one or two of them in the last couple of days.

Larry wasn't going to fire me. He didn't have a letter for me to sign saying I was going to accept the package being offered. He did have an angry scowl, which told me he was probably going to ream me out but I would still collect a regular paycheck.

"Hey, Larry. What's up?" I asked with a light tone in my voice.

"Sit down and shut up," he barked.

I sat opposite him, also realizing that since he didn't ask me to shut the door it meant my job was safe. He would swear at me, call me an idiot or something like that, threaten to fire me, but he wouldn't actually do it.

"What the fuck is wrong with you?" he demanded, waving a few sheets of paper at me. "You disappear for five days without contact and then show up in the middle of the night, write your piece, disappear again, and then show up at work today as if nothing has happened?"

I waited for a few seconds and then raised my eyebrows. "Is that a rhetorical question?"

He threw the papers at me but they just fluttered across the desk to fall on the floor. "Fuck you, Leo. I should fire you right now. I should kick your ass out the door."

I didn't know what to say at the moment because I wasn't sure what role I was supposed to play. So I shrugged.

Larry's face turned red at my response and for a couple of seconds I thought he was having a stroke. Then the pressure lessened and I saw the rage fade away. He was still angry, but in a different way.

"I know because of our past you're not afraid of me, but you could at least act like it, you know," he said with deep sigh. "At least give me that satisfaction, so the next time I call someone into my office, they'll be afraid."

"I'm sorry, Larry. I can't act afraid of you if I'm not. I understand if you want to scream at me for not staying in contact, and I will not only apologize, I will mean it. I'm sorry and I hope it will never happen again."

"You hope? That's it?"

I shrugged. "You and I both know that there will come a time when you will lose contact with me and it won't be because I got too involved in a story. It will be because I am gone."

And it was true. I was doing much better than I had been for years, despite my visit to the casino and the experience with the VLTs at the Cecil. But experience told me that those were only small blips in response to the recent tough events in my life, the death of Marvin and the confusion with being on the street again. I had gone too far into the role.

But there were two things that still kept me from completely falling apart. One of them was this job. The other was the relationship I was building with my son, Peter.

Still, I knew that there would come a time when it would all fall apart again. It could be a month, a year, even a decade, but I would fall again. In a weird way, knowing that made me feel lighter. It was like knowing when you would die. Because if you knew that, then you didn't have to worry about much before then. It would be the perfect life for a journalist because you knew when your deadline was so you could get your story completed in the time required.

Larry sighed again, his scowl deepening into disappointment. "I should fire you just for that, you know. I should let you go now so I don't have to deal with the disappointment."

"You have every right to, Larry. And I wouldn't be angry if you did."

"Yeah, but I would. And unlike you, I don't give up. I won't give you the satisfaction of giving up and blaming it on me. I'll keep kicking your ass back to your desk, even call the cops if I have to, make sure you show up for work so I can kick your ass again. Also, I need you because not only are you a good reporter, you work for cheap. Which is what the head office likes."

"Thanks, Larry," I said sarcastically. "I appreciate that."

He almost smiled at that but caught himself in time. "No. You don't. Because if you did, you wouldn't be the pathetic dick who keeps telling himself he's going to fail even when he's succeeding." He pointed at the sheets of paper that he had thrown at me. "This is a decent story you wrote about life on the street, some real nice stuff that we're going to run on Saturday."

I was about to say thank you again, but he cut me off. "But that story's over. As you know, Franke is gone, good riddance to that sad bastard, and we're not replacing him. So we won't have time for any of these kinds of stories unless you get your real work done, which is to write about who died in what car accident, what house burned down, and once in a while, who murdered whom. Are you able to do that?"

I offered a mock salute. "Yes, sir. And I actually have a story that I found when I was working on the life on the street."

I told him about Marvin, how he had disappeared, how I found him, the role of the native gangs, the other couple of killings by the gang, and how I was looking to approach the whole thing.

Larry listened but when I was done, he shook his head. "Fuck the bit about him being a nice guy trying to get his life back. The story's simple in this one: native gang member is killed; probably by his own gang. That's the story with a bit of an interesting side on how he was killed. Because of the native angle, we'll list you as the aboriginal issues writer on this story."

"I don't know, Larry. I get the part about the gang angle, but this story isn't just about a kid being murdered."

"Actually it's a bunch of kids as you noted earlier. Don't forget to find information on those other deaths. And in these times, that's it. With our present staffing levels, we have little time to spend researching another dead kid's life. If the story breaks into something else, like a gang war or other murders, you can follow it. But for now, get that gang killing done for tomorrow's issue and then put yourself back on the rotation. I'll let Mandy know what's happening so she doesn't assign you something today."

I nodded, knowing that I could argue more about expanding the story, but also knowing that it was a waste of time. Marvin was now going to be just another murder victim, written about in a perfunctory manner and then filed away in the paper's morgue of dead stories unless something popped up to bring it back to life. At least I knew I had a scoop and some inside info from Detective McKinley that no other journalist in the city would have. If I wrote it nice, Mandy could argue for A-1 coverage.

"About Mandy," I said before I left the office. "I think you should promote her."

Larry gave me an incredulous look, like I was telling him the best way to make love to his wife. "Do you know what a recession is? Do you realize how many people I've had to let go in the last month? If you think I've made cuts in the newsroom, you should see what I've done in production and ad sales. And now you are telling me to promote someone? That's the stupidest thing I've ever heard. Get the fuck out of my office."

"No, it's actually smart. Every time you walk out of your office, everyone out there is wondering who's going to be offered a package," I said. "If you promote her to city editor, it will get rid of that feeling and everyone will relax. And Mandy doesn't really want more money, she just wants the title of city editor, so you'll look good without ruining your bottom line. And you also know that she deserves it, so be a good guy and make an honest woman out of her."

Behind his annoyed expression, I could tell that he was thinking about it. After a second, he actually smiled. Not a big one; he didn't show his teeth but his eyes came along for the ride.

"That's why I don't give up on you, Leo. You're too smart to be a fuckup. Don't say anything about it to Mandy but I think you've got a good idea."

He stood up and came around the desk, putting a hand on my shoulder. "And I'm really sorry your friend died. I really am. If you want someone else to write the story from your notes, I'm okay with that. I'll still put your name first on the byline since you did all the work on it."

It was a tempting offer because I knew it would be a tough slog to write. But I figured I couldn't start running away from things like this. If I kept running, then I wouldn't stop and I would be lost much earlier than I was expecting. Marvin's story was mine for the moment. Besides, I didn't really have notes for a good chunk of it, especially the bits from McKinley.

"Thanks, Larry. But I think it would be best if I write this."

"You sure? You've had a tough few months and I don't want to burn you out. I need you out there, not just as another reporter, but as a friend."

It was the second time in as many days that one of my work colleagues was calling me a friend. It was odd, but probably only to me. Many people had friends at work, but since this was my first job in such a long time, it felt unusual. Having friends was good; I felt a welling up of emotion when Larry said it, just like when Mandy told me the same thing.

It was good to have friends again. It made me feel like I belonged somewhere. I had been alone and lost for so long that it was a joy to have people in my life who liked me, who wanted to be with me. I enjoyed the conversation, the banter, the support, and just knowing that if I needed something from them, they would do whatever they could to help. I also enjoyed that lack of judgment because of my past.

But at the same time, having friends was bad, especially for me. Having friends meant that some time in the future, I would disappoint them, I would let them down when I fell back into the abyss.

14

It was very tough to write this story. Twice during its production I felt a wave of nausea flow over me, and dashed to the men's room to ride it out. Both times, I thought about going to the casino or finding a downtown bar with VLTs. There were plenty within walking distance.

But I made it back and told myself to finish it off. I did, but when I reread it, I felt it was missing something. I knew exactly what that was, but I had put off getting that part of the story in the hope that it would be fine without. It wasn't.

I sighed. Last time we talked, Marvin had mentioned his uncle Norman. I went into my browser and found a Norman Threefingers living near the town of Wetaskiwin, about forty minutes south of the city. I called the number, hoping that this Norman Threefingers was not his uncle and I could write the line "Family members could not be reached for comment."

The voice that answered the phone did not say hello. It was gruff and impatient when it answered, "What?"

I introduced myself.

"Yeah, so what the fuck do you want?"

I was in a tough spot. Even though I had told McKinley that Marvin had an uncle, I had no idea if he had been told about Marvin's death. I didn't want to be the one to break the news to him, but I also knew I had to get some kind of family comment or Mandy and Larry would be on my ass about it. The journalist in me won out.

"I was just wondering if you heard any news about your nephew Mar—"

"Those sonsabitches!" he screamed into the phone, confirming that he knew what had happened to Marvin. "They deserve to die for what they did to Marvin, they deserve to have their hearts cut out and their bodies fed to the coyotes and crows . . ." He screamed incoherently for several more seconds.

"Who deserves to die?" I said, interrupting him.

"Who?" he screamed. "Those fucking gangbangers who killed him. Those assholes who take our kids and feed them drugs and money so they can turn their backs on their people. And if you say no to them, they kill you like they killed Marvin. Those are the fuckers who deserve to die!"

"But the police say Marvin was a gang member himself." Even though I now knew what Marvin's tattoo signified, I still found it hard to believe.

"He was never a gang member!" Norman screamed again. "Marvin had his problems, sure, but he was a good kid, he was a smart kid, he was a wonder—"

Norman broke down in a fit of crying. It was a sound that reached into my chest and squeezed my heart as hard as it could. I tried to wait for it to stop so I could ask more questions, but I couldn't. I put the phone down and for the second time during the writing of this story I escaped to the bathroom.

I stayed only long enough to catch my breath and then I left. I started down the hallway to the elevators. I would have completed my trip out of the building and back into gambling, but I ran into Brent Anderson.

"Leo, where you going?" he asked, his face showing that he was glad to see me but concerned to see that I was leaving.

"I was going to get some air," I stammered. "I'm feeling a bit under the weather."

"Well, you can't go out there. It's a bitch out there."

I nodded, remembering my time in the street, only a couple of days ago but seemingly almost a lifetime. "I know, but I still need to get some air."

"Yeah, but you don't want to go out there," he said, placing a hand on my shoulder and slowly turning me around. He steered me away from the elevator back into the newsroom, and I realized that he'd probably figured out I had some kind of problem. What kind, he probably wasn't sure, but that didn't make a difference to him. I was in need of help and he was going to offer it. He didn't mention that he was helping me, just said he knew it was close to deadline, that we both had stories to file and it would make sense if we got them done, regardless of how hard it was.

I knew he had finished his work but he waited until I finished my story. With his help, I was even able to include a short paragraph about Norman's reaction. Out of respect, I didn't include his name. I quoted him as a family member who wished to remain anonymous.

With the story out of the way, I felt that it was now time to get some gambling done. I pulled on my jacket, decided where I should lose myself, when my phone rang. I stared at it for several seconds, thinking it was Norman returning my call, so I was intent on ignoring it, until Brent snapped me out of my trace.

"You gonna get that?" he asked.

I nodded and grabbed the phone. "Desroches here," I barked, annoyed at Brent for making me take the call.

"Hey, Dad." It was my son, Peter. And when I heard his voice, all my anger and fear, worries and sadness, plus the desire to gamble, disappeared. It was a joy to hear his voice, but an instant later I began to worry because he had never called me at work.

"Hey, Peter, what's up?" I said, trying not to sound too worried. "Did your mother ask you to call me?"

"Naw. Mom's still at work," he said a little too nonchalantly, seemingly trying to act as if nothing was wrong when there was.

"So she has no idea you are calling me?"

He paused, telling me that the answer was no.

"She's not going to like that. Is everything okay?"

He paused and I imagined the worst. I imagined that he was at a police station because he'd gotten involved with the wrong crowd. I imagined he was about to fail at school and needed a way to tell his mother. I imagined that he was about to tell me that his older cousin Hunter had been abusing him all these years and he was going to kill himself, but he first wanted to say good-bye. I imagined he was at the hospital, suffering from some kind of injury that made him lucid but would kill him in a couple of hours.

Some of these theories were no doubt preposterous but they nevertheless came into my mind. I may have been a terrible, absent father but I still thought bad things could happen to my kids. I was also a journalist, at the moment a crime reporter, so I had heard and written about horrific things that could happen to kids. Brent was also a father, and when he heard what I said and the tone of my voice, he immediately stopped writing and turned with a look of concern on his face. He, no doubt, was running through his own child endangerment scenarios.

"I'm okay, Dad. Nothing's gone wrong," he said. For a second I felt a sadness come over me. Because he was my boy, still barely ten years old but already understanding that parents need to be protected in this way. "It's just that—"

He took a breath and I wanted to jump in to find out what the hell was wrong. But I knew if I did, he might turn away. He was taking a big chance calling me without his mother's permission. My forays into gambling had almost destroyed our family, and the only way I had been able to prevent that from happening was to leave. But that also shattered the lives of everyone—Joan, Peter, and my now teenaged daughter, Eileen. A few months ago, I made an attempt to reconnect with them, and even though she was reluctant Joan allowed it. Eileen refused to have anything to do with me but Peter showed some interest.

Joan had been extremely vigilant. Understandably, she didn't trust me and she was highly protective of her children by setting strict rules for how events would unfold. I was never to come to their house. I could meet Peter only in a public place, agreed upon in advance. If we were to go somewhere like a movie or a hockey game, we had to tell Joan exactly where we were, and when we were going to come back. Any violation of the rules would mean an immediate cutoff of the relationship with no chance of restitution.

So Peter knew the consequences of phoning me without her permission. This must be important and I had to let it unfold.

"Uhh, there are these guys at school," he said, drawing out the words slowly. Like me, my son isn't the best at verbal communication. I can write a new story that can inform, entertain, and create an emotional response, and do it seemingly without effort, and in a short period of time. But if I tried to tell that same story in a conversation, it would always die an uninteresting death.

So Peter was working hard, describing what was happening at school and how these older junior high school kids were coming down and hassling the younger kids. He didn't say so, but I knew from the crack in his voice that he had been a target many times.

"Have you told anyone. A teacher?" I asked, but right away I knew that was the wrong thing to ask. I hadn't been a kid for decades, and even though this was a time when schools actually did something about bullies when they were aware of such situations, I knew that no kid wanted to squeal to the authorities.

I knew that even calling me was tough for Peter because he let loose a defeated sigh. He was only a second or two from hanging up so I jumped in. "Okay, screw that. Forget the teachers. No one wants to be a squealer."

"Yeah. No one," he muttered.

"Okay, how many kids are there?"

"Three of them."

"And what grade are they in?"

"Seven."

"You sure?"

"Yeah, 'cause a couple of them graduated from our school last year."

"So you know these kids?"

"Yeah, a couple. The other one came from another school."

"Do you know where they live?"

"Yeah, but Dad, I'm not going to tell their parents."

"No, no. I'm not saying that. I'm just asking if you know where they live."

"Yeah, I do."

"Okay, here's what you do. Get as many of your friends as you can. You'll probably only get two or three. And then after school, follow one of these guys home, or meet him on the way home. He'll be surprised to see all of you, but he'll act tough. Tell you to get lost."

"Right. And then we tell him to leave us alone or we'll get him?" he asked in an excited voice.

"No, you don't say anything, because if you guys are quiet, it'll be even scarier."

"Then what do we do? Do we hit him?" He asked the question with incredulity.

"That's exactly what you do. All of you. You hit him. Several times if you want, enough to hurt him but not enough to really hurt him, if you get what I mean."

"Yeah." It was a drawn-out noise, barely a word because here was a parent doing the unthinkable, promoting violence.

"But the trick is to not say anything. Just hit him, knock him down, and leave."

"But what about the other guys?"

"Don't worry about the other guys. They'll get the message. In fact, every kid in the area will get the message. And no one will bother you and your friends again. Ever."

"I don't know if I can hit someone, Dad."

"I know, it's tough to hit someone because we're told it's not a good thing to do. And you know, it's not. You'll probably feel bad about doing this, but you'll feel worse if you let these kids keep pushing you around."

"What do I tell Mom?"

"You tell Mom what you want to tell Mom."

"She'll get mad."

"Probably. But she loves you so she'll get over it."

"She'll get mad at you. And she doesn't love you anymore."

He was right, on both counts. But that was okay. She had been mad at me before and I had already accepted the second one.

15

After talking with Peter, I knew I couldn't continue down the path I was heading. I had to stay out of the casinos. It wouldn't be easy, but as long as I kept myself busy I could do it. So when I finished filing my assigned story for the day, I looked into the story about native gangs. Except for the information I got from McKinley about Marvin, his tattoo and all that, I knew nothing about native gangs. Up until that point I didn't really think they existed.

So I called someone I thought might know something and set up a meeting.

Francis Cardinal was a local aboriginal elder that I had met a few months ago. I had been working on a story about a murdered prostitute named Grace and he got involved. He owned a car repair shop near the old Westmount Mall, but in his off time, he offered a wide variety of assistance to many members of Edmonton's urban aboriginal population.

Most of the thirty thousand natives in Edmonton came from one of the many bands that lived within a hundred-mile radius of the city, and while they didn't have many of the official services and established social support networks that the reserves offered, there was a loose group of organizations that worked together to provide connections.

Like many native elders, Francis didn't have an official title like president of the Aboriginal Business Leaders Group; he was just there, offering advice, knowledge, and acknowledgment to those natives who lived within the city limits.

I was aboriginal myself but I had grown up in the white world with little or no exposure to native culture—and so Francis saw me as one of his pet projects. He jumped at any opportunity to expose me to native culture, or to bring me a deeper understanding of where I came from.

So when I called and asked if he would meet me for coffee, he quickly agreed. I wasn't completely against finding out more about who I was and where I came from, but I was also at the point in my life where I felt set in my ways. I also didn't want to explore too deeply into my psyche, because that might make me question my other assumptions about myself. Such as why I gambled. Or why did I know deep down that sometime in the future I would be lost? And despite my inclination to ask questions of others, I hated asking questions of myself.

So I didn't tell Francis that I wanted to talk about native gangs. Because if I had, he probably wouldn't have agreed to meet me for coffee.

And when I surprised him with a question about native gangs, he gave me such a look of disappointment that I felt the same way I did when I was ten and I had been caught shoplifting by the old pharmacist who owned the drugstore down the street from Currie Barracks in Calgary.

"Leo, what the hell?" he said, shaking his head. "This is why you called me?"

"No, not really. It's only partly why I called," I stammered. "I also wanted to see how you were doing. It's been a few months since we last talked."

"And as I remember it wasn't a good talk." It wasn't. I had accused him of killing Grace, but then he told me the true story. I left him weeping in his office at the repair shop, full of grief and guilt. This was the first time we had met since then, and again, I wasn't doing a good job of connecting.

"Yeah, I'm sorry about that. If I could take that time back, I would. But I can't. And now they've got me working on this story about native gangs. It's connected to that kid that was killed a few days ago. The one with the gang tattoo on his hand? Did you read the story?"

Francis nodded but his face showed that he wasn't pleased. "Yes, and once again many members of our community, myself included, are not happy that most of the stories written by the aboriginal issues writers deal more with the negative aspect of native life in the city. After the entire series on Grace and her terrible life, we were hoping for some more positive stories. More stories about aboriginal successes rather than the other side of urban native life."

"But I can't deny that side, can I? I can't ignore the fact that Marvin Threefingers was a member of a native gang and was murdered. The same way that I couldn't ignore that Grace Cardinal was also native, and a prostitute, and was murdered. You can't just have the good without the bad."

"I know, but it seems that most of the stories concerning urban aboriginals focus on the bad rather than the good," he said, jabbing his finger into the table. "We were hoping for more balance."

"It's not up to the newspapers to give balance. We just report the news, and the news, whether it's white, native, black, Asian, or any other race, is usually bad."

"Bad news sells newspapers, good news doesn't."

"That's right. I won't deny that." And it was true. People didn't read the newspaper to read stories about good news unless it was related to sports, entertainment, or lifestyle. And even then, what they really wanted was the bad news, the stories about the difficult professional hockey player or the actor who cheated on his wife, or how parenting today was harder than it was in the old days.

A lot of people complained that newspapers and other media were only interested in the hard, bad news, and ignored the stories about the good things people did. But that was only because the readership demanded it. Fill a paper with feel-good stories about how great the world was and how all these people had succeeded, and that paper would fold within a month. Sure, it was good to have a few of these stories scattered throughout an issue, but what made people read papers, watch the TV news, or click on a certain news site was the stuff that made you feel your life wasn't as bad as other people's.

So when you read or watched a news story about some guy who got killed in a car accident on the Whitemud Freeway, you felt bad about it, but at the same time you also were glad it wasn't you.

I could have argued that point with Francis all day, but I would have gotten nowhere. There was a key to every interview and the key to this one was to get information about native gangs. So I told him the story I was working on and asked him politely if he knew anything about native gangs. Redd Alert especially.

His face dropped when I mentioned the name of the gang. His voice became a whisper.

"That's not a good place to go, Leo. You don't want to deal with those guys."

"So you do know something about native gangs, then," I said, ignoring his warning.

"I don't know much, but I know enough to stay away from those guys. They're a tough bunch and they don't mess around."

"Do you know anybody willing to talk about them?"

His face got even darker and more filled with concern. "Why? Why would anyone want to talk about them? They're dangerous;

they're thugs and criminals who prey on their own people for profit and power."

"And that's why people should talk about them!" I said, a bit more triumph in my voice than I had wanted. "If we ignore evil, it doesn't go away, it just gets stronger. But if we bring it into the light, then we expose it for what it is and that will help get rid of it. Or at least slow it down so it has a more difficult time preying on its people."

When Francis said nothing for several moments, I knew he was thinking about it. He didn't like what I'd said, but he was thinking about it. He finished his coffee, set the cup down and started playing with his keys.

"I might know someone who knows someone," he said with reluctance.

"Find out if they're willing to talk and get back to me."

He nodded, slowly, and with a tilt to his head that was almost a shake. "It might take a while. More than a few days, even more than a week."

"I can wait."

He nodded again, a nod that said, "Yes," but also said, "After all these centuries of living with them, I don't think I'll ever understand the white man."

He gathered up his keys and stood to leave the coffee shop. I got up to shake his hand but he placed a hand on my shoulder and gently pushed me down. "This is not a good thing, so don't be happy about it. These are dangerous people."

"Don't worry, Francis," I said, putting a hand on his. "I'll be careful."

"I know that. But that probably won't be enough. I know these people because they are my people. I know where they come from. I know the world that created them because that same world created me. I understand them because I understand their anger, their futility. They have had everything taken away from them—and many of them started with nothing. These are dangerous people not because they are evil and wish to harm others. They are dangerous because they feel they have nothing left to lose. You have to understand that."

I told Francis that I did understand that. And he gave a shake of his head, meaning that he believed I didn't.

But I did. I knew exactly what it was like to lose everything. But the difference between the guys Francis was talking about and me was that no one had really taken anything from me. I had simply lost it. I would probably lose it again.

16

A few days later, I was coming in from covering a car accident. Although the damage to the two cars was extensive, it was a nonfatal. There were injuries, one of them serious, but since no one had died and it happened in the middle of the day and didn't cause any major traffic tie-ups, it probably wouldn't get any play in the next issue. I would write it up and file it, just in case. But unless it was a very slow news day, it wouldn't run.

It was part and parcel of being a police-beat reporter at a metro Canadian daily. A lot of stuff happened during your average day: beatings, fires, accidents, all those little bits of mayhem, but you didn't read about them in the paper. We did write about them, sometimes we wrote three of these pieces a day. But many times, there just wasn't enough space to include them.

Unless somebody died. Then it would run. But again, depending on what else happened, it could cover several column inches or it could only run two or three.

I plopped down at my desk, took off my winter gear, and started working on the story. A few minutes later, Brent came in from a story. I grunted a greeting at him and he grunted back. He sat down and began to work on his story. We worked silently, side by side.

"Hey, guys," Larry said from behind, startling both of us. Brent was taking a sip of water and looked like he almost spit it out.

"Jesus, Larry, give a guy a bit of notice, will ya," I said.

"Listen, guys, I need a favor from one of you."

"Sorry, Larry, I'm not helping you move," I said with a smirk. "I did that for you once twenty years ago and that was enough."

He looked at me with annoyance. "Keep it up, Desroches, and I'll have you working as an assistant for the rim pigs." *Rim pigs* was a term describing the group of editors who sat at desks along the perimeter of the various department desks. Even though they were called senior editors, they were only glorified copy editors with little or no power. They were once reviled and even feared in the old days of the daily newspaper, but with the proliferation of computers, stories filed online, and cuts made to overpaid staff, rim pigs were an endangered species. To become an assistant for them would be like inhabiting one of the inner circles of hell.

But I knew that Larry wasn't serious. He needed me on the crime beat. Still, it wouldn't look good to undermine his authority.

"Sorry, boss," I said with some sincerity. "What you got for us?"

"This isn't a team request," Larry growled. "I only need one of you. I was going to assign it to one of you but I thought that it might be better for morale if I asked for a volunteer first."

"What do you need, Larry?" Brent chimed in. I glanced over at Brent, a bit surprised at his response. He rarely addressed Larry.

For a second, Larry was taken aback, as well. But he recovered and rubbed his hands twice before explaining his request. "I need a crime blogger," he said.

I tried my best to withhold my reaction but I couldn't keep a bit of a groan from coming out. For the past few years or so, newspapers had been working on their online presence in order to attract new readers or, at the very least, keep the few readers they had from abandoning them altogether. And having news blogs was one way of doing it. It was designed to give immediacy to a story, to show that we were on the ball, ready to break news to our followers the instant it happened. Sometimes it worked, but regular citizens using Twitter on their smartphone could break a story faster than any newspaper, even through our online portals.

And a lot of newspaper blogs, even newspaper Twitter feeds, were just comments about a story that had appeared or was to appear in the issue of a paper, usually one written by another writer. We even had a few reporters who were doing video blogs, but it was mostly amateur hour over there.

"Nice to see your usual enthusiasm, Leo," Larry said.

"Oh, come on, Larry. You can't be serious with this idea of a crime blog," I said. "What are we going to write about?"

"What are you writing about now?"

"I got a three-car pileup on the Wayne Gretzky Freeway?"

"Fatal?" Larry asked.

"No, but one of the drivers is in critical but stable condition."

He turned to Brent. "How about you, Anderson? What do you got?"

"Uhhh, I got a small drug bust," he said with a bit of a stammer. "Undercover operation that ran for a couple of months. They used female cops to lure low-end drug dealers."

"Do you think it's going to run today?"

Brent shrugged. "Depends on Mandy and what else happens today."

"His will, mine won't," I said, jumping in. "No one dies in mine but his has that weird angle of using female cops as bait for small-time drug dealers."

"So there," Larry, said pointing at me. "Your story is something we could run in a crime blog."

"That's what you want to run? A story that's not good enough to make it in to the real issue of the paper?" I asked.

"Of course. One of the biggest complaints the paper gets is

that we don't run enough of the small stories. We only focus on stories where people die in car accidents, we don't write about the stories where people survive car accidents."

"That's because people survive car accidents all the time, at least more times than they are killed in them. So that makes them less newsworthy."

"But they're not," Larry said. "People want to read about them, people want to hear about other things, as well, especially about all the stuff that happens in a newsroom that doesn't get into the newspaper. Such as what's it really like being a crime-beat reporter, how do we find these stories, how do we decide what's newsworthy . . . what's it really like inside a crime-scene tent?"

The last one was a dig at me and my stories on the life and death of Grace Cardinal. But I didn't flinch. "And those stories worked because you let me pursue them, not worrying about the column inches it took or how the advertisers, readers, or the CEO felt about it. You weren't after me to make sure I stayed on the assignment rotation because there was enough staff to back me up. Those stories worked and attracted a lot of attention from almost everyone because you were smart enough to run this paper the way an actual newspaper should be run."

"Well, times have changed," Larry said. He tried to sound strong but I could sense there was a little defeat in his voice. But that tone only lasted for a second. "And because times have changed, what we need now is a crime-beat blog. And based on your reaction, Leo, I'm seriously thinking of reconsidering my idea to look for a volunteer and assigning you the job just to piss you off."

I was going to say something, but Brent cut me off. "I'll do it," he said, raising his hand like he was in school.

Larry and I were both so surprised that there was a five-second pause before anyone spoke.

"I'll do it," Brent repeated. "I think it's a good idea."

"That's the spirit, Anderson," Larry said, raising a fist in support. "Talk to the online folks and get yourself set up by the end of the week. Then run a quick intro piece past Mandy and me and file at least one blog post a day, more if it's needed. Use your judgment."

Brent seemed pleased with the idea but I was still annoyed. "Does he get any extra money for this extra work?" I asked.

Larry pointed his finger at me. "Get back to work, Desroches. I'm going to personally look over your stuff for the next few days to make sure you're doing the job I'm paying you to do."

And with that he turned and walked away.

"Are you serious with this, Brent?" I asked a second later, not caring if Larry heard me. "They're just using you to do more work."

"I have to do this, Leo," he whispered. "They've let five people go in the past two weeks and almost fifteen since New Year's. If I don't do something to make me look more valuable, then I'm going to be the next Franke. And because I haven't been here as long as he was, my package is going to be a lot smaller."

"You got nothing to worry about, Brent," I said, knowing that I was lying. "They'll fire you before they let you go."

"No they won't," he said. He smiled to show that he knew I wasn't telling the truth.

Before we could talk more about it, and I could figure out how to help make Brent's new responsibilities easier, Larry's voice roared out again.

"Everyone listen up," he shouted, standing by Mandy's desk. "As of now, this fine journalist is our official city editor. As I speak, changes are to be made on the masthead and in the paper to signify this change. She'll also be getting new business cards with her new title. So listen to her and do what she says because I have given her the power to do so. If you fuck with her, you are fucking with me. Everyone got that?"

The entire newsroom was stunned into silence for at least a whole second; an extremely rare occurrence. Mandy's face was bright with happiness but also red with embarrassment. Larry leaned toward her and whispered something that made her smile become brighter and her face turn even more red.

A second later, a great cheer went up and many staffers rushed to her desk to congratulate her. Some of her female friends leaned in to hug her while her male counterparts were content to tap her on the shoulder.

I turned to Brent, who was smiling from ear to ear, and bringing down his coffee cup after making some kind of toast. "Hey, Leo! Great news, eh?" He then turned to the crowd and raised his coffee mug again.

"Let's hear it for Mandy!" he shouted. And the rest of the crowd joined in. A scattered version of "For She's a Jolly Good Fellow" started but then petered out. Some yelled, "Speech," and that captured the crowd.

Mandy blushed at all the excitement. For a brief second, our eyes met and she smiled at me. I returned the smile and gave her a congratulatory nod. After more than thirty seconds of people shouting, "Speech, speech," Mandy stood up, holding her hands out to silence the crowd.

"All I really have to say is thank you. Thank you, all. I really appreciate your support," she started in a quiet voice that forced us to really pay attention. "Besides that, the only other thing I have to say is"—she paused for dramatic effect—"get back to work. We've got a paper to put out."

The crowd laughed and there was another cheer, but we quickly realized that she was also being serious. We all went back to work, happier than we had been in a while because we had an actual city editor, which meant we were a real paper again. But we knew she was right; we had a paper to get out.

17

Later that afternoon, I had finished my car accident piece and was putting the finishing touches on my third piece of the day, one about an eighty-seven-year-old sex offender who was being released from prison due to his age and the fact that he had terminal cancer.

I was pretty confident that story would run, especially when I managed to get a comment from one of his victims who said he was "glad the old bastard had cancer. They should have left him in prison to die."

That was the kind of thing that made my job fun.

I filed the story into the system and started to put on my jacket to head home. It had been a good day and I was feeling pretty good. But another reporter, the education writer—Lara, or Sara or Mary, I wasn't sure—came over to the police-beat section. She told us a bunch of them were going out for drinks to celebrate Mandy's promotion and we were invited.

"I can make it," Brent said. "but I can't stay long. My wife's got yoga tonight."

"How about you, Leo? You coming?"

I nodded but waved Lara, Sara, whatever her name was, to come closer. When she did, I whispered, "You are aware that Mandy doesn't drink."

She shook her head at me like I was an idiot. "I've known Mandy since J-school. I'm quite aware of her situation. She's come out for drinks with us many times and had no problem with it."

I nodded but I knew that probably wasn't true. Mandy probably did enjoy her time with her friends when they went out for a drink. But she was probably on edge while she was there. Her friends may have been sympathetic, but only another addict could truly understand what it was like to fight the temptation to fall prey to one's addiction.

So I agreed to come along, not just to celebrate, but to offer Mandy any support she needed.

But in reality, Mandy didn't need my help. Unlike me, Mandy had most of her shit together. She had plenty of fun at the celebration, laughed and joked with all of us, threatening, in a bad impression of Larry's voice, to "kick our asses." All around her, people were drinking, some to excess, but she held her own, sipping soda and cranberry juice, having a hell of a time.

Near the end of the night, when a bunch of staffers came off the dance floor, she plopped down on the couch next to me. Her hair was out of its bun and her face was flushed from the dancing. I knew other people had lives outside the paper, but since mine was in a shambles, I expected that others with addictions like me were the same. I didn't know if I was happy for her or disappointed.

"You having a good time, Leo?" she asked.

I told her I was.

"You sure? 'Cause you've been sitting there like a bump on a log all evening. You remind me of my dad. He was always sitting in the corner at family parties, looking morose and bored. I hope you aren't bored."

"Actually, I wasn't bored. It's kind of neat seeing everybody having a good time, celebrating. It's been really dark in the newspaper the last few months."

"Yeah, the strike really took a lot of wind out of everyone. We were all so confident we were making a big change, fighting the good fight. But in the end we lost. And we're still trying to get over it. And with these cutbacks and layoffs, it's been another kick in the balls while we're down."

"I think you're mixing metaphors there, Mandy."

She laughed, a soft gentle laugh, and gave me a playful tap on the shoulder. "Hey, I'm the city editor in this room. No one gets to criticize language in this room except me. And I'm off duty."

"By the way, congrats on the new job. You deserve it."

She smiled again but there was something mischievous behind it. "Thank you, although a few months ago, I knew you hated me."

"I hated you? You were the one who hated me. I was the evil scab who was old friends with the managing editor coming in and taking a job from the oppressed workers on the picket line."

"That's exactly what we thought of you. Some still do."

"Fuck 'em, I always say."

"Me, too, because scab or not, you're probably one of the best reporters we have on staff. A pain in the ass, but man, can you write a story. I learn a lot from editing your stuff."

"And I learn a lot from the way you edit my stuff."

"You lying prick," she said with a laugh. "You don't even read your stuff when it's been edited and put into the paper. Everyone else reads their stories, sometimes complaining to me that I took out an important piece or ruined the tone of their story. You never read it. You look to see where I've put your story in the paper, check the head, and that's it. You never read what I've done with the mess you've given me. You pay no attention to my edits."

"I don't have to, 'cause you're a good editor," I said with all honesty. "I'll admit that during the first weeks after you guys came back from the strike, I made sure I read every single word in my stories. But I stopped when I realized that you knew what you were doing. I really meant it when I said you deserved this, Mandy. You're a damn fine editor, and one day you'll have Larry's job."

"Ugh," she said, a sickened look on her face. "I would hate to have Larry's job. He can be a jerk, but a lot of times, I really feel sorry for him. I really feel bad about the stuff he has to do."

"Don't. He loves his job, every bit of it. It's what he was born to do."

She nodded several times. "I know, I know, but it's not something I would like to do. I'm happy being the city editor. The official city editor." She raised her fist in the air.

"And in case you didn't hear me the first time, congrats. You deserve it."

"Thank you. And thank you for talking to Larry about it. I don't know what you said to him to get him to move, but thank you. It was one of the nicest things anybody's ever done for me."

She then turned to me and her face got all serious. "Would you mind if I asked you a question, Leo?"

People had asked this question before and I always knew what it was. Something along the lines of "Why do you gamble?" or "What's it really like being homeless?" And they didn't care if I minded, because whenever I said I minded, they would ask the question a few minutes later, but without the preamble. I was a little disappointed that Mandy was about to do the typical thing, but I had no choice.

I told her I didn't mind and in my head I prepared a stock answer.

"What's the best story you've ever written?"

"What?" I asked, surprised. It was the first time anybody had ever asked me that question.

"What's the best story you've ever written?" she asked again. "I know it's probably a hard thing to answer because you've been at this for a long time and you've probably written thousands of stories. But I was wondering what story in your career stands out for you."

It wasn't a hard question to answer. I had written a lot of stories, the one about Grace Cardinal a few months ago was one of the best. But as soon as she asked the question, I knew what my answer was.

"The best story I ever wrote was a simple auto fatal I wrote more than fifteen years ago," I told her.

"You're kidding me, aren't you?" she said, a look of incredulity on her face. "All those stories including the Cardinal ones and your life on the street, and all you can come up with is a fatal from fifteen years ago? You can do better than that."

"Okay, it wasn't the story per se that stands out, because it was just a basic fatal," I said. "I was working in Didsbury, my second job in journalism. It was a small paper, the *Review,* a weekly with a circulation of about three thousand. It was run by a couple of weird brothers, but it was a decent paper. One winter day there's this fatal accident. Mother of two is driving to work on Highway 2A and another car is coming the other way, a bit out of control because the roads were icy. So she does what she's supposed to do, she drives her car into the ditch to get away. But the out-of-control car goes into the same ditch and crashes into her. She dies immediately."

"That's very sad."

"Yeah, it's sad because she's a mother of two and she was just going to work. But it's really nothing new; it happens all the time. So I write it up and since it's a small town and a fatal car accident involving a local woman, it runs on the front page. Typical stuff."

"And that's it. That's the best story you've ever written," she said, taking a sip of her drink. "It's sad but it's kind of disappointing."

"Well, the story isn't over. The day after it runs, which is a couple of days after the accident, the woman's husband comes into the office. He wants to speak to me. I really didn't want to, because I figure he's grieving and angry and needs to take that out on someone. And that person is me, because I put his wife's death on the front page."

"Understandable. We get a lot of angry calls like that all the time."

"Right. So that's what I'm thinking," I continued. "And I can't really fight back, so to speak, because what can I say to someone whose wife has just died? I don't want to look like a dick being mean to someone like him. But my editor, Peter, this old-school journalist who started in the business as a copy boy back when they had copy boys, tells me that I have to talk to this guy. This was a small-town paper and one of the jobs of a small-town newspaper reporter is to talk to people when they come in the office to talk to you.

"So I sucked it up, headed out and talked to him. I tell him I'm sorry for his loss, all that crap, and I'm waiting for the angry tirade. But instead, he sticks his hand out and says 'I want to thank you for the story you wrote.'"

"Thank you?" Mandy asked, eyes wide. "He wanted to thank you for that? Why?"

"Yeah, I was shocked and that's what I asked. Who wants to thank someone because they wrote a story telling everyone his wife got killed in a car accident?"

"So what did he say?"

"He said he wanted to thank me because 'Now if anybody asks me how Lily died, I don't have to explain what happened and why. I don't have to cry through the details, all I have to do is point to your story and that tells them everything. You've made this really tough time a lot easier and I wanted to thank you for that.'"

"Wow."

"Yeah, wow," I said, tears coming to my eyes as I remembered that husband. "And that is why that story is the best story I've ever written."

She smiled and leaned in, so close I could smell her, a mix of vanilla perfume, cranberry juice, and hot wing sauce. It was a wonderful smell, one that I would file away in my memory. She grabbed my chin with her thumb and forefinger and pulled me close to her. She kissed me, a gentle kiss, the kind you give on the first date when all has gone well and you know there will be a second. I couldn't help but kiss her back.

18

A few days later, I was sitting outside the Native Friendship Centre, drinking a coffee in a car that I had signed out from the tiny fleet of cars available for use by reporters and ad salespeople. The engine was running, and the heater blasting on high, but it was still freezing inside the car. The radio was tuned to the Oilers game against the Blue Jackets, but it had been a long time since the announcer had been able to use his trademark "He scoooooooores" that he would shout whenever the Oilers popped one in the net.

I was waiting for someone, I didn't know who, because Francis didn't tell me. He had phoned me earlier in the day and announced, "Friendship Centre. Tonight at eight thirty." By the tone of his voice, I knew he had meant I was meeting someone to talk about native gangs, but he wouldn't tell me any details.

"They didn't give you a name or anything?" I asked.

"They only gave a location and a time," he said quickly. "I don't know a thing. And to be honest, I don't want to know."

"It's going to be pretty hard to get this off the ground if I don't know who I'm going to be talking to."

"Well, that's too bad, Leo. You asked me to find out if I know anyone who was willing to talk to you about native gangs, and I did. I made a couple of calls, told people what you wanted, and this is the response I got." I could hear the annoyance in his voice.

"Okay, if this is the best you got."

"It's the only thing I got. And to be honest, I'm surprised I got this."

"Should I bring a shooter?"

Francis gasped. "What!"

It took me a second to figure out why he reacted that way.

"Sorry, I meant a photographer. That's what we call them here."

"No. Only you, I was told. If there is anybody else with you or anywhere near you, the meeting is off."

"Okay. I guess." I was a little disappointed and it probably showed in my voice.

"Listen, Leo. You have to be careful with this. These are not nice people, they're criminals—"

"And that's why I want to talk to them. I'm a crime-beat reporter and this is a crime story."

"But you aren't talking to someone because their mom got killed in an accident and you're not getting info from a cop after a bank robbery. These guys are dangerous."

I thought about what happened with Grace Cardinal, Mike Gardiner, Justin Conlee, and the two cops who left me in the middle of nowhere last fall. That wasn't a very nice experience—I even surprised myself with my actions in the end—but I made it out of that. I still had some nightmares and worried that someone would figure things out. But so far, according to my buddy Detective Al Whitford the case was still open but unofficially closed. No one liked a rat in the police, especially a police rat.

"Don't worry about me," I had said with confidence. "I can take care of myself."

Francis offered more warnings but finally got the message and let me go.

And so I waited in my car outside the Native Friendship Centre on 101st, wondering who I was going to meet. It was already nine thirty, and I was getting bored watching the traffic whiz by. I no longer looked up with anticipation whenever a car slowed and I was hoping *something* would happen, even if it was the Blue Jackets scoring on the Oilers.

I was so lost in my boredom that I didn't see the headlights come from behind me until they were blazing in my rearview mirror. The lights were high, so I knew it was some kind of truck but I couldn't make out the make or model. There was also a thumping noise that I first thought was the knock of the engine, but it was too deep. I finally clued in that the thumping was the bass from some hip-hop song that was emanating from the truck.

I waved in the rearview mirror but there was no response. I rolled down my window, the cold wind blasting at me, and stuck out my head. I waved again and yelled "Hey" at the vehicle, but again, no response.

I sighed, turned off my engine and the pathetic Oilers game, and climbed out my car. I pulled my toque over my ears, bundled my jacket closed, and tucked my notebook underneath my arm. I also had a recorder in my pocket and I turned it to record. The thump of music got louder as I got closer.

The vehicle was a giant Hummer, one of those brand-new models; almost every single spot that could be decked out with chrome was decked out with chrome. It was also spotless, glowing with cleanliness, which was almost impossible in the dead of winter with the blowing snow and the constant sanding of the streets. All the windows were heavily tinted, even the front windshield, so I couldn't see inside.

I walked up to the driver's side, waved again. But nothing. I fought the urge to lean forward and peer in, reminding myself that I didn't want to look like an idiot. Also, someone in the truck had a connection with gangs of some kind so I didn't want to provoke a negative reaction.

I stepped back, crossed my arms to stay warm, and waited. Thirty seconds later, the back door on the driver's side opened. The music blared even louder, drowning out everything including the winter wind. Out of the car stepped a huge native kid, about six three, over two hundred fifty pounds. He was dressed like he was straight out of Compton or what he probably thought Compton gangs wore, with oversized jeans, a black hoodie over an old L.A. Raiders jersey, and a large, red ball cap perched on his head and turned sideways. Whether he was a member of Redd Alert, I couldn't confirm but it was pretty obvious. The red cap meant something, his colors.

His face was covered with a black balaclava; I didn't know whether it was to protect against the cold or because he didn't want to be identified. For the first few seconds, he didn't look at me. He scanned the area, like he was a Secret Service agent and the President of the United States was about to step out.

It was a little funny, this big native kid, dressing in gangsta fashion and acting like meeting me was some kind of high end security deal. I stifled the urge to laugh because I didn't want to ruin the meeting. And also, I knew that behind the flash and the image, these guys were not poseurs. Guys like this had set Marvin on fire.

When he finally looked at me, there was no emotion in his eyes. He grunted my name and I nodded. He reached out a hand, and for several seconds I had no idea what he wanted. But then I realized he wanted some kind of confirmation, so I pulled out my wallet and handed him my business card. He spent several long seconds reading it and looking back at me. When he was satisfied, he handed it back and I stuck it into my back pocket.

He pointed at my notebook tucked under my arm, twisted his

wrist and gestured with his index finger for me to hand it over. I did. He flipped through the pages, and I expected him to hand it back. He tossed it away like a Frisbee, the wind pulling it into the dark. He then stepped forward and patted me down. It was a bit rough but I was expecting it. He reached into my right coat pocket and found my recorder. He dropped it to the ground and crushed it under one of his high-tops. On my belt he found my cell phone.

He turned it over in his hand, flipped it open and pushed a few buttons. He held it out, as if he was handing it back, and I reached for it. The second before I could, he dropped it and crushed it underneath his foot.

I looked at him, and even through his balaclava, I could see he was smiling. It was a mean smile but also a mischievous one, the way a little kid looks when he knows he's done something bad but doesn't care.

I replied with a Gallic shrug, something I learned pretty young from my French-Canadian dad. He stepped back and gestured toward the door.

I had no cell phone, no recorder, no notebook. I had no way of contacting anyone and no way of keeping notes for my story. I had signed out the vehicle earlier in the afternoon but told no one where I was going, who I was going to meet, or when I was going to come back.

Francis's voice echoed in my head. "This is not a good thing, so don't be happy about it," he had said. "These are dangerous people."

I could have backed out and left, and no doubt ended up somewhere I could gamble. I had been waiting a long time for something to happen tonight, and the urge was very strong. If I backed out, I'd have to blow off that tension somewhere. So I couldn't leave.

I had to step into the vehicle because, in my mind, the other choice was worse.

And I couldn't let go of the story. If I went with these guys, then someone tonight might let it slip that they had killed Marvin. Or knew someone who did. And if they did, I could let that rest.

So I got into the vehicle.

19

There were three more of them in the Hummer; all three were different versions of the first one: big native guys wearing some kind of gangsta garb. All of them had a piece of red clothing somewhere on their person, either a cap or bandana. The other guy in the backseat to my right had his bandana covering the lower half of his face and mirrored sunglasses covering his eyes.

The two guys in the front only wore sunglasses, but I wasn't going to lean forward to get a better look at their faces; I wasn't that stupid.

The guy who had crushed my cell phone and recorder climbed into the vehicle and shut the door. An instant later, the Hummer pulled out of the parking lot without stopping to see if there was any traffic on 101st. We headed south. I heard a few car horns behind us but said nothing. In fact no one said a thing as we drove through various parts of Edmonton's inner city, along 107th Avenue near my old neighborhood in Kush, back east onto Stony Plain Road, past the casino on the north side of the street and the rest of downtown on the south.

We went past the Police HQ, over through Chinatown and Little Italy, into Norwood and McCauley, along Alberta Avenue and the neighborhoods around there and everything in between.

We made various versions of this circuit many times, even crossing the High Level Bridge to the south side, only to drop down

Walterdale Hill into the river valley, and come across the bridge and back to the Northside.

Throughout the entire trip, no one said anything. The only sound was the sound of the music, the heavy bass of hip-hop pounding through the speakers, filling the air with its weight.

I was not unfamiliar with hip-hop music; Peter was a fan, but this stuff was much harder than the stuff Peter listened to. But there was a strange feel to the songs. In some there was native singing in the background with the hip-hop rhythm, and in one, there was a traditional native flute fused with the beat and the angry, hardcore lyrics.

I knew I should have felt afraid being trapped in a large SUV with four very large and probably dangerous gang members, circling Edmonton's inner city. But in truth I was bored.

At first I'd felt some trepidation, and second-guessed myself, but after a while came boredom and repetition. Even the heavy hip-hop beats started to wear on me.

It felt no different than one of many summer car trips that my family took to Quebec every year after Mom and Dad had just had one of their arguments. We would travel for miles through dull lands around the U.S. interstates of North Dakota and Minnesota—Dad would drive through the northern U.S. states to get to Quebec in order to miss the long ride through the Canadian Shield north of Lake Superior—and no one would say a word.

I knew what these guys were trying to do: to confuse me and to dull me into some kind of submission so whenever it was time to talk, I would be out of sorts and whoever was doing the talking would have the upper hand. Or at least they thought they would. I had lived on these same inner city streets for over two years and I probably knew way more about them than these guys.

I knew not just which street led into what, which ones were one-ways and which ones weren't. I also knew which businesses had the best Dumpsters, where was the best place to get out of the wind, who hung around where, and any other street-level details you could think of. These guys may have been gang members, but like the police, they rolled past in their vehicles, away from what was truly happening.

And these guys had never been on a Desroches cross-country trip to Quebec trapped in the car with a dad who drank beer while he drove and a mother who sulked because Dad drank beer when he drove, and two sisters who kept fighting over unseen borders in the backseat . . . but only when one of them wasn't puking out the side window.

And in that SUV, like in my silent family car when I was a kid, I wanted to say something. I wanted to make a joke, to fart, or burp, or to make some kind of noise to break the tension.

But I didn't.

Not in the family car, because I would get an elbow in the ribs from one of my sisters.

And not in the SUV, because at the very least I would probably get a punch in the mouth from one of the gang members. Or they would toss me out while the vehicle was still moving.

So I waited, silent, knowing that none of these guys was the one I was supposed to meet and talk to. These were only the delivery personnel. They could have sent one, but four made more of an impact, created more of an image of toughness that the gang wanted to impart to me. For all I knew, these were the only guys in the gang. But I doubted that. After Detective McKinley mentioned the name Redd Alert to me, I'd done some research on the group.

There was nothing in Infomat, the paper's in-house search system, which only meant that no one in any of the papers in the chain had mentioned the name in any of their stories.

On the Net, there wasn't much, except some information on a few police, prison, and native gang sites. The gang was formed in the nineties at the Edmonton Max, a federal penitentiary about twenty kilometers north of Edmonton. At that time, the Correctional Service of Canada, the government department that oversaw the federal prison system, decided that the gangs were getting too much power and influence over the prison population. And since the aboriginal population in Canadian prisons was large—very similar to the way the African-American prison population was large compared to the overall population in the real world—many of these gangs were native ones.

So in their infinite wisdom, the Correctional Service had felt that transferring many of the inmates to other prisons across Canada would dilute their power. But instead, it had spread their power, as transferred gang members from areas that had a much bigger native gang population had set up chapters in prisons that didn't have much of a gang presence.

A large number of these inmates had come from the Stony Mountain Penitentiary in Manitoba and were members of the Warriors prison gang. And when they showed up at the Edmonton Max, they decided to take over the in-house drug trade from the local native prisoners.

To fight this, the local native inmates decided to band together and formed Redd Alert, adopting red as their official color to symbolize their native background. In prison, they fought the Warriors for the drug trade and when various members of the respective gangs were released into the Edmonton area, they fought for their bits of the drug trade in Edmonton.

Because of their Manitoba roots, the Warriors had a tougher time. Released members of Redd Alert had connections to all the reserves in the area and therefore had an easier time attracting recruits. Many of these recruits came from bands around the Hobbema area, which had a controversial way of sharing its proceeds from oil development with its band members.

Oil companies drilling for and removing oil, natural gas, and sour gas from Alberta had to pay royalties on every barrel they removed, either to the province or, if they were drilling in a reserve, to the native bands. They also had to pay for access to these sites and for any environmental impact on traditional native lands.

Deals of this sort brought millions of dollars into native communities, which used the money to develop a wide variety of community services and buildings. They also built housing for native band members. Some offered annual rebates to their band members in the same way Alaskans got a check from the government because of oil exploration. But a few shared the money in a different and highly controversial way.

These bands put the money into a trust fund, and whenever a member turned eighteen, they would get a one-time payment. And these payments weren't small; they could range from $50,000 to over $150,000, depending on how much money was in the trust fund at the time, the prevailing price of oil, and how many people were turning eighteen then.

Most of these kids, who had a much tougher time growing up than the average Canadian kid despite the oil revenues in the community, lived at a lower economic standard, and blew their money within a few months. They bought cars or big trucks that were fully loaded, like the SUV I was riding in. They threw parties and gave lavish gifts to friends and family. Some would put part of the money aside for education, but even those often had a difficult time dealing with a six-figure check as an eighteen-year-old.

And others, those who were involved in gangs, would give a good chunk of their money to their gang. So with this kind of money coming in every year, along with the monies from their criminal activities, Redd Alert became the most prominent and powerful native gang, not just in Alberta, but in all of western Canada. They allied themselves with gangs such as the Hell's Angels and clashed with others such as the strong Asian gangs in Vancouver.

All that information was ready to be used in a story for the paper but I needed someone from Redd Alert or another native gang to talk to me. Driving around in a Hummer would add a nice element but the story wouldn't be complete unless I got some good quotes.

Finally, there was a noise that had nothing to do with hip-hop or the sound of the SUV's heater. Something vibrated and I turned to see that it was a phone that belonged to the guy on my left, the one who had searched me.

He answered it, but said nothing. I could hear a voice on the other side, but couldn't pick up any words. It spoke for only a few seconds and then Balaclava Guy turned and held the phone in front of me. After a second of wondering what was going on, I realized that I was supposed to answer it. I took it from Balaclava Guy.

"Hello?" I said, tentatively.

"Mr. Desroches." It wasn't a question. The voice was male, clear and firm. He also pronounced my last name correctly.

"Speaking."

"I was told you wished to talk to me."

"Yeah, I guess. I'm doing a story on native gangs in the city and I was hoping to talk to someone from Redd Alert or from any other native gang. Is that who I'm talking to now?"

"I wouldn't call us a gang but that would just be an argument for semantics and I don't think a journalist would be interested in that kind of argument."

"I might if you thought it was important," I said. I didn't want to control too much of the interview. If he wanted to talk about why he didn't like his group being called a gang, that might give me some insight into this group. "But is there anyplace we can talk in person? It's really hard to hear you over the sound of the music and the engine."

"Don't worry, Mr. Desroches, we're getting to that," he said with a chuckle. "I'm sorry you've had to experience a long tour of the city but we're in a bit of a conflict with one or two other gangs and we want to make sure we're not being followed before we actually meet."

I was going to say something to the effect that if they didn't want to be followed, they shouldn't be driving one of the most tricked-out Hummers I had ever seen, but thought better of it.

"So what happens now?" I asked instead.

"Give the phone back to our member and we'll take it from there."

I held out the phone to Balaclava Guy, thinking that it was funny how, like the cops, gangbangers used the term *member* to describe another gangbanger. "He wants to talk to you," I said.

He took it from me, listened for a second, and moved to put the phone back into his pocket. At the same time, he tapped the driver on the shoulder. A second later, there was a popping sound.

The window on my left exploded and I was sprayed with glass and some kind of wet material. Something stung me on the left shoulder, like a giant wasp, and I felt another one on the side of my head behind my ear. I didn't have time to react and check to see what had stung me because Balaclava Guy grunted and fell against me, his heavy body pushing me down onto the seat.

More wetness poured onto me, drenching my face and my shoulder.

Someone yelled—"Shit!"—and I felt the SUV lurch to the right, then left. The back window exploded and the Hummer powered forward, the roar of the engine drowning out even the hip-hop. There was a crunch of metal on one side and the SUV jerked back and forth.

Balaclava Guy wrenched back and forth, but only in response to the quick movements of the SUV. He was lifeless, his limbs flailing like a rag doll's.

"Go, go, go!" someone shouted, and there were more popping noises. Bullets battered the side of the vehicle and I heard some whizzing noise overhead. One of the headrests blew into pieces, foam and leather bursting out, then drifting down like a late March snowfall.

I looked up and saw the guy with the bandana on his face pull a large pistol from his pants and start shooting through the opening where the back window used to be. The flashes blinded me, and my ears raged in pain after each blast. But even through that and the ringing that came afterward, I could hear the shattering of glass in the distance and the squeal of rubber as another vehicle swerved away. Our vehicle jerked to the right so quickly that it tilted up on two wheels.

For a second, we were weightless and I waited for the SUV to roll over. But it righted itself in a heavy jolt, and a couple bounces later, we were racing away, the engine roaring. We drove this way for a couple blocks and then the guy in the front passenger seat turned to the back.

"Get him out!" he shouted. I knew he was talking about me and I struggled to push Balaclava Guy off me. But he was too heavy.

The other guy in the backseat stretched over me and popped open the back door. The wind blew it back so hard that it almost snapped off.

The vehicle slowed as we turned a corner but that didn't stop him from reaching underneath me, and heaving me and the dead guy out the door. I felt the blast of the wind, not just from the winter, but from the momentum of our movement. We flew for a second, and I knew the only way for me to survive the landing was to hang on to the body as hard as I could, hoping it would break most of my fall.

There was a crunch of bone and flesh as we hit the pavement. Our heads connected and I felt a flash of pain; then for a second or two, I knew nothing, only darkness.

And then I felt my body rolling, and the pavement was about to come up and hit me. Instead, I got caught in a line of hedges, the branches scratching and tearing at my heavy winter parka. Some of the hedges gave away, several of the branches snapping off, but the whole held—held us, breaking the rest of our fall. Then, slowly, the hedge flexed back against our combined weight and tossed us off. I found myself lying on top of Balaclava Dude on a sidewalk somewhere in the heart of the inner city.

I was covered in blood, but most of it didn't belong to me. Balaclava Guy had a small hole on one side of his head and the other side of it was missing. His arms and legs were bent in odd positions because of the fall.

I pushed off him and patted my body, flexing my arms, hands, and legs, searching for any injuries. One of my wrists seemed a bit tender but I could move it so I knew it wasn't broken. There were two sharp pains on my left side. I felt behind my ear and winced when I touched a shard of glass that was lodged there. It was about the size of a dime, and when I pulled it out, I felt the heat of blood trailing down my neck. I tossed the glass aside.

I checked my shoulder, which felt like it had been stung by something and I saw that my jacket had been torn and there was a two-inch-long wound. It hurt like a bitch but I knew I was lucky. The bullet that went through Balaclava's brain had bounced around enough to give me only a flesh wound. I made a note to tell the doctor who would be treating it so he would make sure I didn't get an infection.

My ears rang, but I could hear the sirens in the distance. I could have waited quietly for them to come but I didn't want to. I had lost my native gang story but if I kept myself focused for a few more minutes, I would have another one.

I patted my pockets, then remembered that my cell phone was in pieces in the parking lot of the Native Friendship Centre. But the guy who had broken my phone had just talked on one, and it had to be around here somewhere. I looked around and was about to pat his pockets the way he had done mine, but I didn't have to. His phone was exactly where it had been before all the shooting started: in his hand. I pried it loose, and as I did, I saw he had the same tattoo as Marvin. I sighed once and then punched in a number. There was an hour or so before the final deadline; the night editor would be surprised to hear from me.

20

The cops that arrived first grabbed the phone from my hand and pushed me to the ground. One of them slipped some plastic twist-tie cuffs around my wrists and then pulled me to a sitting position. This cop was Sikh, sporting a thick black beard and a turban instead of a hat. He was a big man and easily turned me left and right, looking me over. Behind him, the other cop, of Chinese descent, was talking into his shoulder mic, probably calling in more backup, an ambulance, probably both.

"You okay?" the Sikh cop asked in a nonaccented voice.

I nodded because I was too tired to speak. I had used most of my energy to narrate the story to Elizabeth Cash, the night editor. Since she worked late nights we rarely met, but we were aware of each other. She was quick and professional, and would probably replace Mandy once she left her city editor position in a couple of years. Even though she was surprised when I called, after I started reciting the story she didn't interrupt me.

No doubt she was typing everything up while making a mental note to contact the police about the situation, and punching in the number to wake up whatever shooter was on call that night.

When I finished, she efficiently double-checked most of my facts, including my location. When we were done, she asked if I was okay.

I told her I was, and that was when the police arrived and they took away my phone.

Well, not my phone.

"Is this your blood?" the Sikh cop asked me. I shook my head and pointed at the dead gang member on the sidewalk next to me. He glanced over and winced when he saw the condition of Balaclava Dude. His partner stepped over and gave the body a light kick.

He looked over at his partner and shook his head. The Sikh cop swallowed a couple of times and shook his head quickly to clear himself.

"Did you shoot him?"

I shook my head and held out my handcuffed hands to show they were empty.

"Do you know who did?"

Again, I shook my head.

He pulled out his police-issue notebook and made some notes. After a second, he looked back to me. "Can you tell me what happened?"

Another shake.

"Why not?"

" 'Cause it's cold. I'm cold. Put me in the back of your warm car and I'll tell you what happened."

"Tell me what happened first and then I'll put you in the back of the warm car."

"Sorry. Warm car first and then I'll talk. That way we can both be warm and your partner can hang outside, establish a perimeter, and deal with anyone who drives up."

His eyes widened for a second and then he smiled. "Okay then." He pulled me up to a standing position. While we were standing, he gave me another quick pat-down search. He found my wallet in my back pocket and pulled it out. He tucked it into his jacket pocket and guided me to the car.

Over his shoulder he shouted to his partner, who was searching the area for the gun or any other evidence. "Carl. I'm going to interview this guy in the car. Keep an eye out for backup and anyone else."

Carl nodded but gave his partner the finger. "Fuck you, Ravin. You're buying coffee later." The comment wasn't mean, it was a friendly jest, common to coworkers or partners who have known each other for a long time.

Constable Ravin—I didn't know if it was his first or last name because I hadn't checked his name tag yet—smiled and walked me over to the cruiser. He opened the back door and gently set me in, putting his hand on my head so I wouldn't bump myself on the frame.

I normally don't like being put into the backseat of a cruiser, especially considering what happened last fall, when I was shanghaied by two cops and dumped in an industrial zone. This time, it was welcoming. If all my experiences with police cruisers were like this, I would never complain.

Constable Ravin got into the front seat, and rubbed his hands. He reached to the dash, turned up the heat, and sighed as the fan increased the temperature. He turned to look at me, his notebook at the ready, but then he paused.

He set the notebook on the dashboard and pulled out his cell phone. He held it up in front of me, and snapped a couple of photos. Then he reached under his seat. He pulled out a package of wet towelettes, those things I used to use to wipe my kids' butts when I was changing their diapers, and handed it to me.

"Clean yourself off first and then we can talk."

I took the package and pulled one out, but it was covered in blood in a second. It took almost the whole package before there was no blood when I wiped myself. My hair was stuck together because of the blood and I tried to clean it. But it was too sticky and difficult. It was also filled with little bits of debris, glass, and other things I didn't really want to know where or who they came from.

With my last few pieces, I wiped the wound on my arm, hoping that this would help prevent any infection, because the bullet had come through someone's head before it struck me.

There was a pile of used towelettes on the seat next to me and Constable Ravin gave me a small blue plastic bag to put them in. Then he took the bag and tucked it under his seat. By the time this was done, a few more cop cars had pulled up, along with an ambulance. The paramedics went over to the body and looked it over, while the cops started stretching out yellow crime-scene tape around the area. One of the cops started snapping photos but there were also a few more, brighter flashes coming from across the street.

Everyone looked over there and I saw a shooter from the paper, popping shots. I couldn't make out who it was, but I smiled inwardly at the efficiency of Night Editor Cash. Larry would be pleasantly surprised to wake up with an unexpected front page of tomorrow's issue.

"You okay?" Constable Ravin asked. "Do you want some water?" I read his name tag and saw that Ravin was his first name and that I probably couldn't pronounce his last name correctly on the first try.

"No, thanks."

"Okay, we'll get started Mr. . . ." His voice trailed off as he read the name on my driver's license. To his credit, he didn't attempt to pronounce it, probably because people butchered his name all the time, so he didn't like to repeat the offense.

"Desroches," I said. "Leo Desroches."

"Yes. Mr. Desroches. Can you tell me what happened? Can you tell me why we find you covered in blood, sitting beside someone who was obviously shot in the head?"

So I told him who I was, what I was looking for, and everything that had happened, from the time I was picked up to the time my dead companion and I were thrown from the truck. Constable Ravin was patient and took thorough notes. He didn't interrupt, except to ask specific details such as the truck's location when the shooting started, if I knew what time it was when it started, if I saw the car that fired on us, and in which direction both vehicles went after the excitement. He would have made a solid reporter.

I told him where we were when the shooting started—about a block and a half northwest of Giovanni Caboti Park—but I had no idea what the other car looked like or where everyone went afterward.

"Okay, okay. Thanks for being so cooperative with me, Mr. Desroches. I'm going to leave you in the cruiser for a moment. But I'll be sending the paramedics to come take a look at you because it seems you've suffered a couple of minor injuries. Also, I should tell you that someone else, probably from Homicide, will be talking to you and you'll have to tell your story again."

"That's okay. I'm aware of that."

"Okay, then, you sit tight and I'll get you looked at."

There was a brief blast of cold as he opened the door, and I thought if this was an example of the cops they were hiring these days, I would have to change my opinion about the state of the Edmonton Police Service.

I knew it was going to be a long night and I'd be having a lot of shakes and sweats over the next few weeks as I thought about what happened, but for the moment, I basked in the warmth of the cruiser.

21

After the paramedics decided that the guy in the street was dead, they came over to me. Constable Ravin opened the door to let one of them come in to take a look.

She was about five five, fit, as most paramedics are, with her brown hair pulled back in a tight bun. She leaned down to look into the cruiser. She stared at me for several seconds, assessing the situation, before she stood up and turned to Ravin.

"He okay?" she asked with a bit of trepidation in her voice. "He's not dangerous, is he?"

Ravin smiled slightly and shook his head. "He's harmless. He's only a victim and a witness."

"You sure? I don't like working in the backseat of a cruiser even if you do say he's harmless."

"Don't worry, he's harmless."

"If he's harmless why's he handcuffed in the backseat of your cruiser?" she asked. I thought it was a good question and wondered myself.

"I'm not allowed to uncuff him until someone from Homicide comes over to talk to him. Don't worry about this guy. He can't hurt you. I'd bet my life on it."

"Yeah, but would you bet my life on it?" said the paramedic. I didn't blame her for worrying about me. One minute she was probably hanging out at the ambulance station, watching TV, maybe having a snooze. And the next, she was on a call about a shooting in the inner city. And when she showed up, there was a dead body in the street, half his head blown away and his limbs twisted into unnatural positions because his lifeless body had been thrown out of a moving vehicle.

And the only other person the police had in connection to this scene was some guy, handcuffed in the backseat of a cruiser, his head all sticky with blood and other bodily bits, his jacket torn to shreds, an oozy hole the size of a dime on the side of his neck and a flesh wound caused by a bullet that probably also caused all that damage to the dead guy's head.

I wouldn't want to get in the same car with that guy . . . and I *was* that guy.

The paramedic stood her ground. "Sorry. I don't care what you say. I'm not going in there. You gotta bring him out."

"I can't bring him out. Homicide wants to talk to him first."

"So bring him over to the unit. I can work on him there, and when Homicide comes, they can talk to him there."

"I can't bring him out. He's gotta stay in there."

"But he needs to be treated. He's got a nasty oozing wound on his neck and a surface bullet wound on his arm that has a good chance of getting infected."

"So go treat him," Ravin said, pointing at the car.

"I'm not going in there. You have to bring him to the unit."

"I can't do that."

"You have to. I don't care if the pope wants to talk to him, he's got to be treated now. And the only way for him to get treatment is for you to bring him out. Now."

Ravin stared at the much smaller paramedic, giving her his best cop look. But she was having none of it. She stepped back, pointed at the car, and gestured at him to bring me out. He waited for a second and then sighed. He leaned into the car.

"Come on, Mr. Desroches, I gotta take you out," he said.

I scooted over as much as I could, swung my legs out the door, and then Ravin took me the rest of the way, pulling me up by my handcuffed wrists with one hand, while protecting my head with the other. I helped as much as I could with my legs but it hurt like hell.

I smiled at the paramedic when I was standing up straight but she gave me nothing in response. She turned and started walking to her unit. Ravin and I followed.

The paramedic was efficient and quick. She cleaned and patched up my wounds with precision and, I'll admit, a bit more pain than I hoped. But she said nothing to me. Because I was still in custody, they kept the back door of the unit open. Constable Ravin stood watch, like some kind of guardian to the Harimandar Sahib, the Sikh Golden Temple.

She was finishing up with the bullet wound on my shoulder when a plainclothes cop came to stand next to Constable Ravin. The constable stiffened for a second at the sight of a superior and then relaxed. For a minute or so, they conversed quietly, so I couldn't hear what they were saying. Every so often, Ravin pointed at me and the detective nodded.

I knew the plainclothes cop. He was Detective Al Whitford, a Homicide cop who'd dealt with me when I was working on the Grace Cardinal story. In fact, if it wasn't for him, there probably wouldn't have been a Grace Cardinal story. Whitford had broken protocol by letting me into the crime-scene tent that held her body and that had started my quest to find out what happened to her.

I liked Whitford. He was a decent cop, smart and honest. He looked to be in his mid-thirties, wore fashionable wire-rimmed glasses and a triangle-shaped soul patch underneath his lip. Every time I met him, I wanted to pull that little tuft of hair off his face.

He climbed into the paramedic unit and sat down on the bench to the right. The paramedic stopped working on me and gave him an inquiring look. He held out his ID. "Detective Whitford," he said formally. And then added, "Homicide."

She gave it a long look, nodded and continued cleaning my shoulder wound.

I nodded at him but he didn't acknowledge me. "He okay?" he asked the paramedic.

"He'll live," she said as she put a piece of gauze on my shoulder and taped it down. "He's got a small wound on his neck that I patched up, a surface bullet wound that I cleaned up pretty good, and a pretty nasty bruise on his wrist. Could be a minor stress fracture so I was hoping to take him in to get some X-rays just to be safe. We'll be heading out in a minute or so."

"Mind if I come along for the ride?" Whitford asked.

She shrugged. "Suit yourself. Can't give you a ride back, though."

"I'll find my way. If it's possible I'd prefer you ride up front so he and I can talk."

"You're not going to slap him around, are ya? I've made note of his wounds and if I see any more when I pull him out, I'd hate to have to fill in a bunch more paperwork." Her voice was so flat that I couldn't tell if she was joking or not.

Whitford gave her a small smile. "I just wanna talk to him. Leo and I go way back, don't we, Leo?" He looked me in the eye for the first time. He was disappointed, I could tell, but also concerned.

I nodded. "Yes, we do."

She looked at Whitford and then turned to me. "You sure you want me to leave?" she asked, speaking to me for the first time. " 'Cause I don't have to. I can stay."

Despite a tiny bit of roughness in her manner, I was glad there were emergency workers like her around. She might not like me or what I represented but she wasn't going to leave me in the back of her unit with a cop she didn't know.

"That's okay. I've known Al for a long time. He's a good guy."

She stared at me for a long moment to see if I was telling the truth. Then she nodded, and climbed into the front. "Let's go," she said to her partner, who had probably been listening to the entire conversation from the front seat.

Whitford gestured to Constable Ravin, who had been watching all along. He waited for a moment and then shut the back door. Whitford banged gently on the wall and the unit moved forward. Since I wasn't a critical case, we drove at a normal speed without sirens.

Whitford pulled off his glasses and rubbed his eyes. "Leo. What the heck are you doing in the middle of a gang shooting?"

"You know what I was doing. I'm working on a story about native gangs. You got all the information from Constable Ravin," I said. "Nice cop, by the way."

"Yeah, he's a decent sort. But I wanted to hear it from you. I want to hear what you've got yourself involved with and why."

So I gave him a quick rundown, knowing that he already knew most of it but was trying to confirm it or to see if there were any inconsistencies in my story. I knew I would have to tell it again a few more times tonight.

"So who told you to meet the gang tonight?"

"They didn't tell me to meet that gang. I asked to meet someone who wanted to talk about native gangs and I was told someone would meet me in the parking lot of the Friendship Centre. So that's where I went."

"Yeah, but who told you to go there?"

I didn't want to give Francis's name because I knew Whitford would go to interrogate him. "I can't tell you," I said.

"You have to."

"Why? He didn't do anything wrong. He was just a guy I asked to do me a favor, a favor he didn't want to do in the first place, but I pushed him and he did it. I don't want him to get into any trouble."

"I have to know who he is so maybe I can find out who told him they would meet you. And maybe through that I can find out who was involved in this shooting and if anybody knew it was going to happen before it happened."

I sighed, knowing Francis would probably never talk to me again once a Homicide cop came breathing down his neck. But I gave Whitford his name and contact info nevertheless. Whitford wrote it in his notebook.

"But he's an innocent, Al. He's a good guy. An elder in the community. I don't think he expected something like this to happen. And like I said, he didn't want to do this in the first place and told me I should forget it."

"You should have taken his advice," he said, shaking his head. "I don't know how you get mixed up in these things, Leo."

"Just lucky, I guess," I said with a small laugh that didn't have any enthusiasm behind it.

"Fuck you, Leo. You almost got killed tonight. If that bullet had hit you one inch in either direction, we wouldn't be having this conversation. You'd be lying on the street next to that dead gangbanger and I'd be the one that would have to go to your kids and tell them that their dad was dead."

"I'm sorry. I was only working on a story."

"That's always your excuse, isn't it? You got shot in a gang shootout tonight, almost killed, because you were working on a story.

You got the shit beat out of you because you were working on the Grace Cardinal story—"

"That wasn't my fault. You're the one who got me onto that story."

"Yeah, but I didn't tell you to pretend to be a cop so that when someone found you out, they'd beat the shit out of you. You had the story but you had to go deeper. The same thing with Gardiner. Because of your involvement you became a suspect in that case."

This news knocked me back onto my stretcher. I knew what I'd done in the Gardiner story. I still had nightmares about it, but I thought I was okay. Obviously I was wrong and how I responded now would make a big difference.

"I'm a suspect in the Gardiner case?" I asked as innocently as I could.

Whitford caught himself, his expression showing that he had given out too much information. "Not *are* a suspect, *were* a suspect. Past tense."

"But didn't he kill himself? Why would I be a suspect for a suicide?"

"It's just standard procedure. A cop dies, even an ex-cop like Gardiner, and we have to investigate. Even if it's a suicide, we have to investigate. We have to do everything we do for a regular case, try to figure out motives, see if anyone stands to gain from his death, who was close to him before he died, all that stuff, just to make sure.

"And since Gardiner was the one who gave you the information for that story you wrote, that put you on the list of suspects. That's why we had that interview just before Christmas. But like I said, you were on the list, you aren't now."

I sighed deeply, the tension in my body about being a suspect in the Gardiner story fading away. I closed my eyes for a second and felt the ambulance slow and then turn. We were pulling into the Emerg.

I knew I should have let it go and forget about it, but I was the one who had begun the Gardiner story. And I had to find out where it was at the moment.

"So is there anybody else on the suspect list? Or is that it? Is Gardiner a suicide or not?"

Whitford gave me a long look and I couldn't figure out what his expression meant. Was he still disappointed over my actions tonight or was it sadness that I almost died?

"Why you asking? You barely knew the guy."

Yeah, but I knew enough, I thought. Out loud I said, "I'm just curious. He seemed like a decent cop." I added a shrug to complete the picture.

"He was a rat," Whitford said quickly, using the term for a cop who turned in another. It was a surprise to hear him use that expression in that tone of voice but I guess nobody in the police service liked a rat. Even the good cops. "So the Gardiner case is dead. There were some suspicions but all signs point to a suicide."

"Suspicions, what kind of suspicions?"

Whitford paused before he answered, this time sighing as he did. "Doesn't matter. To everyone in the department, Gardiner was a rat. And now he's dead, signs point to a suicide and that's it. Nobody's going to look deeper for a rat."

I hope the relief I felt inside didn't show on the outside.

22

By the time I got through with Whitford and the X-rays, it was too late to go home. At least that was the story I was sticking to. I could have gone home and taken the rest of the day off because of my injuries, but I didn't want to go home. If I did, I would start to think about all that had happened that night, and how close I came to death.

I would look at my bandaged arm and imagine what would have happened if Balaclava Dude had turned his head a fraction of a second earlier. Then the trajectory of the bullet would have changed. And instead of just giving me a nasty flesh wound, and a face full of Balaclava Guy's brains, the bullet would have sliced through my arm and into my chest.

The number of possible scenarios from last night was great, and I had a good imagination. But despite my imagination, every scenario I envisioned resulted in only one outcome: my death.

So I couldn't go home to sleep and recover. I would only fall apart into a mewling mess on my kitchen floor. Or I would attempt to quell the nightmares with other means, such as gambling. Or worse, by hitting a bank.

A few months ago, when I was working on the Grace Cardinal story, I had developed the odd habit of robbing small, strip-mall banks. My life was never in danger, because Canadian security and gun laws meant that most banks didn't have security guards. And if they did, they were never armed.

But there was always the chance that I would get caught. The police were aware that a person of my general description was behind a series of bank robberies. They even had a blurry photo of me in my ball cap at one of these banks. There was no way to discern if it was really me in the photo because my description, Caucasian male, with brownish hair, average height and weight, was pretty generic.

The weird part was that when the police went to the media about this bank robber, I was the one who actually wrote the story. It was then that I thought I'd better step away from hitting banks. But without the thrill of banks, I needed a different source of thrill, so gambling came back into play.

And to keep away from gambling, I had to work on stories about Marvin's death, and the role of native gangs in the city. Which then resulted in me being exposed to guys who drove giant SUVs and got into gunfights.

It was a vicious cycle and I couldn't find a way out, except to head back to work and find an assignment to keep me busy.

Mandy, the city editor, was waiting for me at the reception desk, barring my way into the newsroom. I had a feeling Dr. Sen may have called after he did a quick look-see of my injuries when I came in the front entrance. His medical opinion was for me to go home and rest for a couple of days.

And I have no doubt that when I rebuffed him, he called on a higher power: Mandy.

When she saw me, her face was livid, although there was a touch of concern, as well. And I didn't blame her. I was a mess, both physically and mentally. Not only was some of my hair still caked with dried blood, my jacket was torn in places where I had been shot and had landed in the row of hedges. The wound on my neck was closed with a couple of stitches but the doctor had decided to forgo placing a bandage on them.

My wrist had not been broken in the fall but it was severely bruised, an ugly yellow and purple stain that was slowly spreading to the back of my hand and fingers.

I was also totally exhausted from the intensity of the experience and a lack of sleep, so the usual dark circles under my eyes probably made me look like I had been punched in the face.

"Go home, Leo," Mandy said, stepping in front of me. Her lips were pursed tightly.

"I'm okay, Mandy. It's worse than it looks." But she was having none of it.

"I said go home."

"But you guys are short-staffed. I don't want to let the team down." I tried to walk around her but she stepped in front of me again.

"You already filed your story today so your work is done. Go home."

"But what about tomorrow?"

"Don't worry about tomorrow, we can handle tomorrow. In fact, we can handle it for the next few days, so don't come back until Monday."

"Boy, now that you're the city editor, you're really pushing your weight around, aren't you?" I smiled when I said that so she would know I was only joking, but I saw that it hurt.

"Just go home, Leo. It doesn't look good when our reporters get involved in a gang shooting and then come to work the next day. You did a good job filing the story afterward, but you have to let it go. You need to rest."

I sighed. "Okay, I'll go home. But I got to get something from my desk before I do."

My plan was to get to my desk and then settle in for the day. Even if I didn't have an assignment, I could at least sit in a safe, nongambling place and be part of the action.

"What do you need? I'll have one of the interns get it for you."

"That's okay, they'll never find it. It won't take a sec." I made another move to get by Mandy.

But she was quicker than me. This time, not only did she step in front of me, she placed a hand on my chest and pushed back. It was a hard push, hard enough to knock me back a couple of steps.

"Jeez, Mandy. What the hell? I just wanna get stuff from my desk and then I'll go home."

"No. You'll go home now. Because if you don't, I'll drag you back there myself and lock you in."

"That might be fun."

She slapped me across the face. Not a hard one but enough to get my attention. Normally, it would have only surprised me, but because of my condition, it actually made me black out for a microsecond and I only managed to hold myself upright by grabbing onto the reception desk.

There was an audible gasp from the people in the newsroom but Mandy grabbed me by the shoulders, pushed around the corner to get out of the view of the crowd, and shoved me against the wall.

"Don't you make fun of me," she hissed, her eyes filling up with tears. "Don't you ever make fun of me like that!"

My shoulder flared in pain as she gripped it and I lashed out. "Jesus! Mandy! Don't you know that I just got shot?"

There was a second when I thought she was going to hit me again, so I shut my eyes and prepared for it. But instead, she leaned forward and kissed me. It wasn't a nice first-date kind of kiss like the one she had given me a couple nights before. It was a full, deep-tongued kiss that people give each other just before they tear their clothes off. It lasted only a couple of seconds, but it had been years since a woman kissed me like that. It seemed endless. When she released me, I was out of breath.

She was mad and let me have it. "That's right, Leo. You just got shot. You were in a gunfight where one person was killed and another was seriously wounded." Her voice was hushed and urgent at the same time. Tears were streaming down her face and I could tell that despite the kiss, she was in pain.

"So when somebody gets shot and almost dies, they don't come to work the next day as if nothing happened. They don't pretend they're all right when everyone knows they aren't. And they don't pretend that life will go on as usual when all their friends are worried about them. Worried that they got hurt. Worried that they might have died. You're not allowed to do that! I won't let you."

She stepped back and buried her face in her hands. Her body was shaking with sobs. I wanted to step forward and hug her but I couldn't. I didn't have the strength to hug anybody or to take care of anybody else because I really didn't have the strength to take care of myself. I knew what would happen if I left this building.

"I can't go home, Mandy," I said quietly. "If I go home, I won't go home. You, of all people here, know what I'm talking about."

She looked at me, exhausted by the emotions but with understanding in her eyes. "You just have to fight it then, Leo. Every day you have to fight. Every day. You can't give up."

"But it's hard. It's too hard."

She stepped forward, pulled me into her, and I buried my face in her neck. "I know it's hard. Every day it's hard. Every day you keep wanting it, knowing that it will make you feel good. But that's only for a short time. Life isn't easy in the best of times and it's harder when you're addicted to something. But you've got to fight it, because if you don't, it'll kill you. And no one wants you to die, Leo. Not even yourself, no matter what you tell yourself."

Everything that I had been holding in for the past few hours, for the past few months, escaped. I let it all go. Mandy's neck and arms was a warm and comforting place, a place that I wanted to live in for a long time, but I knew I couldn't. Not for long.

She was right that it was hard. But I didn't want to die. Every time someone or something tried to kill me, I fought back. I would always fight back against dying. My problem was that I couldn't figure out a good way to live.

23

Larry was standing right there when the elevators doors opened on the main floor. His face was red with anger.

"Tell me why I shouldn't fire your sorry ass right now," he growled.

"Because I'm the best reporter you have. I just gave you one of the best front-page stories you've had in a long time."

He stepped forward, his face just six inches from mine. "That's not good enough."

"It should be."

"It should, but it's not 'cause you're a crazy fucking asshole who thinks he knows better than everyone else, and you're so determined to prove it that you almost got yourself killed in the process."

"Well, that part wasn't my fault."

"Not your fault," he said with disbelief in his voice. "You were in an SUV in the middle of the inner city with a bunch of gangbangers, what did you expect?"

"There was no way I could have foreseen these guys would get in a firefight."

"There was no way *I* could have foreseen that, either, but at least *I'm* smart enough to realize that if I climb into a Hummer full of native gangbangers, there's a strong possibility that something violent might happen. Jesus, Leo, what the hell were you thinking?"

There was only one answer to that question. "I was on a story."

"A story! There was no fucking story!" Larry's voice rose in pitch and he looked as if he was going to have a coronary. Dr. Sen watched with concern from his security station and I could see there were a couple of people at the customer service desk. They had turned at the sound of Larry's voice. But Larry didn't care if there were thousands watching. That was one of his strengths; if he had something to say to you, he would say it, no matter how harsh it was or who was watching. "There was only you and your dumbass 'trying to turn nothing into something' even when you were told specifically to drop the story in the first place."

"I didn't think that was the right decision."

"But that's not your fucking decision to make, is it? Decisions on what kind of story you are assigned to cover aren't up to you. That's why we call them assignments."

"It should be," I replied, my voice rising in tone with his. "If I left it up to you to decide what makes a good story all the time, then I might as well quit right now. If we're all going to sit at our desks, do phoners all the time, and pound out the same generic three-hundred-word stories that everyone else is doing in order to save money and to please our advertisers and the useless board of directors in Toronto, then we might as well pack it in today and leave it to the bloggers to cover the news."

"Well, that's already happening right now with the bloggers, and if we're not careful, we are going to *have* to pack it in. And it doesn't help that I have to deal with someone like you all the time. It makes it much harder."

"Guys like me give you front-page stories that you haven't seen in years."

"That was just luck, Leo, and you know it," he said, leaning in again. "You were lucky not to get killed, let alone get that story."

"I got the story, didn't I? That's all that counts, isn't it?"

He backed away and thought I saw a small smile come across his face. But it was fleeting and his face was very serious again. "Not anymore, Leo. Not anymore. Maybe ten or fifteen years ago this kind of journalism would work, but with Canadian soldiers dying in Afghanistan, your actions last night, regardless of the story you got, smack of recklessness and stupidity. You not only put your life at risk, you've damaged the reputation of the newspaper, making us look like a bunch of yahoos who would do anything for a good story. And that's not what we're about. We're about good, solid journalism, and getting in the middle of a gangbanger firefight is not good, solid journalism."

"But neither is sitting on my ass writing the same boring story over and over again. If you want to stand out against the bloggers and the Internet news sites, we've got to reaffirm why people used to turn to us for news, even if they could get the same story off the TV and the radio. We can't just do what everyone else is doing because playing it safe will only make it worse."

Larry stepped back and sighed. I don't know if he heard me or understood what I was saying. For years, newspapers had been playing it safe, assuming that their history and standing in the community would keep them alive during the Internet revolution. And now that they were suffering, nearing their demise, many newspapers jumped on the Internet bandwagon, using Twitter, Facebook, Web and video blog posts to capture some of their lost market. But in their zeal to appeal to the vast Internet audience they also forgot that newspapers had a lot of strengths, such as great writers who had the ability to tell a great story using rich, resonant language that could reach out and touch the readers. So instead of using those strengths and creating something new and powerful, they just acted like lemmings and did what everyone else was already doing.

"Okay, Leo. This is what is going to happen," Larry said, after a moment of thought. "First, you are going to go home, take tomorrow and the weekend off and recover from what happened last night. Got that?"

I nodded.

Larry shook his head. "I need you to say it. I need you to say that you are going to go home and take care of yourself."

"Okay, Larry," I said with a sigh. "I am going to go home and take care of myself."

"And when you get back to work on Monday, we might think about you pursuing your friend's story a bit more."

"Thanks, Larry, that—"

"I said might. That doesn't mean it will happen. I have to think about it. But if you do this story, I'm still going to need you to do all of your other work that is assigned to you. You of all people know that kind of work still has got to be done. Modern-day journalism isn't getting thrown out of a SUV after a firefight. There's a lot of grunt work that needs to be done and many times it's that grunt work that leads you to bigger stories."

"I hear you. You're right and I'm sorry I forgot about that."

"Apology is not accepted. What you did last night was inexcusable. Which brings me to my next condition. If you are going to work on some kind of story or go to any kind of interview or event after hours or after your regular shift, you have to tell someone at the paper where you are going, who you are going to meet—if you can—and when we can expect you to come back. And when you are back, you must call and tell someone that you are back. You got that?"

"Yes, boss. I do."

"I'm not joking here," Larry said with a deep frown. "If you don't fulfill any of that, I don't care who you are, how long we've been friends, or whether it will cause you to end up in the street again, I will fire you instantly. You got that? Instantly."

"I got that." I really did, because I knew he meant it.

"Okay, one other thing. If I find out you've been gambling again, I will also fire you instantly. And there is no way you can claim that I've treated you unfairly because of your addiction. I already have enough cause to fire you right now."

"Okay, Larry. I hear you. I promise to be good."

"You better be, because this is your last chance." He slapped me on the shoulder with the back of his hand. "Now get the fuck out of my sight before I change my mind."

"Okay. See you Monday," I said as I walked toward the front door. I was reaching for the handle when Larry called out to me.

"Oh, yeah, Leo. One last thing."

I paused and turned toward him. "What? What else?"

"That was one hell of a story you wrote. Can't believe you managed to file that sucker after you got shot at and tossed out of an SUV. That's incredible fucking journalism. Don't let it happen again."

24

Despite Mandy's assurance that if I worked hard enough I would be fine, and Larry's threats, I went to the casino. I went there in the same way an animal finds a safe den after it has been wounded. It was comfortable, unthreatening; a place where I could move about without worrying or questioning whether my life made sense, or if I should do anything about it.

Nobody bothered me, even though I wore the same torn winter jacket, as long as I kept gambling and didn't bother anyone else.

It was a wonderful trance, in which the only things that really mattered were the spin of the slots, the drop of the cards, and the clattering of the chips as they passed from hand to hand, and in and out of their holding carrels.

When the casino closed, I grabbed a cab home, cleaned up, and fell asleep.

The next morning I had the day off so I was back at the casino just before it opened. The doors opened at nine thirty, and every day there was a queue of people waiting to get in.

There was something pathetic about a casino in the morning. The lights still flashed and flared, the slots still emitted the falling-cash sound effects of enticement, the staff and security were all cleaned, pressed, and wide-eyed. But the picture seemed wrong.

Like finding a photo of a funeral in a wedding album. Incongruous and sad.

The only people gambling at that time were diehard addicts like me, all shapes, sizes, and ages, all moving about in the same way, like death row inmates on their way to the lethal injection, our feet dragging in a slow, deliberate shuffle.

In the casino during the morning, the people drifted about like lazy moths, moving lackadaisically toward the flame, although unlike real moths, we knew the fire would consume us. But we still refused to fly away.

After finishing my breakfast at the casino restaurant, never later than ten thirty, I changed a hundred dollars and took my bucket of coins to the video slots, killing time until the tables opened. Unlike most of my fellow patrons, I played only one machine at a time, moving between games every ten to fifteen minutes.

Around one, having given time for the cards, chips, and dealers to warm up after their opening at noon, I headed over to the tables.

I played all the games—blackjack, Caribbean poker, Let It Ride, and pai gow—moving from one table to the next whenever there was a dealer change. I ate again when my stomach told me to eat. When the casino closed, I went home. And for the next few days, I came back.

I won and lost, not really keeping track. The key was to keep playing as long as possible. I developed a rhythm. The point was to become a part of the regular scene, something you knew was there, but not something that stood out and demanded attention. My only connection with time was the opening and closing of the casino and how the crowds increased during the peak hours after supper.

I didn't think about anybody or anything; didn't think about Marvin, Mandy, Peter, Larry, or my job at the paper. I knew there would come a time when I had to go back to work but I still hadn't decided if I would.

A few days earlier, I had been battling against returning to this life, but now that I was in it, I had no desire to leave. I was happy to stay in my trance for as long as I could.

25

One night after closing, there were no cabs outside to take me home.

So I walked into the northern part of the downtown area just west of City Hall, hoping to find something outside one of the hotels. The closest hotel was the Crowne Plaza, but there were no cabs. I waited for a moment in the lobby, but since I was still wearing my torn winter coat, I didn't look the part of a hotel guest.

The night bellman, a skinny kid in his early twenties, came up to me.

"Sorry, buddy. You can't hang out here," he said in a resigned and unthreatening tone.

"It's pretty cold out."

"Yeah, I know. But the night manager says you gotta move on. The Churchill station's open for you so you can head there."

I looked outside and then I looked at him. "You gonna make me go outside and walk to the Churchill?"

He sighed. "Guess not. But you can't hang around here. I'll unlock the back entrance so you can reach the City Centre Mall and you can make your way from there."

"Thanks. I appreciate that."

"No worries, man. Can't let you freeze out in the cold. Come on, follow me."

He did what he said he would and I thanked him. I could have stayed in the mall area but I knew that if I hung around too long, mall security would be on me and they probably wouldn't be as accommodating as the night bellman. So I quickly made my way to the only nearby place that was open for someone who looked like me: the Churchill LRT station.

A couple of rent-a-cops sporting angry-schoolteacher frowns patrolled the area, but much to their chagrin, they had little power. Because opening this LRT station to the homeless on cold nights was a humanitarian gesture on the part of the city, they couldn't kick people out for minor infractions, and certain rules were relaxed.

A cloud of smoke drifted in the air, in defiance of the city's anti-smoking bylaw. And they didn't really mind if people brought in bottles or whatever to drink, as long as they didn't get unruly.

Since I had nothing to do, I decided that I might as well stay here. Maybe I would meet someone that I knew from before and we'd have a nice conversation. Or maybe I would meet someone who had seen Marvin before he died and I'd get some confirmation that he had been killed by his fellow gang members.

Despite what McKinley had said about Marvin's tattoo and how he died, I was still having a hard time believing that he had belonged to the same group that those four guys in the SUV belonged to.

I noticed there was a long table near the exit to the Winspear Centre. It was manned by a city worker, probably somebody in the social services department, so I headed there. With the state of my jacket, I could easily pass for a street person, at least to workers and the guards. The folks sleeping here would see through me, maybe pick me out as someone who had lived on the streets but didn't anymore. But if I didn't bother them too much, they wouldn't care. They had more important things to worry about.

The young social worker was flanked by a security guard who tensed as I walked up to the table. The worker noticed the guard's reaction and looked up from her book. She was dressed in social worker casual, a cardigan over a dark print blouse, a pair of black jeans, and brown hair pulled into a firm but not stern ponytail. She must have been in her twenties, but she had a little button nose and cute chubby chipmunk cheeks that immediately reminded me of my daughter, Eileen.

"May I help you?" the worker asked.

"I'd like a room for the night," I said with a smile, and got one in return, a dimple appearing in her right cheek. The security guard groaned. He did, however, relax his posture.

"Of course, we've got plenty of rooms available tonight," said the worker. "Although I can't offer you a nonsmoking spot, if that's what you're looking for; we're pretty much all smoking tonight, I'm sorry to say."

"That's all right. I think I can find a quiet corner somewhere."

"And there are also some refreshments, coffee and some buns and muffins," she said, pointing to the south toward the entrance of the Citadel Theatre. "Although there's enough to go around, we ask that you limit yourself to two cups of coffee and two snacks per person, please."

"Right. I'll practice some restraint. Do I need to sign a register?"

She shook her head. "Obviously, names are not required; we understand a person's right to privacy. We only ask that you don't bother your fellow guests, passersby, or anybody else. As you'll notice, we have plenty of security nearby, along with regular patrols of our police service, and no unruly activity will be tolerated. Do you understand, sir?" Despite some of her words, her tone was friendly.

I nodded, but the security guard stepped forward. "Yeah, no fucking around or you'll be—"

The worker cut him off with a wave of her hand. "That's quite enough, Brian. There's no need to be offensive. I'm sure our guest understands the rules."

Brian clamped his mouth shut, but his eyes told me that there were other, unspoken rules for this hotel. He stared at me, his eyes daring me to challenge his authority.

I looked away and nodded at the worker. "Don't worry, I'm not going to cause any trouble, I just need a place to sleep. What else do you need from me?"

She turned in her chair and ducked underneath the table. A second later she brought out a piece of rolled-up blue foam, the kind campers use, and a gray blanket sporting the city emblem.

"Please return these to us in the morning. If you feel you really need another blanket, then we'll do what we can. We don't know how many people are going to be in tonight, so we're asking our guests to be patient if they need another blanket."

I took the blanket and the piece of foam. "Thanks. I should be fine with just one blanket," I said. "I'm a pretty warm guy."

She smiled again, but the guard gave me a look that told me to fuck off. I took his advice and started to walk away.

"Thanks again," I said. "I should be fine."

"Have a nice evening," the worker called out to me as I turned away. I gave her a wave over my shoulder, and pretended to look for a spot to sleep.

26

I strolled through the station, trying to find someone to talk to about Marvin. There were about forty people spread throughout the upper part of the station, some sleeping alone, others gathered in groups of four to six, their backs facing out so they could do what they wanted—smoke, drink, sniff, or just talk—in peace.

One time a civilian entered the area from the north where the law courts are, no doubt heading to his car parked underneath the library or somewhere farther south. He was mid-thirties, dressed in a suit, his winter coat draped over his arm and the boxy legal suitcase he carried. A Crown lawyer working late on a case.

He froze for a second when he realized there were people sleeping, smoking, and hanging around the station. Since it was a couple hours after midnight on a Friday night, he probably thought it was going to be empty. He spent a couple of seconds taking in the scene and then made his way through, his pace quickening, his head down.

Because most of the people were already asleep or had their backs to me, I had a tough time finding the right person. I was looking for some around Marvin's age, late teens, preferably alone, because it was hard to get one kid to talk about another when there was a bunch of them.

But street kids didn't usually hang out alone. It was safer to stay in a pack. So I began to think that I was wasting my time.

Marvin was dead. I knew that for sure. And despite his helpfulness toward others, he was, or had been, a member of Redd Alert. The tattoo on his hand confirmed that. And McKinley had said that gangs were known to kill their own members for a number of reasons. Being a traitor for another gang or a rat to the cops, I could understand. But wanting to quit the gang? I wasn't so sure.

Maybe there was another reason they killed him, I didn't know. I also didn't know why I kept pursuing this. I didn't understand why I kept banging my head against the wall about Marvin.

Maybe I was doing it because I'd become bored if I was just filing typical police-beat stories. Larry was right, the grunt stories were the lifeblood of a paper, but I needed more of a challenge.

Or maybe I just liked Marvin, thought he was a decent kid, and wanted to confirm why he died. I knew McKinley said it was his own gang, and that was enough for him to let the case lie. But it wasn't enough for me. I needed someone from Redd Alert to tell me that they had killed Marvin and why. As my mind worked all these things through, I walked aimlessly around the area and it finally got on the nerves of security.

"Can we help you?" a gruff voice said to me. I snapped out of my thoughts; I was facing two of the guards. They were both the size of football players, with buzz cuts and suspicious looks. The one with the glasses was asking the questions.

"Is there a problem?"

I backed away a step, clutching my blanket and foam to my chest. "I was just looking for a spot to sleep."

"Most of the people are sleeping back there," he said, using his baton to point at the main station area behind me. "We'd prefer that you stay in that area."

"Yeah, I figured. But I'm not really keen on the smoke, it bothers my asthma," I lied.

"There is a bylaw, but for some reason the city doesn't want us enforcing that bylaw at the moment, so there's really nothing we can do to help you there. Please, we'd prefer that you remain in the main area."

"Is it really necessary?"

There was a pause but then he shook his head. "No, it's not really necessary," he said, giving my shoulder a slight touch with his baton. "But it's something we prefer."

I looked at the ground for a few seconds to appease the guard. "I just need a quiet, nonsmoking place to sleep. I'm not going to cause any trouble."

There was another pause, and I could feel the baton move away. I took the opportunity to look up and saw the two guards looking at each other. The one without the glasses seemed confused and shrugged at his partner. Glasses Guy looked away from his partner and his lips tightened in thought.

"Listen, to be honest, I'm really uncomfortable with the drinking going on back there," I lied. "I got nothing against people drinking but it's tough for me. I'm forty-seven days sober, trying to get back on my feet, but it's going to be really hard to sleep back there."

"Trying to get sober, eh?" the other guard said with a grim smile.

"Hoping to, but a few of those guys are my old drinking buddies, if you know what I mean, so if I head back there, I'm afraid they'll just wear me down. Come on. I'm only one guy and I'll be quiet. It'll be only me down here. I won't be any trouble."

"Sorry, no," said the guard with the glasses after a pause, once again tapping me on the shoulder with his baton. "Back you go to the main area."

"Oh, come on, I won't be any trouble."

"You're already trouble, buddy," he said, pushing the end of the baton into my shoulder, forcing me to take a step backward. "So don't make it any worse than it already is. I don't give a shit if you're forty-seven years sober, deal with it and head back. You hear me?"

There was no winning this battle; some rent-a-cops got a hard-on for stuff like this, and if it came to any problems, the guy in the uniform, no matter how flimsy, would always win over the guy with the NFA, No Fixed Address.

So I turned and headed back. I started to look for a decent spot to sleep but then it dawned on me that I didn't have to sleep here. I had my own place. I had worked hard to get my own place, but if I kept on gambling, I *would* end up here, forced to sleep in the LRT station on cold nights, my movements limited by the whim of rent-a-cops who barely had the smarts to make it through high school. I had known all that but I had gotten lazy, allowing myself to un-consciously drift back to my old life, to prevent me from moving forward in the new one.

I dropped my blanket and roll off at the desk and headed into the library parkade. I found the closest exit and came out at the northeast corner of the library, just across the street from the Cita-del. The Westin Hotel was only a block away to the south.

And there I found a cab to take me home.

27

At home I did the things regular people did. I slept for eight hours, I ate, I did laundry, and argued with my wife. Actually it was my ex-wife, and she wasn't too happy about the advice I'd given Peter.

She had left me a number of messages at home. So had Brent, Larry, and Mandy. I called Mandy first, thanked her for her calls and told her I was fine. I apologized for not getting back to her but declined her offer to come over. I told her I had to talk to my ex-wife about my son, who, based on the messages my wife had left me, was in a little trouble at school.

So I told Mandy I would see her at work on Monday—I had to promise on the lives of my children that I would be in—and called Joan.

She was, simply put, pissed.

"What the hell were you thinking, Leo? How can you tell a nine-year-old kid to get in a fight with another kid? Do you know how much trouble he is in at school? They're talking about suspending him!"

"He got in a fight at school?"

"Duh. Yeah, he got in a fight at school, just like you told him."

"I didn't tell him to get in a fight at school."

"You didn't tell him to fight this kid at school?"

"No. I told him to follow the kid home and then fight him."

"What!" she hissed into the phone. I knew she wanted to scream but if she did, she would wake up the kids. "How could you tell him that?"

"Because that kid and his friends were bullying him."

"That doesn't make it right. If he was being bullied he should have told someone."

"He told me."

"You don't count," she said quickly. It hurt. It was a bit true but it still hurt. "I meant a teacher, a principal, someone, like . . ." Her voice trailed off.

"Like you. You're mad that he didn't tell you."

"Of course I'm mad he didn't tell me. I'm his mother, he should be able to tell me everything."

I smiled inwardly knowing that though Joan was a terrific mother and my kids were lucky to have her, there were a large number of things that Peter wouldn't tell her. Soon, new, different things would be happening to his body and she would try to talk to him about it, but he would be repulsed. Some things a boy just couldn't talk about to his mom, no matter how close they were.

"And if he told you, what would you tell him to do? What would you tell Peter to do if he came to you and told you that someone was bullying him?"

"I'd tell him to go talk to a teacher or the principal."

"He wouldn't do that. He's not a squealer."

"It's not squealing. It's called standing up for yourself. It's called getting help from people who will help you."

"Well, to a kid, it's squealing. And even though the other kid will probably get into some trouble, it won't stop. In fact, it will get worse because instead of picking on a bunch of kids, they'll start picking on only him. And that's when it gets really bad."

"So violence begets violence. An eye for an eye and the whole world blind."

"No, it's not an eye for an eye," I said. "It's one kid standing up for himself to another kid who can only understand violence."

"But he might be suspended." I could hear her voice cracking. She was an educational administrator and to have her son get into this kind of trouble was probably harder on her than it would be on most mothers.

"Yeah, but not for long. He'll be back in school in no time."

"But it'll go on his record."

"Who cares? So he has one mark on his record? He's a good kid. You know it, I know it, his teachers know it. The smart ones already know why he did what he did and won't hold it against him. The ones who don't are idiots."

I could hear her breathing heavily: I figured she was not sure what to say.

"So how's he doing anyway? Is he okay?" I asked.

"He's fine. A little too proud of himself but I took care of that and took away his PS3 for a month."

"Good. But I meant physically. How's he doing?"

"Oh, he's got a couple split knuckles that hurt, but he's fine."

"That's it? Some split knuckles?" I couldn't help but chuckle.

"Stop laughing. It's not funny. He shouldn't be fighting. I don't like it at all."

"He wasn't fighting, Joan. He was protecting himself. There's a difference. And based on the fact that he only has split knuckles, he won't have to do it again, Nobody is going to mess with him now."

"You're pretty proud of yourself, aren't you?"

"No. I'm not. I'm proud of him. I should have called you when I found out he was being bullied. I'm sorry for that."

"Thanks. And you shouldn't have called our house. That's a big no-no as you know."

"I didn't call your house. He called me."

There was a pause as she took in my comment. "He called you? Where did he call you?"

"He called me at work."

"At work?"

"Yeah."

"He's not supposed to do that."

"I know, but please don't give him a hard time about it. He was a scared kid being bullied and he needed to talk to someone who could relate to his problem. So he called me."

"It must have made you happy."

"It did."

"Well, I'm glad," she said, sounding like she meant it. "But next time he does something like that you have to tell me about it. I don't want to deal with this again."

"Then be thankful Eileen doesn't call me, because teenaged girls usually have more problems. I know, I had two older sisters."

"Oh, God. I don't want to talk about her. At least Peter still says *Good night* and *I love you,* even after I punish him. Eileen keeps giving me these looks like I've ruined her life."

I let Joan vent about our daughter. It was good to hear her talk, good to hear about my daughter who still hated my guts because I had left them. It was good to feel normal again. For a moment, I could understand why Brent lived this way. And I wondered if I ever would again.

28

After hanging up with Joan, it was early in the evening, so I took a quick bath and watched a bit of TV in a T-shirt and a pair of sweatpants. About a half hour into some reality show, I heard a knock on my door.

I was a bit confused because in the few weeks I had been here, no one had ever knocked on my door, not even the building manager. I slowly made my way to the door and looked through the peephole. It was dark. Someone was blocking it.

"Who is it?" I asked.

Nobody answered. But I could hear breathing and see someone's shadow from underneath the door. I imagined members of Redd Alert coming to talk to me, telling me to stay away from the Marvin Threefingers case. I also thought that maybe someone finally had recognized me in that blurry bank surveillance photo and the police were coming to arrest me.

Whoever it was banged on the door harder, and I knew if it was either some gangbangers or cops, they wouldn't continue knocking. They would kick in the door. So in case it was gangbangers, I needed to find some way to protect myself. I grabbed one of my heavy boots and realized that that wouldn't stop anyone.

So I grabbed my phone, dialed 91, and then held my finger over the second 1, just in case someone was coming to harm me. I undid the lock and the chain, and slowly opened the door.

I was so surprised when I saw who was on the other side, I dropped the phone.

"Surprise," Mandy shouted, smiling brightly, and pushing her way in. "What took you so long?"

"Mandy?" I said. "What the heck are you doing here?" I bent to pick up the phone and shut it off.

"I know you said you had to call your ex-wife about your son but I wanted to make sure you were all right. I also brought some presents." She held up a plastic Safeway bag and pulled out some chocolates and a liter of milk. "I always see you eating a chocolate bar and drinking milk at the office in the morning, so I figured you wouldn't mind if I brought some over. How's your son, by the way? Is he okay?"

I looked at her, incredulous that she was here. Shocked but happy. "Yeah, he's fine, he got into a fight and—"

I couldn't finish because my phone rang. I looked at the call display and it said unknown number. It rang three times and Mandy's expression told me I could get it. She turned to put the milk into my fridge and I did.

"Hello."

"This is Edmonton's emergency service. Someone from this line called 911. Was that you, sir?"

"What?" I asked, confused for a second, but then I realized that when I dropped the phone, it must have accidently dialed the second 1. "Oh, yeah, I hit the speed dial by mistake but I hung up. You didn't have to call back."

"Yes, sir, we do. Anytime someone calls 911 and hangs up without saying anything we have to call back. Is everything okay, sir?"

"Yes, everything's fine. I just hit the wrong button. Sorry."

"No problem, sir. You have a nice day. But please be very careful."

I hung up the phone and glanced up to see Mandy looking at

me, her hands on her hips. There was an expression of annoyance on her face.

"You called 911 on me. I know you said you didn't want me to come over but I didn't think you'd call 911 on me. Aren't you glad to see me?"

I looked at her, and tonight, probably for the first time, I really saw her. She wore her hair down and it had some body to it, a bit of a wave. Instead of a loose skirt or business slacks, she wore a pair of jeans, low cut, and a black sweater that clung to her body, but wasn't tight. She wore some light makeup, a bit of pale green eye shadow and lipstick that was subtly red but definitely there. The scent of vanilla and baby powder hung in the air.

She was gorgeous and I was really glad to see her. So I told her, but not the gorgeous bit because I thought that might be too forward. Just that bit about being glad to see her.

"Good," she said with a smile and a little jump of her toes. "Now let me have a tour of the place." She turned and I watched her walk away. It had been a long time since I had watched a woman walk away and had the kind of thoughts that I was now thinking.

I shook my head and followed her in. When I came in she was looking out my balcony window at the building across the street. She turned and smiled at me. "It's a nice little place. The kind of place I imagined you would live."

"Really?"

"No. Actually, I imagined you lived in a dump, with stacks of old newspapers all over the place, plates of old food, a mangy cat slinking about, and maybe a theremin somewhere."

"I sold the theremin on Kijiji the other day and I managed to spend my time off cleaning up."

She smiled but I could tell she wasn't that happy. "Really? Is that what you did on your time off?"

I didn't know what to say to her. I thought about lying so she wouldn't be disappointed in me, but I didn't feel like lying to her. I didn't know what we were doing or where we were going with this and I didn't want to start it all by lying. So I said nothing.

She figured it out on her own. "Oh, Leo," she said mournfully. "That's too bad."

"Don't judge me," I snapped. "If you've come here to judge me, then I'm going to ask you to leave."

She took a step forward and I knew she was thinking about hugging me. But she stopped herself. "I didn't come here to judge you. I'm the last person in the world to do that. I know where you've been and what it's like being there. I'm just sad that you went that way. And also that you didn't call anyone before you did."

"I'm sorry I didn't call anyone, but I just don't like to bother people."

"Well, I don't mind being bothered. So next time I insist that you call me."

"So you wanna be my sponsor then?"

"No, I want to be your friend. I like you, Leo. You're smart and funny and a little bit fucked up, but then again, who isn't? I know I am. After the party the other night, I went home. And you know what else? I stopped at the liquor store, bought a bottle of wine and drank the whole thing. I don't know why I did it, I just did. It felt good, nice and warm being drunk again, being in that safe and comfortable place, because things are getting challenging at work now. You know that feeling, Leo? Don't you? That safe and homey feeling you get? Do you get that when you gamble?"

I nodded. I definitely knew that feeling.

"I knew you would. I love that feeling," she said wistfully. "But it also feels like shit. Like I know I can do better than this. But there I was, in my apartment, drunk, comfortable, and miserable."

"You could have called me."

"Yeah, I could have. But I didn't. Next time I will." She stopped and raised a finger in the air.

"Actually," she continued, drawing out the word. "I did call you. But you had to talk to your ex-wife about your son. And I knew that was important. So instead of calling you back, I decided to come over." She flopped on the couch like a teenager. "What do you think of that?"

I laughed and sat down on the arm of the couch. I ruffled her hair. "So is that why you came over? Because I'm your new sponsor?"

"Naw, I already have a sponsor. And she's boring." She reached out and placed her hand on my thigh. I put my hand on hers and we entwined fingers.

"I also came over because you promised you'd be at work Monday morning," she said. "And I came over to help you keep that promise."

It took me only a few seconds to figure out what she was talking about.

29

I spent about a couple of weeks happily working on the assignment rotation. There were interesting stories and there were dull ones. Larry said I could pursue Marvin's story but only if I had the time. But I was so busy that I didn't have the time. I could have made the time, but to be honest, I didn't want to. I had other things going on, with Mandy.

Mandy came over once in a while but not every day. We took things slowly because we each knew the other had a lot of baggage in the back room.

At work, she treated me no differently: she criticized me when I didn't do justice to my stories and she praised me when I did. There were no secret smiles, no quick touches as she walked by my desk, no trysts in the lunchroom when no one was around.

It was obvious that she had been through this before, having a relationship with someone at work. Journalism was an insular profession; the long and sometimes unusual hours created a situation where it was hard to meet someone in the real world, so there were many couples in the newsroom.

Brent's wife may have been a stay-at-home mom, but before they had kids, she used to be one of our legislative reporters.

So I didn't hold it against Mandy for not treating me differently, because she had a job to do. And I did my best not to watch her too much, or follow her with my eyes as she made her way around the newsroom. It was hard because I hadn't been with a woman for a few years. Living on the street wasn't really conducive to romance, because there were more important things to worry about, such as finding something to eat, a place to sleep, or a quiet place to go to the bathroom. Sure, there were couples who lived together on the street, but in my experience it was more for a combining of resources rather than a romantic venture.

Apparently, I wasn't doing a good job because one Friday morning, I was watching Mandy talking to one of our City Hall columnists when Brent tapped me on the top of the head.

"Hey, Leo. Wake up," he said.

I snapped out of my daydream and turned to him. "Wha . . . Yeah, Brent. What's up?"

He wasn't looking at me, but instead in the direction I had been looking. Fortunately, there were a number of other reporters and editors in my line of view so he probably couldn't figure out that I was watching Mandy. Or he might have. He was a smart guy, well connected in the newsroom, and he knew who was single or not, so it probably wouldn't take him long. And although his wife was no longer at the paper, she was still in touch with many of the female staffers, so if he really wanted to find out something, she would help.

"Yeah, take a look at this," he said, holding out a sheet of paper.

I reached for it but he snapped it back. "Sorry, buddy, I know you're interested in native gangs but this story is mine."

"Come on, Brent, what you got?"

"It's another shooting, around 107th Avenue and 113th Street. One dead. Shot while driving his car and then he smashed into the side of a walk-up. We got a shooter out there already and I'm about to join him." He started putting on his jacket. "That is, once I talk to the new boss and tell her where I'm going."

I thought about the address and realized that it was half a block from my old place, my little room in the basement. While Brent was getting ready, I snapped the information from him.

"Hey, come on, man. That's my story," he said, trying to get the paper.

I read the few details that Brent had written down. There wasn't much, just a location and a short description of what had happened. Once I finished reading it, I held it to my chest. "Come on, Brent. This should be my story. I was the one on the gang thing."

"Sorry, buddy, this is my turn to be A-1. And there's no info on whether the victim's native or not. He could be Asian for all we know."

He zipped up his jacket, grabbed his notebook and recorder. "Besides, based on what happened to you last time, I don't think the new boss is going to let you cover this one."

I sighed and handed him back the information, even though he probably had it all memorized. He was right. Even if we weren't romantically involved, Mandy wouldn't let me near this story. If I had gotten the information first, she would have taken it away from me and handed it to someone like Brent. Larry probably would have backed her, as well. No one wanted Leo Desroches anywhere near another gang shooting. Even one that was obviously over.

"Okay, you have yourself a good time, Brent," I said begrudgingly. "I really hope the Oilers make a trade while you're gone."

He smiled at me and flipped me the finger. "Makes no difference, buddy. Shooting and a car accident at the same time will make A-1 no matter what else happens." He dashed away, heading to Mandy to tell her what was going on.

"If we get a chinook, then you're screwed," I shouted at him. A chinook is a warm winter wind, known to increase temperatures by twenty or thirty degrees in a day. They were more common in the southern half of the province, but every few years, Edmonton would get one. And as one former editor had told me early in my career: "A big weather story trumps everything. Every time."

Brent gave me a wave over his shoulder and told Mandy where he was going. She asked him a few questions but when she was satisfied with his answers, she nodded and he was off. She went back to her conversation with the City Hall correspondent but gave me a quick look.

I could see there was some relief in her face that Brent was on the story. I offered a short shrug and then went back to writing a series of police-beat briefs, short pieces about minor incidents that had occurred in the last twenty-four hours. I knew not all of them would run, but we needed a few written up just in case it ended up being a slow news day or someone pulled an ad at the last minute.

It was still before noon when I finished with that, so I told Mandy I was heading out for an early lunch. I also told her that since I had finished the news briefs, I might be gone for an hour or so afterward.

"It's Friday, and your work is done, so why don't you take the rest of the day off," she said, not knowing what I had planned.

"You sure? What happens if something comes up? If a story breaks?"

She shrugged. "I think we can handle it. Go have lunch, catch a movie or something."

"You want me to get you something and bring it back?"

"Naw. I brought a lunch. I'll eat it later, probably. Go, before I change my mind and give you something to do like tidy your desk." She smiled her smile, one that sent a shiver down the back of my neck.

"Okay, you're the boss," I said, smiling back. I didn't want to ask her if I would see her later but I wanted to know. So I raised my eyebrows, hoping she would get the message.

She winked, showing that she understood, but said nothing. Instead, she flashed a quick hand signal, extending her thumb and her pinkie, telling me she would call me. I nodded, wished her a nice weekend, and after I gathered up my stuff, I left the building.

It was still cold outside, relative to the rest of the world, but since the daytime temperatures were now hovering around minus seventeen instead of in the low minus thirties, it was practically a heat wave. I still had to wear a winter coat but I could wear it open.

While I was standing at the light to cross Jasper, my phone buzzed. I answered and it was Mandy. She was whispering slightly so no one in the newsroom would overhear her.

"Sorry, Leo. I'm going to be busy all weekend. Kerry, the style editor, is having one of those jewelry parties at her house and then my brother wants me over for supper with his family. You going to be okay?"

That question had two meanings, the first innocuous, the second wondering if I would be gambling. "I'll be okay," I told her, meaning I knew I wasn't going to be gambling. But I didn't know what else would happen. Because of the gang shooting Brent was covering, I knew I wouldn't be going home after lunch. I knew I still needed to find out about Marvin, and I had a bit of a plan but I didn't know how it would pan out.

I wasn't planning anything dangerous, only to go over to Marvin's apartment to see if anybody was living there and if anyone had seen anything before he died. It wasn't much, but I had to investigate. If I found nothing, I told myself, I would let it go. I at least had to give it one more shot.

Mandy and I exchanged some more pleasantries, nothing too blatant because she was still at work, but I told her I would miss her. And I would.

I actually did get something to eat, so I wouldn't be lying to

Mandy. I got a plate of rice and chicken at a popular downtown takeout place that everyone had nicknamed "Crack Chicken" after the drug, because of how many downtown office people ate there every day, as if they were addicted to it. The food was decent; not earth-shattering, but it was better than most fast-food places in the downtown area.

Its signature was the middle-aged Chinese woman who owned the place with her family and took everyone's order. It was reported, even in our paper a couple of times, that she remembered all her customers' orders, even if you had been there only once.

I had been there only three times since I had been working for the paper this past year, and every time I ordered she told me, "You always order that. I'll give you something else."

And every time she was wrong. I didn't know if it was a sign or not.

30

Marvin's apartment was on the fourteenth floor of Lloyd Manor, a run-down high-rise apartment building that was probably built during the late seventies' oil boom. Back then it probably housed middle-management oil company workers, government employees who worked at the legislature a few blocks to the west, and a wide variety of single, blue-collar types who were drawn to the high-paying jobs of the booming oil patch at the time.

Many blue-collar types still probably lived there but the building was also home to a lower socioeconomic set like students who couldn't find a better or cheaper place, folks living on social assistance, and people like Marvin who had enough money for a place but couldn't afford something better.

I made it into the building with relative ease. I punched a bunch of buttons on the downstairs intercom, and when someone answered, I just said, "It's me." And I was let into the building.

The elevator stank of sweat, cigarettes, and cleaning products. As it slowly lurched upward, the smell of marijuana wafted in every few floors. When I finally got up to the fourteenth floor, it bounced a couple of times and the doors took so long to open that I thought I was stuck.

Marvin's apartment was to the left, about two-thirds of the way down the hall. When I got there, the door was open. I peeked through, worried that I might run into those Redd Alert guys from the SUV, but I couldn't see anyone in the apartment.

The entire place was empty: no furniture, no garbage, no one crashing on the floor. It was a clean slate, ready for the next tenant. There were a couple of boxes on the floor by the door but that was it.

I stepped in, calling out, "Hello."

A middle-aged native man stood up from behind the counter that separated the kitchen from the main living area. He was holding a spray bottle and a sponge made out of steel, like he was working hard to get some kind of stain out of the floor. He pointed the spray bottle in my direction, like a weapon. He looked surprised but angry and threatening.

"Who the fuck are you?" he demanded.

I held one hand up while the other reached into my pocket to get one of my cards. "My name is Leo Desroches. I'm a reporter for the local paper. I was the guy who wrote the story about Marvin when he died." I put my card on the counter and, without moving any closer to him, I slid it across.

He looked at the card, then at me, then back to the card. He took a wary step forward, picked up the card without putting down the steel wool. He studied it for several seconds, turning it over and feeling the stock to see if it was real.

When he finally decided it was, he set down the spray bottle, still holding the card in his hand. "You're the guy who called when Marvin died, aren't you?"

His question confirmed what I was thinking: This was Marvin's uncle. I nodded but said nothing.

He put the card in his pocket. "I'd like to thank you for not including my name in the story. I wasn't right in the head at the moment, so I said some things in anger."

"That's okay. I didn't think Marvin's family needed more stress."

"Well, when someone you love dies, there's always a lot of stress, regardless." He looked at me for several seconds, his eyes searching for something in me, something he thought I was hiding.

"So you wrote that first story. And now you're here," he said. "Why is that?" His voice still had a menacing and suspicious tone.

"Well, I did the story on Marvin's death, and the paper was hoping to do a much deeper story on him, so I wanted to find some of his friends or someone that knew him better and get more information about him, not just that he was a gang member who got killed."

"Marvin wasn't a gang member!" he said quickly. "He quit and those fuckers killed him for it."

"Yeah, yeah. I know that. That's why I was hoping to get more about him for the story. More on why he left the gang, and how he was trying to get his life back together but they wouldn't let him. We're trying to do a larger piece on the impact native gangs are having on the lives of young natives, and I'm sorry to say, Marvin is a good place to start."

"And you are the aboriginal issues writer," he said slowly, reading my card.

"Right. We're trying to offer more stories on aboriginals who live in Edmonton. To give a sense of what it's like to be an urban aboriginal in Canada."

"Interesting that they've given that kind of job to a white man," he said with a huff. "Doesn't your paper have any native journalists that can write about aboriginal issues?"

"Actually, my mother is a status Cree. From Norway House, in northern Manitoba."

A look of quick surprise came across his face but then he smiled. "Fish eaters, eh?"

I nodded. Many bands from across Canada called themselves

Cree and they were a diverse people with diverse cultures, lives, and dialects. Since my mother's people lived in an area with lots of lakes and rivers, they ate a lot of fish. They also hunted other animals but the predominant part of their diet was fish. They were also called Swampy Cree because of the muskeg that made up a large part of Canada's northern boreal forest.

"Yeah, but I don't like fish," I said. "I'm more of a meat and potatoes man myself."

The native man laughed, removing all the tension in the room. He put down the card and reached a hand across the counter.

"Norman Threefingers," he said, holding out his hand.

I shook it and hoped that he could help me figure out what happened to Marvin.

31

Norman's truck was dark brown, but it was so new that it sparkled. It was parked in the loading zone in front of the building.

He put the two boxes he had carried down from the apartment into the back of the truck and then climbed in the driver's side. I stood on the other side wondering what was going to happen next, when the passenger side window slid down.

"You coming or what?" Norman said, slipping his belt on.

"In the truck?"

"Yeah. You said you wanted to know more about Marvin. So get in and I'll tell you all about him."

I stood for a second, wondering if I should go with him. Considering what had happened the last time I climbed into a brand-new vehicle being driven by somebody who was native, I was a bit reluctant. But this was Marvin's uncle, not a bunch of gangbangers in a tricked-out Hummer. And I did have permission to further pursue Marvin's story, and Norman was the perfect source on Marvin's life, especially his years as a kid. And since my work was done for the day and I didn't have to be at work until Monday, I was covered on that side, as well.

This also gave me something to do, and that was good, because I wasn't sure if I could make it through the weekend without gambling. I had been fine for the past couple of weeks but Mandy had been around. This was the first time since we started our relationship that I would not see her during the weekend.

The truck had that plastic new-car smell and the seat, although new, was soft leather, like a well-worn jacket. There was also a warm spot underneath my butt, which created a disconcerting sensation, as if I was sitting on warm liquid. I felt my sphincter tighten and I shifted back and forth.

"Heated seats," Norman said. "Takes a bit of getting used to, because we're so used to sitting on cold seats in the winter, but they get to be nice after a while. Comes as part of the whole package. Leather, air, heated seats, power windows, V-8, the whole deal. Couldn't afford it if I was paying for it myself, but then again, I wasn't paying for it myself, so why the hell not? If someone's paying to buy something for you, there's no need to worry about cost."

I found that when I settled into the seat, the heat would move from a single point and spread out over my entire butt. And then the sensation became soothing, like a warm bath, especially with the baby-soft leather that molded around my body. If casinos wanted people to stay in their seats longer, they should install seats like this.

Then again, they didn't need to; folk like me would stay at a casino even if we were losing and we had to stand all day.

"It's a heck of a truck. You win the lottery or something?" I asked.

Norman laughed, and the way he let his body relax into humor reminded me a bit of Marvin. "Naw, this is one of the leftover perks from being chief," he said.

He went on to say he was entitled to a few side benefits from all the work he did during his tenure. "Those houses don't get built on their own," he said. "And tendering those contracts and deciding who deserves a new house this year, and who doesn't, isn't as easy as it seems. And then there's dealing with all those government lackeys who want to sit on their budgets like it's their own money and hoping those fucking oil companies aren't ripping you off on the royalty payments. It takes a lot out of a guy after three years, so I think I deserve something, too, you know. And just because I'm an ex-chief doesn't mean my work is done. It's my duty as a former chief to continue to help my people any way I can, so that's almost a full-time job, especially since the new band council is a bunch of fuckups who can't tell a paving contract from a building reconstitution form. 'Cleaning house,' they said. What a bunch of shit. They couldn't clean their own goddamn bathrooms, that group. So that's why I made a few final decisions before they took over. They're still trying to get my truck back, but they know they can't. They're just causing trouble to make me look bad."

Norman liked to look at me while he talked, looking out the front window every so often so he could pull the truck back into its own lane when it drifted. Horns honked, and I could see the angry gestures of various drivers all around us, but Norman was oblivious to all that.

It seemed that he thought he literally owned the road. I thanked God that we were in a larger vehicle, made sure my seat belt was tight, and stared out the side window.

He also told me a lot about Marvin, about how he was a great kid and student before his parents died in a car accident when he was twelve. And then afterward how he changed, started hanging around the wrong kind of people, people from gangs like Redd Alert. And how he moved into the city when he was only seventeen. Norman said he tried to get Marvin listed as a runaway but the police didn't listen. Nobody cared about a teenaged native kid who left the reserve to live in the city. If he was white, yeah, they might have done something, but a native kid, nobody cared.

He also talked about how Marvin had got ahold of him about a year ago, said he wanted to leave Redd Alert, come back to the reserve and start a new life. Maybe go to school with the money he would get when he turned twenty-one.

"But then those fuckers killed him," he said angrily. "Those fuckers set him on fire before he had the chance to walk away."

We were out of the city by then, just south of Leduc before the Glen Park exit on Queen E 2 Highway to Calgary. Norman stopped talking. And he said nothing for the rest of the trip.

But the truck still drifted back and forth, even on the four-lane highway out of town and on the two-lane secondary that led to his reserve.

32

The forest had thickened and farmyard entrances diminished when Norman, who had been very quiet since we left downtown, banged his fist on the dash and shouted.

"Goddamn sons of bitches!"

The road had been mesmerizing and I was in a half doze, so I jumped in surprise. The tires squealed in a four-wheel skid—I flew forward in the seat, banging my palms on the dashboard to protect myself—as he slammed both feet on the brakes.

The seat belt kicked in and snapped me back, but Norman shouted again—"Stupid fuckers!"—and jammed the gearshift into reverse, wheeling the truck back without even checking for traffic behind us. The momentum of the truck threw me back into my seat, flopping me around as Norman yanked the steering wheel, snapping the front end over into a neck-wrenching turn.

My head jerked back and my side slammed into the door armrest, and an instant later the tires squealed again as Norman gunned the truck forward, onto a gravel side road that I had not seen from my side of the truck. I was again thrown back into the seat, and when I recovered a few seconds later, he hit the brakes again, the tires grinding gravel as the truck slid forward in another four-wheel stop.

The forward momentum was less pronounced this time because of the slide on the gravel, but that only delayed the seat belt mechanism. I almost flew into the dashboard before I was jerked back.

Norman yanked his belt off, slapped me on the shoulder—"Stay in the fucking truck and look pissed off"—threw the door open, and jumped out of the truck. His face was bright red underneath his cap, and his fists were so tightly clenched that they had turned white.

We had stopped in a small clearing. Scattered around us were two bulldozers, two backhoes, one trailer, two other pieces of equipment that I couldn't identify, and several pickups of various ages and conditions. The trucks were all painted the same color, robin's egg blue, each with the name JOHNSON'S OILFIELD SERVICES on the driver's door.

A bunch of men dressed like Norman were also scattered throughout the clearing, frozen in surprise, staring at Norman storming toward them. Near the trailer three guys gathered around a fourth, who was holding a clipboard in one hand and a pen in the other. He was the oldest guy around.

When he saw Norman coming directly toward him, he squinted at us and shook his head. After their initial shock, the rest of the guys relaxed, slouching against their equipment, one or two reaching into a pocket for smokes; but even from the truck I could see an underlying anger in their faces, like Norman was a recurring evil in their lives.

The only one who wasn't angry was the older guy with the clipboard. He slapped it against the chest of one of his guys and waved his other hand to the other guys, as a signal to stay where they were, and then moved, right hand outstretched, to intercept Norman.

I did what Norman ordered, I stayed in the truck, but I was so confused by the scene in front of me that I forgot to look pissed off. Nobody was really looking at me anyway. Even though they seemed to accept the interruption as a chance for a quick break, they still watched intently as the two men met at a point about three meters in front of Norman's truck. I pushed the button to roll down the window.

"What the fuck are you doing here?" Norman shouted, waving his hand at all the equipment.

"Norman! How the hell are you?" replied the older guy, sounding as if he was meeting an old friend. He still held out his hand.

Norman stopped and stood with his hands on his hips, ignoring the outstretched hand. "I asked what the fuck are you doing here, Brad? You guys aren't supposed to be here."

Brad pulled back his hand and held up the clipboard. "I only go where they send me, Norman, and this paper says this is where I'm supposed to be."

"That's a load of bullshit, Brad, and you know it. This is our contract, not yours."

"Sorry, Norman, that's not true. We were awarded the contract fair and square. Got the papers and decision notice in the truck, if you want to see them."

"Fair and square's got nothing to do with it, Brad. This is our land, so it's our contract. You guys shouldn't be out here."

"Actually, this is Crown land. Reserve's still a few miles away, so there's no laws concerning aboriginal businesses for this patch."

Norman stepped forward and jabbed Brad in the chest with his finger. "Fuck you. This is our traditional land. It may not be part of the official reserve, but it's been a traditional hunting and trapping area for my people long before you goddamn fucks discovered the wheel."

As soon as I heard the words "traditional land," I pulled my recorder out of my pocket, hit record, and hung my hand out the window.

Brad stepped back from Norman's jab and shook his head. "If

we see any trap lines, we'll be respectful of them and back away as far as we can, but we did a survey around the area and didn't spot any, so there shouldn't be any problem. And so that we put back into your community because we're so close to your reserve, I made sure at least one third of the guys hired for this project come from your own band."

"Fuck that, Brad. I don't care if you hired the whole fucking band," Norman said. "This was supposed to be our contract. We had promises."

"I don't know what to say about that, Norman. I don't know a thing about any deals you may have had with the oil company, but I only go where they tell me to, and today they told me to go here. You got any problems with that, you should call the company."

"Fuck the oil company. You're here, so you better be prepared to cover the compensation deal, or there'll be trouble."

Brad took another step back, dropping the clipboard by his side. His expression, which had been friendly and affable, turned serious and angry. "What are you talking about, Norman? I hope you aren't going to take that next step, because so far we've had a good relationship with your band. Like I said, we made sure we hired some of your guys, been doing that for years, even before the oil companies put that stipulation in their contracts."

Norman stepped forward, his face only inches away from Brad's. "Anybody working for you has turned their back on the band and don't belong anymore. This was supposed to be our contract, but if you're going to get it, then you got to make compensation for the band. Normally it's fifteen percent, but since you've been such a good supporter of aboriginal people, we'll knock it down to ten percent. Got that?"

"Fuck, Norman, that's goddamn blackmail, that's what that is. That pretty much takes all my profit out of this project."

"How you run your business is no concern of mine and you can call it what you like. It's what the deal is."

"You can't do that. You're not even chief anymore; your own people threw you out."

"Makes no difference, Brad. I'm still the chief to a lot of people, and what those people have been telling me is that they want you out of here, unless you make compensation to our people. There's just no two ways about it. For years and years and years, we've watched the oil companies and guys like you tear up our country, destroying our traditional hunting areas. And the government may say that the oil isn't ours, that we're not on the reserve and so they don't have to compensate us. But if you check the treaty you know we got rights on our traditional lands, and we're going to get something back somehow. Any way we can. You either pay, Brad, or we'll run you the fuck out of here." Norman took two steps back, and then turned to walk to the truck.

"That's a load of shit, Norman, and you know it," Brad shouted after him. "We're not going anywhere, and we're not going to pay your fucking blackmail."

Norman turned back just as he reached the truck. "It's your funeral then, Brad. You run your company the way you think you have to, but we natives have had enough. I make no apologies for what happens next."

Brad shouted something else, about fair play and contracts, but Norman ignored him and climbed back into the truck. I drew my hand back in and turned off the recorder, surreptitiously putting it back into my pocket.

Norman backed out of the clearing, roaring onto the highway

without looking. A few seconds later, we were back where we had been several minutes before.

I had no idea what to think about what had happened, but Norman was shaking his head as we drove on. "That was fun," he said with a smile.

33

A few minutes later, Norman was no longer smiling. He whipped his phone out of his pocket and stabbed at a few numbers. He drove with one hand, phone tucked in his ear, weaving back and forth across the striped yellow line.

"Melvin," he said into the phone. "We got a situation out near Black Creek. . . . Yeah, it seems like another one, so can you meet me at the band office in a couple hours? . . . Thanks, Melvin, I knew I could count on you. Bring anybody you think should be invited. . . . Naw, I'll call him myself. Don't worry, I'll be nice, you just show up at the band office and I'll fill you in. . . . Right, later. Thanks."

Norman made several more phone calls similar to that one, and we made two rights, a couple of lefts, and then another right.

I quietly thanked God we were on a quiet country road heading toward a reserve, with no traffic to be seen.

There was no sign announcing our entrance into Norman's reserve, but when the truck started to bounce, hitting the swells and waves of a rough, ill-maintained road, and the trees started to press in, unrestrained by shoulders and the regulated twelve-foot cut line, I knew we had crossed over.

We pulled into the center of the reserve, a four-way stop, with what looked like brand-new community buildings on each corner. Norman ignored the stop sign and made a sharp right, so I only caught a glimpse of what seemed to be a combination gas station and restaurant on one corner, a long, low redbrick building, probably a school, on another, and a high hangarlike building on a third. We went a few more kilometers down the road and then Norman turned onto a newly paved road that had a beautifully carved sign that featured a dreamcatcher and the words THE HEIGHTS.

The subdivision looked like one of those new developments that sprang up all around the outskirts of Edmonton during the boom times in the early years of the twenty-first century. The streets were wide, with newly laid concrete sidewalks, and there were large lots and houses with big two-car garages at the front.

Some of the houses were in good shape, with lawns and fences like you would find in a suburban neighborhood. They even had cars in the drive and things like tricycles, swing sets, and other kid-friendly stuff in their yards.

Other houses were a bit run-down, they had no grass, their yards nothing more than empty lots.

And some, maybe a third of the entire subdivision, could only be called dumps. Many of them had graffiti painted on all the walls, gang tags and other comments. Most of the windows were boarded up, and the few left unboarded had holes and cracks in the glass. Many didn't have a front door, just a large sheet of plywood leaning against the opening, while others had heavy-duty steel doors, the kind you'd see at the back of a bank or something.

There were also a number of burned-out houses, without windows or doors, the exterior walls stained black where the flames must have come out through the windows. But even in these, I could see the silhouettes of people shuffling about and the glow of a fire burning in what was the middle of the living room.

I filed the images away in case I could use them for a story, to give a sense of the community where Marvin grew up.

It was sad and frustrating at the same time. These people had so much money to spend on their houses, so much money to help build community centers, social service agencies. They were part owners of one of the largest banks in western Canada, had the possibility of free university education, or at least the money to pay for it, and yet there was all this waste.

I knew there were a lot of issues involved, issues such as the destruction of a millennia-old culture, the genocide of a people, the theft of children for forced religious conversion, theft of land and its resources, denial of legal rights and language and self-government. But my first reaction was anger at all the waste.

Even so, the landscape was beautiful. The subdivision was surrounded by virgin forest of mostly deciduous trees, their bare and exposed trunks offering a tinge of green in the bark, with a smattering of spruce and pine trees scattered throughout. Property like this went for huge bucks near the city, and would hold houses several times as large.

Most folks would have cut back the trees and replaced the forest with some kind of perfectly manicured park with a playground and walkways, even a man-made lake, and called it a green space.

As we made another turn, a pack of dogs, a collection of mangy mongrels and grimy mutts, came bounding toward the truck. They were intent on their prey, barking and howling.

Norman, though he couldn't have missed seeing the rowdy pack on a collision course with us, didn't slow or turn the wheel. I was sure several of the dogs would be struck by the truck, and I shut my eyes in expectation of a fleshy thump and a quick yelp of pain.

But the dogs knew what they were doing; they knew how to hunt as a pack, and they skillfully parted as a group when they came even with the truck. They surrounded us, keeping pace for a few seconds, like remoras with a shark, but then fell back, most turning and heading off the road. A few stragglers got caught up in the chase and continued to pursue us, barking at the cloud of dust.

Norman's house had a lawn but no fence. He parked the truck outside the garage, jumped out, and gestured for me to follow him into the house. He stopped in the front foyer and then disappeared into the house, but even from there I could tell it was not your average reserve home.

Of course, there are many natives who have nice new furniture, but the minimalist design elements, the black leather couch and chairs, matching coffee and end tables, black-and-white photos on the wall, and scattered accessories were out of the price range of even your average white family with two working parents. This was the house of a bachelor executive, someone high up in the corporation with plenty of disposable income to spend on all the twenty-first-century frills.

But the house was empty, soulless. Everything was in its proper place, beautifully designed and created, but lacking any human warmth. There were no indentations in the couch and chairs, no layers of dirt on the furniture, no dust bunnies tucked under the tables, no lingering smells of cooking, no scents of life; just a persistent odor of stale cleaning fluid and the chemical aroma of fresh paint and new construction.

I had no idea how old the house was, but it felt like it had been built and furnished only yesterday, and had yet to accumulate the detritus of human habitation. Even the tiny room under some basement stairs I called home several months ago seemed more alive than this house.

I followed him into the kitchen, but kept a respectable distance. He popped some bread into the toaster and then walked over to the fridge to get a tub of margarine. When the toast popped, he covered it vigorously with the margarine, a drummer swatting at his cymbals. He took big bites and ate with his mouth open, until a heap of crumbs lay at his feet and were scattered about his face and chest.

"What's happening, Norman?" I asked, worried that he was like one of those mutts that had chased down his truck, angry, relentless, and ready to bite.

He made a noise at me, a mixture of a cat's purr and a dog's growl, and bent over the sink to drink in lusty gulps from the tap. Finished, he wiped his face with the back of his hand, and then strode out of the kitchen toward the front door. I followed, keeping a good distance between us, saying nothing, shocked and concerned about the scene of animal hunger in the kitchen, but afraid and unsure of what to do about it.

"Wait here for a few hours," he said. "There's a TV, and you can help yourself to anything in the kitchen, even the beer."

"I don't know, Norman. I need to get back to the city."

"Right, and you will, but at the moment I need you to stay here." I could tell it wasn't a request, because he started heading toward the door.

"Where are you going, Norman? What's going on?"

He swung open the door but before he left, he turned to me. "You're really a journalist, right? You really are the aboriginal issues reporter for that rag, right? That's not bullshit?"

"That's not bullshit. And I really have to get back to the city."

"You will, you will. But there's a great story about to happen out there. A great aboriginal issues story that will make your front page," he said. "But you just gotta wait for a couple of hours."

And then he dashed out the door, the sound of his truck pulling away.

I had no idea what was happening, and though I was open to many more native things than the average person, I didn't feel safe in a neighborhood where a third of the houses were dumps. I also wasn't sure there was a story here, even one about Marvin.

Almost everyone and their dog thought what was happening to them was a news story, a front-page news story, but in reality, most of what happened in the world wouldn't even make it to a spot that had to be filled when someone pulled an ad. There was always a more newsworthy story waiting in the wings.

I didn't want to wait but I had no choice. So I sat down and watched TV. The size of Norman's TV, almost the width of a living room wall, was both amazing and disconcerting. I spent almost ten minutes running the TV gauntlet, flipping from show to show like an attention deficit child. No visual image was good enough for me to watch for more than several seconds, and I only stopped when the microwave beeped to let me know my dinner was ready.

I found the hockey game from the east coast, Rangers versus Bruins—*Five bucks on the Bruins, Dad,* I said in my head—and went to pick up my meal.

The kitchen was modern, black granite countertops and brand-new stainless steel appliances placed between cupboards that contained not only plates, bowls, cups, glasses, utensils, and pots and pans, but almost every single cooking device, tool, or gadget designed by man.

Norman had all the basics: butter, flour, sugar, bread, cereal, peanut butter, honey, and so on.; but little in the way of real food. He had no vegetables, no meat, no rice, no pasta, no spices except salt and pepper, nothing you could make a real meal from. There was actually nothing you could even make a basic lunch from: no canned soups, no cold cuts, no boxes of Kraft Dinner macaroni and cheese

His basic food group seemed to be frozen meals, TV dinners, pizzas, and fast-food items, all of which could be cooked in a microwave that had more buttons than a 747 cockpit. I had randomly chosen a TV dinner out of the pile, and I took it out of the micro-wave when the beep told me it was done. I put the steaming meal tray onto a large plate, and since Norman also had a large supply of soda and beer, I grabbed a can of beer and settled into his comfy black leather couch to watch the rerun of the game.

The coffee table had an ingenious set of hinges so that you could raise the top, like a jumbo, stylish TV tray. The meal wasn't that good, a bit chewy and too much salt, but I was bored and nervous, so eating seemed like a good thing to do to pass the time.

I must have dozed off because when the lights of a truck coming to the house woke me up, the game was over. I heard footsteps crunch up to the front and the door flew open. Norman came in but only halfway, his hand still clinging to the knob. There was a long pause during which Norman seemed on the verge of saying something, but he didn't speak for several seconds, leaving the silence to swing and twist, like a hanging victim.

And then, as if it had never existed, he brushed the silence away. "Get dressed and get in the truck. I need your help."

34

Norman drove the same way he had made and buttered his toast—with a vengeance. Both hands gripped the top of the steering wheel as he leaned forward, his nose just inches away from his hands, his eyes seeming to search for the meaning of life in the road ahead.

Overcast clouds hung above us, the soft light of the city to the north casting a gray glow in the air. The sound of rushing wind and the crunch of gravel against the tires filled the cab with noise, but there was a silence in the moment, an expectant quiet that bred an urge in me to say something, anything. Talk about the weather, ask about the Oilers, offer a compliment on his truck, any sort of small talk to lighten the mood, but I seemed to have forgotten how to speak English.

We drove for five, maybe ten minutes, making a couple of quick turns. I was completely lost, but Norman seemed divinely aware of where we were going.

We hit hardtop for a bit, the low-pitched scraping of gravel replaced by the higher-pitched whine of asphalt, and then Norman started to slow the truck, coming almost to a complete stop, before he turned into a side road that only he seemed to know existed. He leaned even farther forward, resting his chin on his hands, his eyes scanning the area.

Through the trees I could see various pieces of heavy equipment and a trailer, telling me we were in the same clearing where Norman had had the argument with the foreman of the company. The scene looked exactly the same, except there were no workers or pickups in the clearing. Also, lying across the road, blocking the way, was a large, freshly cut log. Norman sighed with deep relief, and the air in the truck became less stifling.

"Thank God. I made it back in time," he said, deflating the tension.

"Back in time for what?"

He said nothing in reply, only smiling with a crooked and innocent grin that made me want to forgive all his trespasses. He made a three-point turn, the branches of trees scraping the truck as we moved back and forth, in and out of the woods. Once he had the truck turned around, he backed the truck up slowly until the back bumper nudged the log.

He shut off the truck and stretched and twisted his back and shoulders, like a dad at the end of a long road trip with the family, and then turned and reached into the backseat. He grabbed something, but didn't bring it over to the front quite yet. He lifted his head, looking me in the eye.

"You ever handle a rifle?" he asked casually, as if he was asking me if I knew how to drive.

I knew neighborhood kids who hunted, and during clandestine late-night walks in the river valley, they had showed me how to load, hold, and shoot their twenty-tows. We shot trees, cans from rocks, and fleeting shadows in the woods, and we ran from angry voices and searching flashlights, our hearts beating and mouths gasping, half laughing, half crying in excitement, fear, and glee. I nodded, but that same sense of thrilling alarm filled my senses.

"Excellent," Norman said, and pulled out a rifle bigger than any of those twenty-twos my friends had. It was a .30-30, a typical rural Alberta rifle, used to hunt deer or to shoot coyotes. He handed it to me, stock first. I reached out for it, but just as I was going to take it from him, I held back.

"What the hell is going on?" I said. "What are we doing out here, and why do I need a gun?"

"Don't worry about it," Norman said. "It's only a prop. Go on, take it." He pushed the stock into my hand, and even though I didn't remove my hand, I didn't close my fingers on the gun.

"That's not a prop. That's a real gun."

"Yeah, but I don't expect you to use it. Just hold it like you mean it."

"What the hell for, Norman?" I asked, my voice cracking and stammering. "What the hell is going on here?"

Norman shrugged, still holding the gun out to me. "We've decided that we're sick of the oil companies stealing from us, so we're blockading this project."

"Who's we? The band?"

Norman shook his head. "Ha! Those idiots think we should talk and negotiate, but we've been talking and negotiating since you white fuckers showed up on our land, and look what's happened to us. Stolen land, residential schools, third world reserves, some of the worst poverty on earth, and more broken promises than an unfaithful husband. We're a dead people, Leo, my people, dead to the world and doomed to be trampled underneath the white man's boot if we continue to negotiate and talk. And I'm not going to let my people die. I'm not going to let your people kill my people, so this is where we start to take a stand. This is where we stop talking and negotiating and accepting lies as the truth, and start closing our legs, because we're sick of getting fucked."

He thrust the gun into my hand and let go. I was forced to grab it, to keep it from falling to the seat or the floor and possibly going off.

I tried to hold the gun firmly, pointing the barrel toward the floor, but my hand shook so much I almost dropped it. I added my other hand to the grip and stared, eyes wide with shock and terror, at Norman.

"Relax, Leo. Don't look at me like that. We might be blockading this project, but everything's under control," he said, his voice sounding calm and reassuring, although his words did little to calm or reassure me. "Despite the blockade, there is talk going on between us and the oil company, but they still think we're bluffing, so we got to at least look like we're serious. I can't sit out here alone tonight, and a lot of the other guys with me on this spent most of the day out here, so I need your help. And besides, there are two other things to make you feel better.

"Number one: I doubt anybody's going to be coming by tonight. They're in so much shock about the whole blockade concept that they haven't started to think sneaky thoughts, like trying to break in at night. But we have to be here anyway, you know, just in case.

"And number two: the gun's not loaded."

I hefted the rifle, trying to feel the weight, but I couldn't tell if he was telling the truth.

35

The seats of the new truck may have been made of supple leather, but after a few hours, that leather became too soft and yielding. When I leaned for too long on one part of my body, a painful cramp would begin, and if I let that go for too long, the area would tingle and then turn numb.

So when one butt cheek went numb, I shifted to the other, but then that, too, would go numb, so I would shift back and repeat the cycle. Later, the nerves in one of my legs fired signals to the muscles, creating an irresistible need for movement, but since I was stuck in the truck, there was little I could except jerk, twist, and shake my leg at irregular intervals.

I attempted to keep my leg still, but the nerves kept on firing, and the pressure built up to an intensity that bordered on pain, and with a gasp of frustration and relief, I released my muscles, shaking my foot back and forth as if it was on fire.

Norman wouldn't keep the engine running because that would drain the gas tank. He didn't want us to freeze, so he would start the truck every thirty minutes or so, snapping me out of a doze with the roar of the engine and a blast of cold air from the vents.

But I must have finally fallen asleep, because one minute I was blind in the dark and mentally cursing Norman, Marvin, and their people, for putting me in this unpleasant situation, and the next minute, Norman was nudging me—"Hey. There's a truck, wake up"—and when I opened my eyes, a pale light hung in front of me.

The sun hadn't risen, yet there was a natural glow rising in the air. I had a mild pressure headache from resting the corner of my forehead against the window, and my face was covered in a clammy sweat, because sometime while I slept I had pulled the balaclava over my face. The rifle rested against my thighs. The corners of my eyes clung together with clumps of eye goop, and I wiped that and sleep from my eyes.

A mist hung in the air, and for a second or two, there was nothing in front of us save the outline of trees and the line of the road, but then one of those baby blue pickup trucks appeared, pushing the curtains of fog aside.

The truck moved slowly but purposefully, coming within a foot of our truck, the two front ends almost kissing, before it stopped. I sat up, stretching out the stiffness in my back, and since I was still holding on to the rifle, it came up with me, the barrel rising above the dash and in plain view of the people in the other truck.

The driver was one of those workers from the previous day, maybe twenty years old, wearing coveralls. He had native features and long hair tucked up underneath a ratty ball cap. At first he sported a frown of disgust at me, but that quickly changed to one of surprise, and then, when he saw the rifle, anger. He leaned forward, eyes blinking rapidly, as he tried to determine if he could recognize me.

The damp coolness against my face made me want to lift up the balaclava, but the look on the driver's face changed my mind.

His passenger was the foreman, Brad, and while he, too, responded to the sight of the gun with a shake of his head, he looked more disappointed than angry. He also had a cell phone tucked to his ear, his mouth moving in a conversation I couldn't hear. Norman adjusted his ball cap and opened his door, the repeating musical tone warning him the keys were still in the truck.

"Stay here," he said. "Keep that rifle in sight. But get ready to be the aboriginal issues writer. And try to look more native."

Norman stood just outside the truck, hands on his hips. I didn't know if there was some way I was supposed to sit, or some aura I was supposed to project to look more or less native, so I just sat as I normally did when two trucks faced each other in the woods at the edge of a blockade.

I didn't like the way I was holding the gun, as if I was expecting trouble, so I set it down, pointing the barrel toward the floor and leaning the stock against the seat. I also checked the charge of the batteries on my digital recorder. They were fine but I had another couple of backup AAs in my pocket. I didn't have a notebook, but I had written many stories and quoted many people without the use of a notebook.

However, no one was really looking at me. The driver rolled down his window a crack and sparked a smoke, but he kept his eyes on Norman. Brad nodded in response to something said to him over his phone and then tucked his cell into a chest pocket.

A second later, there was a ringing from Norman. He reached into his pocket and pulled his phone to his ear. I leaned over and pulled the keys out of the ignition to stop the incessant beeping so I could hear what was being said.

"Phillip, how the hell are you? It's a nice beautiful morning out here. A little cold but there's something comforting about dawn. . . . I told you yesterday we were serious about this, but you didn't believe me. And don't believe what they're saying at the band office, this action is backed by the majority of my people. We've decided that we've been pushed around enough, that we've had enough taken from us and this is the first step. . . . I know it's Crown land,

Phil, but it's still our traditional land, land we still use and hunt on, and the treaty says if you're going to use some of our traditional land, you're going to have to come up with some kind of fair compensation. What you've offered us for destroying this piece of traditional land can't be considered fair compensation. . . . Yeah, yeah, good on you, Phillip. You got some of our people hired, and you bought the scoreboard at our community center and the sod for our sporting fields, and don't get me wrong, we appreciate all that, but you can no longer buy my people off with your trinkets and beads. We've been demanding our fair share of our mineral rights as outlined in the treaty for years, but it seems that nobody really cares about those deals, they feel that they can just take what they like."

"Oh, yeah, I've also got a member of the media with me, a reporter named Leo Desroches. Works as the aboriginal issues reporter, and he's here to see what's what and he'd like to talk to you."

He handed the phone to me and I reluctantly took it. I introduced myself, including my media affiliation. I found out his name was Phillip Thornton and he was the president and CEO of Ennaturan Resources, a mid-sized exploration company out of Calgary.

Once I forgot about the rifle, and the angry look from the driver and the foreman, and Marvin, I began to realize that with the combination of oil companies, a native blockade, and the odd gun there was a good story here.

"Am I being recorded right now?" Thornton asked, his voice sounding worried.

"Not recorded, no, but I am taking notes as we talk." I gestured to Norman for a pen and he found one in his pocket and handed it over. He also gave me a paper bag from the floor of his truck as something to write on. It wasn't great but I had used worse.

I didn't write verbatim what Thornton said, but only the gist. He talked about how important dealing with the local aboriginal community was, and how he understood about the importance of their traditional land but he didn't like the blockade. He defended his company, saying that they have gone through all the regulatory steps and made sure the subcontractors had hired enough native employees from the region.

He was right and no doubt he had done nothing legally wrong, but it didn't take much to get approval for drilling in Alberta. All you had to do was fill out the forms, apply to the Energy Conservation Board for approval, and if you weren't drilling in the middle of a school yard, or in the center of a town or city, you pretty much got the approval.

The ERCB was pretty much a big giant rubber stamp made up of oil industry types and Tory party members who needed be rewarded for their loyalty to the ruling party of Alberta.

Whether Norman was right was another story. There did seem to be a lot of natives hired to work on the project and no doubt the contract was awarded with due diligence. But the issue of natives, traditional lands, and oil, gas, mining, and other industrial development was a huge landscape of gray area, filled with metaphorical landmines that could go off at any moment and holes that could swallow you and drown you in a sea of genocide baggage and government bureaucracy.

But I didn't care who was in the right, I had something worth writing about. I just had to get home or someplace where I could file the story.

When I finished with Thornton, I handed the phone back to Norman. After he spent a few minutes haranguing the oil exec, he handed the phone to foreman Brad.

As he listened for the first few minutes, the foreman's face turned red with anger. He started shouting at the phone, arguing with the voice on the other side. The sound of his voice carried, so I could hear the anger but none of the actual words. Some seconds later, Brad slapped the phone with the palm of his hand and tossed it back to Norman.

He stared at Norman, eyes burning with anger, and for a bit I thought he would jump out of the truck. I imagined the worst sort of violence, but he said something to the driver and the truck lurched into gear.

But it wasn't reverse. The driver, ignoring Norman and looking me directly in the eyes, allowed his truck to drift forward. He touched our bumper, giving us a little nudge, and cocked his finger and thumb, like a gun, at me.

The gesture caught all of us by surprise, even Brad. By the time anybody reacted, Brad with a slap on the driver's shoulder, Norman with a "Son of a bitch" and a fist on the hood, the young native slipped the truck into reverse and backed away.

Norman followed the truck, walking all the way to the end of the road. He was like a well-trained guard dog, making no aggressive moves, no threatening sounds, just quietly yet sternly staking out his territory.

36

"I need to get back to the city so I can file this story," I told Norman.

He agreed but said he couldn't leave. We were the only ones on the site, and if we left, the company would just come in and start work again. And then they would order twenty-four-hour security to prevent anything from happening again. So I would have to wait.

We waited about an hour and half. Two more trucks came by, and there was a second when both of us flinched at the sight of them. But Norman immediately relaxed when he saw that they didn't match the color of the company truck.

The first truck was blue and white with three people in the cab, an older model spotted with rust, while the other was similar to Norman's, new, racing green, and carrying two people.

"Thank God, the cavalry has arrived," Norman said, as the trucks pulled to the side of the road and parked. The men got out. All of them were native, dressed either in coveralls or jeans and jean jackets, but all wearing ball caps. Norman went out to meet them, and they all gathered at the back end of the older-model pickup. They conversed for several minutes; I didn't hear what anybody said, but from the look of Norman's animated movements, I figured he was telling them about our recent visitors.

One of the guys raised a chin at Norman's truck, and then they all turned to look. Norman shrugged, said something, and then there were a few nods of acknowledgment to me from the group. Two of the guys waved at me, so I waved back.

Norman continued talking and pointed at several spots in the area, and most of the guys nodded. One of the guys raised his hands to stop Norman, and placed an arm around his shoulder, smiling and laughing. He gave Norman a gentle push, but there was no harm in it. It seemed like a friendly gesture meaning, "Yeah, thanks, we appreciate your advice, but we know what we're doing."

Norman took the gesture in the manner it was intended, slapped a couple of the guys on the shoulder, and walked away. As soon as he did, three of them started to unload chairs, canvas bags, coolers, chain saws, and rolls upon rolls of thick cables and chains from the back of the blue and white pickup, while the other two went to scout out the area.

Norman climbed back in the truck, started it up, and began to drive away. He gave a wave to the guys unloading the truck, but only one of them saw it. He distractedly waved back. Some had powered up their chain saws and were walking into the bush while the others started to unroll the chains and cables.

Back at Norman's house, I used his computer to file my story. The weekend editor, Steve Sericin, was surprised to get my e-mail, but pleased when he saw what I was sending him. He promised to send a shooter, so I let Norman give him directions on how to get there.

Norman clapped his hands with glee when he heard what was going to happen.

I also called Mandy on her cell and told her what was happening.

"How did you get out there?" she asked.

"After I had lunch, I got to talking to this ex-chief that I know and he told me about it. I had nothing better to do so I figured since I'm the aboriginal issues writer, it would make a good story."

"Okay, Leo, I guess." I could tell from her voice that she wasn't buying the whole thing, but since a story was being filed, there had to be some truth to what I was saying. "Don't expect to get any overtime out of this."

"Don't worry, Mandy. I won't. And I'm about to come back into the city. I'll drop by the paper and talk to Serecin about it when I get in."

"Okay. Good work, Leo. But get back to the city."

And then she added, "I miss you."

"I miss you, too, Mandy," I said. And I did. The only people I really missed seeing these last few months were my kids, Peter and Eileen. I saw Peter from time to time but not Eileen. I probably wouldn't recognize her if I did. But I did miss Mandy now. And I discovered that I also missed Larry. And Brent. But in different ways.

I hung up with Mandy and turned to Norman, who was doing his best to look like he was not listening. "I need to get back to the city," I told him. "You got your story, and who knows, maybe the TV cameras will come out once they read my piece, so you'll have more media. But my work is done and I want to go home."

He nodded. "Okay. I can't do it 'cause I gotta help the guys on the blockade. I'll find someone to come get you."

He started heading toward the door and I went after him. "Come on, Norman, you can't leave me here. I did what you want and now I got to get back to the city."

But he was already out the door and shouted back at me, "Don't worry. Someone will be here in a few minutes and he'll drive you home. Promise." He jumped in his truck and drove away.

I slammed the door behind him, swore and cursed for a few seconds but then collapsed on the couch. I turned on the TV, running through the channels, expecting to wait several hours.

But it was only a few minutes. I heard tires on the gravel and went to the door. A pickup had parked out in front; it was relatively new but looked like it had been well used. A young native kid, barely twenty, stepped out of the truck. He waved at me.

"Are you Leo?"

"Yeah. You my ride into the city?"

"You bet. My name's Greg," he said with a smile and walked over to the house.

I stepped out of Norman's house and shut the door. I turned away from the house and Greg was right in front of me.

"Hey," I said.

He drove his forearm into my face. My head snapped back, hitting Norman's front door, and it all went black.

37

I woke up coughing, a retching that started deep in my lungs and burst out in gusts that jerked at my diaphragm and snapped my head forward and back, sending wrenches of pain up and down my neck and spine.

My father had been a two-pack-a-day smoker for over forty years and there were days in my childhood when he would wake up the entire house with a series of deep coughs and barks that would last for what seemed forever. None of those incidents came even close to what I was doing right now.

There was a second when the hacking paused, a short second of relief. But with the coughing gone, there were other pains, a throbbing in the front of my head where Greg had straight-armed me and a sharp stabbing in the back where I hit the door.

My vision was clouded but I couldn't tell if it was due to the blows I had suffered or because my eyes were burning as if I was standing downwind from a campfire of wet wood.

But even in that short moment of time, I was able to figure out a few things.

I was lying facedown on something soft, a couch or maybe a mattress. The air was cool but not as cold as I remembered the day being. So that told me I was inside, in some kind of building. And it was a small building, probably a house, because I could hear the scuffling of feet and there wasn't any echo to the sound.

There was a whooshing noise, a quick flare of golden light coming from somewhere nearby. Someone shouted, "Shit! Jesus Christ!" Footsteps ran across the floor in front of me and a second later, there was the silhouette of a figure standing in the opening of a doorway. I reached out to it, pleading for it to help me, but as I stretched out, I rolled off whatever I had been lying on and fell onto a hard surface, the front of my head banging against it.

Another flash of light, this time without a whooshing noise, and I blacked out again. But this time it was short, barely a second, because when I came to, I couldn't see much but I could feel the hard floor and hear the quick slam of a door.

And then the coughing came back and for the next several minutes I was lost in that.

When that stopped, I finally figured out why my lungs were bursting with pain and my eyes were seething: I was in a house that was on fire. I couldn't see any actual flames but I could feel the heat coming from somewhere else in the building and smell the acrid scent of burning gasoline and wood.

I pushed myself up to a seated position and the hacks came back. Even so I forced myself to look about as best as I could.

There was light but it was not a welcome light source. It emanated from an adjoining room, and it flickered, giving the space I was in an eerie dancing glow. I knew from that and from the intense heat that radiated from that area, that the fire had been set there. Whoever had dumped me in this house had also set the fire and knew that this fire would catch and burn fast. So they had set it in another room because they didn't want to get caught in it.

I could hear the crackling and snapping of wood and plastic, and knew that the fire would spread quickly, engulf that room in a few minutes and then spread to the rest of the house, including the room I was in. The whole house would probably burn to the ground in about ten minutes.

But I had less time than that.

The smoke that had filled up most of my room had been gray, and even though it raged into my lungs, this smoke was mostly harmless. Darker smoke was now starting to blow in from the adjoining room, rolling along the ceiling in billows that got darker and darker.

This was what would kill me faster than any flames. This was probably what killed Marvin before the flames got to him. Detective McKinley had said that Marvin had been unconscious when he died, so while I didn't have a lot of time to save my life, at least I had more time than he did.

I held my breath and used all my will to hold back the coughs in my lungs, and stood up. My head spun but I managed to hold myself upright. The temperature increased substantially and the smoke thickened. Even though I was holding my breath, I could feel the smoke forcing its way into my nose, mouth, and lungs, sucking out the little oxygen I had left in my system. I knew I had to move much faster than I was moving.

I remembered where I had seen the figure standing by the doorway and I quickly twisted to head in that direction. But when I took a step, my foot landed on whatever I had been originally lying on and it slid out from underneath me. I fell to the ground hard, my teeth banging against each other. My hands had gone out to break my fall and my right wrist bent back sharply with a snap of pain.

There was a second of disorientation, but I came back quickly, feeling my wrist to see if it was broken. There was pain but it wasn't sharp, only a throb, so I figured it was only sprained. I also realized that my head was a bit clearer, that the temperature had dropped some and the intensity of the smoke had lessened. It was still hot and stifling but not as much as when I was standing.

I mentally kicked myself for forgetting that one of the basic rules of fire safety we learned as kids in school was to stay low. So I crawled toward the door, pulling myself along with my good wrist and pushing with my feet.

The heat intensified as I crawled and I could hear things shattering and crashing down in the adjoining room. But I did my best to ignore it. If I focused on the things that were trying to kill me, I'd never escape. I knew the odds of surviving this fire were against me, but terrible odds never did stop me.

Professional gamblers and those who did it for fun once in a while always weighed the odds. They measured how much they could risk based on how much they stood to gain. Or lose. They always thought about it and even calculated their bets before they made them.

But degenerate gamblers like me don't act that way. Even though all gambling venues, be it casinos, tracks, or bookie lounges, listed their odds so they could determine how much they paid out, we didn't care about them. It wasn't how much we expected to win or even how much we expected to lose that counted in a wager; the making of the wager was always more important.

So even if Marvin had woken up while the fire that had killed him was burning, he might have thought that he didn't have a chance and given up. He probably wouldn't have made the bet on trying to escape. He might have gone partway, but at some point he probably gave it up.

But not me. With a gambler like me, you never gave up, no matter how the odds were stacked against you, until you ran out of money. And even when the money was gone, there was always some way to make the bet. I had robbed bank after bank for about six months in the past year, using only a ball cap and sunglasses to disguise my identity. Even though the odds of my getting caught kept increasing, I still continued to rob banks. And when the police asked the media for help in solving these bank robberies, I wrote the story, my byline right next to the security camera photo of me robbing a bank.

A few months ago, I not only discovered who had been killing prostitutes, I killed the person responsible. Sure, it was a bit of self-defense, but just barely. And to hide my involvement in that crime, I made that death look like a suicide. It was a huge gamble, especially because of the detailed forensics that many police departments employed.

I had made these huge gambles with my life and had won. This time, I won again because I made it to the door. The flames and the smoke billowed and raged above me. The heat reached down, singeing my skin, licking at the walls alongside of me.

I stayed low, out of their reach, and stretched upward with my good hand. I had to push with my injured wrist and the pain almost brought me down, but I fought through the pain. I grabbed the doorknob, the hot metal burning into my skin, and I jerked my hand away. But not for long. My shirt had been torn somehow, probably when I was knocked out and dragged into the house, so I ripped a strip of material from that, and quickly wrapped it around my hand. The burned skin screamed in pain but I accepted it and moved on.

I had no choice. The flames were starting on the door and I only had thirty seconds, probably less, before they would engulf me. I started to reach up but then I stopped as I saw what was happening.

Instead of grabbing the door in hopes that it was unlocked, I decided to make an even more dangerous bet. I pulled my hand back and slowly pushed myself to a small crouching position. I tried to take another breath to prepare myself but there was no more oxygen in the house. The acrid, burning smoke tore at my lungs and I coughed it out. But as I did, I forced part of my brain to watch the door and hold my body in position.

From behind me I could hear walls crashing and the roar of flames. The smoke thickened and I could barely see in front of me. But there was enough light from the fire on the door. I waited, watched for the right time to move, because if I moved too soon, I would be knocked back. And I would have no more strength to try again.

But if I moved too late, the fire would consume me. And even though I could probably roll away from the building, I would take some of the fire with me. And it would burn me up.

So I saw my chance and tensed my body to move. But instead of jumping, I waited another couple of seconds.

And then I jumped, my arms in front of me, my head tucked in as much as I could.

The door, weakened by the fire, burst apart. There was a rush of fresh air and an explosion of fire that helped propel me farther along.

I landed on my left shoulder and rolled. I almost blacked out but the part of my brain that had kept me alive and came up with the idea to wait for the door to weaken forced me to roll again and again.

And when I felt I was far enough away to be safe, I stopped, sucking in the freezing air of the winter, basking in the joy of a winning bet. With fresh oxygen in my lungs, my body rejoiced in life, and my brain, which had kept functioning far longer than it should have, finally shut down.

I dropped into a blackness, but before I slipped completely away, I felt a pair of hands grab me. By then, I was too weak to care. I had escaped but I had no fight left in me if they wanted to throw me back into the fire.

38

My throat was aching, it felt like my lungs were full of cotton, and I couldn't stop coughing. But I was still alive. There was no fire.

Still, every time I coughed, I retched. A thin stream of yellow spittle dripped out of my mouth. Pain was everywhere, and I felt burned skin on my right arm and shoulder, where I had bashed through the burning door.

I was on my hands and knees on a carpeted floor but I couldn't see where I was. My head throbbed like I was coming off a week-long bender, and my eyes burned.

"Give him water," said a voice in the distance. I heard some rustling and then some footsteps. Someone put a hand on my shoulder, and I blindly stuck my hands out, expecting them to hand me water to drink. But he pulled my head back, and dumped a rush of water over my face.

My body jerked several times with the shock of the cold, and the water poured into my nose and mouth. I retched again. But as time passed, I realized that my lungs were beginning to recover. My breath came in halting gasps, but each one became deeper than the one before until I was taking in full breaths. My body started relaxing as oxygen filled my system. And my eyes, while still in pain, started to clear.

I was in a house, the floor covered wall to wall with pale Berber carpet, and several pieces of furniture that looked to be couches and chairs covered in black leather. I saw there was a slight mess of vomit on the floor in front of me but I ignored it.

I could see six figures, four of them standing a ways away, one right next to me, and another sitting in one of the leather chairs. It was still night out and for some reason there was only one light on, a tall, skinny modern lamp that was turned to a low setting.

"Help him up and give him a seat," the same voice said. Someone roughly pulled me up and tossed me onto the couch. The pain in my body flared again, especially the burning of my hands, and I had trouble breathing again. But my recovery time was faster.

"Do you want some water?" the voice asked again. And then he added, "To drink this time."

There was some laughter and I tried to speak but couldn't get any words out. So I nodded. The guy who tossed me on the couch handed me a bottle of water. I drank it slowly, almost throwing it up after the first swallow. But I held it down and finished it off. The dryness in my throat faded away and having some liquid in my body helped things clear up further.

The five guys who were standing were dressed in the same gangbanger fashion as the guys in the SUV several days ago. They also all had sunglasses and bandanas on their faces. All of the bandanas were red. A couple wore red ball caps.

The one sitting on the chair was older than the rest by about a decade. He wore a pair of jeans and a cowboy shirt. He also had a red ball cap on his head, but unlike the gangbangers, he wore it like a farmer. He had glasses, but they were regular prescription glasses with no tinting. His face was round, not broad like many natives, and with a skinny nose. But his eyes had the right shape and his lips were naturally pursed together. Because of the shape of his head and the roundness of his glasses, he looked like an aboriginal version of Malcolm X. I realized with a start that this was the look he was going for.

"Are you okay, Mr. Desroches?" he asked, leaning forward. "Are you feeling better?" He had the flow of a native accent, but none of the slur. That told me he had lived outside the reserve in the white world for a while, maybe for university. Or maybe like me, he grew up in the white world. He also pronounced my name correctly.

"I've been better," I croaked through a couple of coughs. "Who the hell are you?"

He waved his hand at the group. "I think you can figure out who we are."

I didn't have to look. I knew who they were. I recognized his voice from the phone in the SUV before the shooting. "You're members of Redd Alert."

"Very astute, Mr. Desroches."

"Not really," I said, still coughing now and then. "I recognized your voice from the phone a few weeks ago."

"Again, very astute, Mr. Desroches," he said with a nod

"Also, you guys aren't really subtle with how you wear your gang colors."

He laughed, leaning back in his chair. A couple of the other guys also laughed but it was forced so I could tell they didn't get the joke.

"I like you, Mr. Desroches. I really do," he said, pointing at me. "You're one heck of an Indian and a credit to our people."

"Thanks," I said sarcastically. "Is that why you tried to set me on fire?"

"We didn't set you on fire," he said, spreading his arms, palms toward me in a pose of innocence. "We saved you."

He pointed at the guy standing next to me. "In fact, Robert there saved your life. He risked his life to pull you away from the house before it all fell down."

I flashed back to the fire and remembered someone grabbing

me. But at the time, I thought it was someone who would throw me back into the flames.

I looked up at Robert. He was looking down at me, but due to his sunglasses and his bandana, I couldn't see his face. But I could see that his pants and his shirt had scorch marks on them and that the smell of smoke wasn't coming just from me.

I stood up, looked directly at his sunglasses, and held my hand up in front of him. "Thank you, Robert," I said as clearly as I could. "For saving my life."

He looked at the hand for a second, probably not knowing how to respond to this genuine offer of thanks. But then he took it and shook. "You're welcome," he said in a voice that told me he was barely an adult.

That done, I sat back down, turned to the one seated, who was obviously in charge.

"So who did try to kill me?" I asked.

He shrugged. "Don't know," he said quickly, almost as one word. "There are a lot of different factions in this area battling each other. You were seen with one of them at the blockade site, so another saw an opportunity to make a statement and you became an innocent pawn."

"Norman Threefingers's group is a gang like yours?"

"They're more of a political entity. However, many gang members belong to it, some of them Redd Alert members, but in a more clandestine way."

"So Norman doesn't know he has gang members in his group."

"Oh, no, he does. He just doesn't know which ones belong to gangs. More importantly, no one knows that Redd Alert members are involved. We're trying to be more discreet."

I looked about the room. "Yeah, I can see that."

He smiled. "This is only a PR exercise," he said, taking off his hat to show me. "I don't normally wear this around in public, but I'm doing it now because I wish to show solidarity with my fellow frontline warriors. If you saw me on the street, even on the streets of Edmonton, you would have no idea I was a member of any gang. I bet it would take a few seconds to figure out I was native. We're here in all our native colors because we knew you were doing a story on native gangs so we wanted to show you one. We also wanted to tell you something."

"Get out of town, Whitey, and leave us alone?" I asked sarcastically.

He laughed and put the hat back on his head. The other guys got the joke this time and they laughed.

"Yeah, if you could, because you'll only get hurt again. But there was something more important we wanted to tell you."

"I'm all ears," I said. "If any of you guys have my recorder, I could quote you for the paper."

He smiled but it didn't reach his eyes. "I don't think you'll need to take notes for this. I'm pretty sure you'll remember this word for word."

I shrugged, a sign telling him to get on with it.

He leaned forward, and though his voice got a little quiet, it was very clear.

"We didn't kill Marvin Threefingers."

39

I couldn't help but laugh. And from the look on the leader's face and how his henchmen stiffened, I knew they weren't too happy with my reaction. It turned into a series of major coughs but I got through it. And when I did, I chuckled again.

"You don't seriously expect me to believe that, do you?"

"I'm very serious about that. We didn't kill Marvin."

"Of course you didn't," I said with sarcasm.

"You don't believe us."

"I don't. You're a street gang. You're a bunch of thugs and criminals who will do whatever to make more money. You might have a lot of members and some organization, but you're still a street gang. Nothing more, nothing less."

He laughed. "Good, very good. That's exactly what we want everyone to think. And I'll admit, we did start as a street gang and still have many aspects"—he waved a hand at the rest of the group—"of a street gang. We deal in drugs and other bits of crime but that's just the tip of the iceberg. As I said, that's just PR so no one will think they really have to worry about us."

"I think a lot of people do worry about you guys."

"True, but only as a street gang. In reality, we are different from any one of those so-called gangs out there. We aren't a bunch of drugged-up toughs with nothing to do.

"We are warriors, proud descendents of a great people, once vanquished, but now rising soon to be even greater and more powerful than we ever were before. We have members everywhere, members like these gentlemen here, members in organizations like the one Norman Threefingers runs, and in other established and respectable native groups like his. We have people across the country, on the street, in the band offices. In the native political groups, in the native corporate world, and in many levels of white corporate business such as the oil and gas industry. They are young men like these. They are women. They are elders.

"In a few years, a few will run for political office and become part of the band council. One day we'll have a chief and when that happens we will control one of the largest native banking companies in North America. We will control almost a billion dollars in business."

His voice grew in power and I could tell he had wanted to make this speech for a long time. "And with that, we will bring our nation to real power, give pride back to our people, and then you will see what we can do. Norman's blockade and things like Oka will be nothing compared to what will happen, because we will not only have the money to back our warriors, we will have the political connections to bring a revolution to our land and our people."

He was like a James Bond villain, telling me his whole crazy plan. But in a strange sort of way, it made sense. And I wasn't too sure if I was in complete disagreement with him. Native people had suffered much since the white man arrived in North America. And here these guys were, planning to use the white man's methods to regain power. I didn't like the fact that they were dealing in drugs and crime and killing people, but I knew they would justify it by saying that there was always collateral damage in a revolution.

But they were being impatient. I knew that natives were slowly gaining power, slowly regaining their culture. People like Francis Cardinal and all those others fought for native rights and justice, and proved that natives in Canada were strong in their honest and hardworking day-to-day existence. They were the true warriors of their people, not Redd Alert.

"So why tell me all this? So I can go back to my newspaper and write all about it? Or are you going to make sure I never go back to my newspaper?"

"We're not going to stop you from going back to your newspaper and we won't stop you from writing this story. Heck, you can quote me word for word if you want."

He leaned forward and smiled at me. "But who's going to believe you? Nobody. Because the truth is, everyone, including many of our people, believe that we're a bunch of fuckups, a bunch of stupid, drunk Indians who can't even keep themselves sober for a couple of days, let alone take care of their own communities. So go ahead and write what you want."

He was right there. Canadian white society didn't have a good view of natives; they only saw the negative aspects of native life. The people living on the street, the hookers, gang members, the reserves filled with homes falling apart. They never saw the positive side of natives, except in the powwows or ceremonies with burning sweet grass and praises to the creator. They never saw the average natives down the street who were just like the average white folks down the street. People who only wanted to live their lives and help make a better future for their kids.

And I realized I was also responsible for that because in the few months I had been the aboriginal issues writer, I only wrote about crime stories involving natives, or political controversies that involved natives. There were a lot of positive native stories out there and, as Francis Cardinal had said, I was ignoring them in the name of hard journalism.

"So you're going to let me go?" I asked, hoping that it was true and I could get back to my life.

"Yes, we've delivered our message so now you can go."

"Right, you will rise up and take over Canada. I got it."

He smiled and shook his head. "No. That was just a corollary to the main message. What we really wanted to tell you is that we didn't kill Marvin Threefingers."

"Yeah, you said that. I hope you forgave me when I said I didn't believe you."

"Marvin was one of our best young warriors. Why would we kill him?"

"Because he wanted to quit. That's why."

"Marvin didn't want to quit. He loved being a part of Redd Alert. He loved what we were about, what we were planning to do in the future."

"That's not true. Marvin was a good kid. He helped people. He helped a lot of street kids."

"He did. He did help them," he said with a nod. "He was great with the young native kids in the city. That's why he was one of the best recruiters we ever had. He was so good, I wanted to give him a gold watch for all his hard work. But we don't work that way, yet."

"No, no. Marvin wasn't a recruiter," I said in disbelief. "He liked to help people."

"And he did help them. Some kids, he helped them kick drugs. Others, he got them to stop selling their bodies to the white man and found them a place to stay."

"But he didn't just help native kids. He helped a whole bunch of other street kids."

"That's true, he did. He just liked helping kids. But when he helped a native kid get back on his feet, he pointed him in our direction. He, in fact, helped some of these gentlemen, like David over here." He pointed at the gangbanger standing next to him.

"David here was a drug addict and a glue-sniffer, and to make ends meet and pay off his drug debts, he sometimes sold his body to old white men. I know it pains him for me to tell you this, but Marvin helped him. Marvin helped David find his way back to his people and now he's a proud warrior of Redd Alert. Isn't that right, David?"

David stiffened, but nodded slowly.

I couldn't believe it, I didn't want to believe, but it made sense. Marvin did help people get back on their feet, he had been helping them for a while. And with that tattoo on his hand, he must have been a member of Redd Alert at some time in his life. The only person who said he probably quit was Detective McKinley.

"But the police said you killed him because he was a traitor or he wanted to quit."

"The police have it wrong. All of us here have the Redd Alert tattoo somewhere on our body and all of us know if we do cross our fellow warriors by going to the police, or work for another gang, or kill or hurt someone who is not supposed to be harmed, then before we die, we will lose our tattoos. We will be stripped of our status as warriors before we die."

He looked at me for several seconds and then took off his glasses again. He rubbed his eyes, and when he put the glasses back on, his face showed resigned determination.

He turned to David and nodded his head. David and another gang member left the room. In the distance, I heard a door open and the sound of struggling. There were a couple of grunts, some thuds against the floor. A while later, they returned to the room through the other way. Behind them they dragged someone; at first I thought it was a dead body. It wasn't.

They tossed it in front of me and I saw Greg, the guy from Norman's group who was supposed to give me a ride home. His ankles were tied together, his wrists were lashed behind his back, and his mouth was gagged with a red bandana. There was blood coming out of his nose and his right eye was swollen shut. His other eye looked about with horror, and when he saw me, he started grunting, pleading with me to help him.

I wanted to help, but I didn't know what to do. There was no way I could take on five of these guys to save him.

The leader got off his chair and knelt before Greg. "As you know, Mr. Desroches, this is the man that was supposed to drive you back to the city. But Gregory was under orders to bring you to me before that, so I could give you our message. He didn't follow my orders. He listened to someone else, another faction, another leader, I don't know who. And he tried to kill you by locking you into that house and starting the fire."

I looked at Greg and he shook his head back and forth. He struggled against his bonds and grunted something that sounded like "No, I didn't" through his gag. But David reached over to him and slapped his face. He stopped struggling but continued to weep.

The leader leaned forward, grabbed Greg's shirt and ripped it. On the right side of his chest, just below the clavicle, there was the Redd Alert tattoo, the red stylized *R* and *N*.

The leader nodded and David knelt on Greg's chest to hold him down. Greg started struggling, kicking his legs, screaming through his gag. The other gangbangers came over to hold him down. He pushed against them, weeping, pleading, his good eye filled with terror. But there was no way he was escaping.

From his back pocket, the leader pulled out a cheese grater, three inches wide, four inches in length. It was the kind for grating larger pieces of food. When Greg saw it, he struggled even harder but David hit him again.

The leader held the grater against the skin, right over the tattoo. And before he scraped it away, he looked me in the eyes. He showed no emotion; it was if he was preparing dinner for his family.

"This is what we do to traitors. This is what happens before Redd Alert kills one of its own."

40

I sat in a pickup truck making its way through the reserve. I was alone in the vehicle with the gang leader. With his hat, even with the glasses, he looked like a young small-town Alberta farmer, not some gang member who had just scraped a tattoo off the chest of a screaming gang traitor with a cheese grater.

I worked very hard to put the images of that scene from my head but I knew they would come back over and over again. I had witnessed a lot of gruesome scenes in my time. About a decade ago, I was invited to be a spectator for an experimental surgical procedure for cancer, but what had happened in that house a few moments before was the worst thing I had seen in my entire life.

I made a mental reminder that if I got home, the first thing I would do was throw away my cheese grater. I would never use a cheese grater again.

"You look a little pale, Mr. Desroches. At least pale for a white man."

"Was that entirely necessary?"

"Of course. I told you we don't take kindly to traitors so we must send a message to others about what happens to traitors."

"I meant, did you have to do it in front of me?"

He reached an arm across the seat and slapped me on the shoulder. "Of course I had to do it in front of you. You had to know that we didn't kill Marvin Threefingers, and since you didn't believe me when I told you, I had to show you that we didn't."

"Okay, okay. I believe you. Redd Alert didn't kill Marvin Threefingers."

"Good. I'm glad we got that cleared up."

We drove a little while longer until we got to a secondary highway. He made a left turn and we headed north.

"So if Redd Alert didn't kill Marvin, who did?" I asked.

"Ahh. A very good question. Unfortunately, the answer isn't clear to me or anyone else but there is always one way to find out who killed someone."

I was getting tired of these cryptic clues and was almost to the point where I didn't care who killed Marvin. I just wanted to get home. But the journalist in me couldn't stop myself from asking what the hell he was talking about.

"As you probably guessed, I've witnessed a lot of crime in my life. And despite my speech about our great warriors and how we will bring power to our people, the main motivation behind it all comes down to one thing: money. The only way we can gain power is to gain money, first by criminal means and then by taking over this band and controlling their finances. And the reason Marvin was killed was because of money. That's it."

"Marvin didn't have any money. Or at least that's how it seemed to me. Unless you guys were funneling him some. But it probably wasn't enough to kill him."

"I've seen someone killed for less than ten dollars, Mr. Desroches. It doesn't have to be a lot of money for someone to die."

He was right. There were a lot of stories in the paper about people being killed for minuscule amounts of money.

"But in this case," he continued. "There was a lot of money involved."

"But Marvin didn't have that kind of money."

"Yeah, but he was about to come into a lot of money. Before he died, he was only a couple weeks away from his eighteenth birthday and—"

"He gets his oil trust fund money," I cut in. Marvin was a member of a band that distributed some of their oil revenues directly to their band members in a lump-sum payment when they turned eighteen.

"That's right. Marvin was due to get a large amount of money when he turned eighteen. And as a faithful member of Redd Alert, he was going to give us a good chunk," he said, as we passed a sign saying we had left the reserve and were now in the county of Wetaskiwin. "We would allow him to purchase some goodies of his own, a truck, some other luxuries, maybe make a down payment on a house. I mean, our people deserve this money to make up for how the oil companies have raped our traditional lands, so we let them buy some things that make them happy. But the rest they give to us."

That was one of the reasons why Redd Alert was stronger than many other native gangs in the country; they had a reliable supply of money coming from their members. It was probably why they were keen on recruiting members who were still in their teens.

"But it was Marvin's money," I said. "He could do with it what he wanted. If he wanted to give it to Redd Alert, he could give it to Redd Alert. If he wanted to blow it on a new truck, drinks for all his friends, whatever, he could do that."

"Yeah, but Marvin's family wasn't happy with his plans for his money. They weren't happy with Marvin being in Redd Alert because Redd Alert has become a strong force in this community and some of the other, established political groups in this reserve don't like sharing power, even with each other."

I thought about that for a second but it didn't make sense. Marvin's parents were dead. He had no brothers or sisters. "He had no—" I started to say but then it hit me. I was so stunned that I sat there with my mouth open for several seconds.

And when I came back, I asked if he would turn the truck around.

He slowed down so he could face me. "Are you sure? It might not be a good idea."

"Turn the fucking truck around," I shouted.

So he did.

41

He left me at the side of the highway about a hundred yards away from the entrance to the blockade. As he drove away he wished me luck, but I ignored him. I knew their plans were doomed. It didn't matter what he hoped they would accomplish and how high-minded they thought they were, his actions with the cheese grater meant they would never succeed. No matter how pretty the words they used to describe themselves, they were only a street gang.

The weather was still nasty, the wind biting and harsh, but the weather was nothing to me. This winter would not kill me.

When I came around the corner onto the approach road my feet crunched on the snow and gravel. I held my hands over my head to show that I wasn't dangerous. I made it halfway in and then a set of headlights flashed on me. A voice shouted in the wind.

"Who is it? What the fuck do you want?" It was Norman's voice.

I waved my arms to show I meant no harm. I had no idea what I was planning to do, but it wasn't the first time I had decided to confront a killer. I had killed that time and I had no idea if I could kill again. It all depended on the circumstances.

"It's me, Norman," I shouted, and I wasn't sure if my voice carried in the wind. "It's Leo."

There was a pause and then the truck started and moved forward. I first thought he was going to run me down so I got ready to jump away and dash into the woods.

But he wasn't trying to run me down; he was just pulling closer. When the truck came even with me, he rolled down the driver's window. His face was full of shock but not guilty shock. He was just surprised to see me out there.

"Leo? What the fuck you doing out here? I thought you went home?"

"Naw, I just went into Wetaskiwin for a bit and decided to come back and see how things were going," I said as nonchalantly as I could. "My editor wants me to hang around for an update. He's pretty sure this story is going to break nationally and he wanted someone here."

"Wow, that's pretty cool. So you think there might be more media?"

"There might," I said with a shrug. "Uh, Norman, if you don't mind, could we continue this in the truck? Pretty cold out here."

"Yeah, yeah, sure. Come on around."

I walked around to the passenger side and climbed in. The heat was blasting out of the vents and it felt nice to be out of the wind. The truck smelled of sweat and stale coffee. I adjusted my feet so each was on a different side of the rifle. I was glad the gun was still there.

"You okay?" Norman asked, and I could tell he actually meant it. He was also still surprised.

"Yeah, I'm fine. Just a bit tired," I said, acting uncomfortable with the gun between my legs. I grabbed the barrel, brought it up to my lap, and pretended to adjust myself so I could settle in. "You here alone?"

"Yeah, for a couple of hours. The guys have done a pretty solid job making sure the perimeter is secure and no one's going to bother us in this cold."

"Oh. Cool," I said. I put my hand around the trigger hold and adjusted the rifle so that the barrel was pointed toward Norman.

He saw it and backed away a bit. "Whoa, Leo. Be careful with that. I know it's only supposed to be a prop but it's still loaded."

I looked down at it but didn't move. "Yeah, I know it's loaded. That's why I have it on my lap. I wanted to ask you a couple questions."

"Yeah, sure," he said with a bit of a stammer. "But I'd be more comfortable if you moved the gun. It's a bit dangerous like that."

"I know. But I also need to know if you killed Marvin."

His eyes went wide with shock. And it looked like it was actual shock. "What! Kill Marvin? I didn't kill Marvin. Those gang types killed Marvin. Those Redd Alert fuckers killed Marvin. He was going to quit, and they didn't like it so they killed him."

"That's not what they told me."

"They're a bunch of goddamn liars, a bunch of criminals, a stain on a community like ours. They aren't true natives, they're traitors to their own people."

"Yeah, I'll agree with you on that, and when they told me they didn't kill Marvin, I didn't believe them, either. But then they showed me something that convinced me they didn't kill Marvin."

I adjusted the gun to point it a bit to the left, toward his stomach. He noticed and shifted but there was really no way he would get away if I pulled the trigger. "They said he was still a good gang member when he died. So they had no reason to kill him."

"Those bastards are lying. They're criminals, so of course they would say they didn't kill him. Of course they would say he didn't want to quit."

"Not really," I said with a shake of my head. "When these guys kill someone for stuff like that, they like to let people know they did it, so everyone understands they're badasses. That's the way these guys work. If they could they'd take out an ad in my paper."

"Well, they're lying."

"Not about that. I'm pretty sure about that." I shifted and held the rifle even closer to Norman. He backed away but there was nowhere for him to go, except out the door. And he didn't know how serious I was. He didn't know if I would get a shot off as he tried to escape.

"So I'll ask you again, Norman: Did you kill Marvin?"

He whimpered a bit, looking at the gun. But he said nothing.

"Did you kill him?" I asked again.

He backed away and then he made a grab for the door handle but couldn't get it open. I slid toward him quickly, my finger on the trigger and the barrel shoved against his stomach.

"Did you kill Marvin?" I demanded, my voice echoing in the cab of the truck. I shoved the barrel deeper into his gut and tears came to his eyes. I looked at him, stared in his eyes, and knew that I could kill him. I had done it once before; it would make no difference if I did it again.

I probably wouldn't get away with this one because there was no way to make this one look like a suicide the way I'd made Gardiner's. But at that moment, I didn't care. I didn't worry about what would happen if I did. That's why capital punishment never worked and why Canada didn't have it; we knew it wasn't a deterrent. We knew most people didn't think before they killed someone, they just did it.

Finally, Norman broke, his body bursting into a series of spasms. "Okay, okay. I killed Marvin. I did it." I was so shocked by his admission that I pulled away. "But I didn't mean it. It was an accident." He started sobbing and couldn't speak anymore.

I leaned back, at once happy that I knew who killed Marvin but also devastated to know that Norman did it.

"Tell me how it happened," I said.

"I don't know how it happened. It was an accident. We were at his place and we were arguing about what he was going to do about his trust fund money. He wanted to give it to his gang, those god-damn Redd Alert assholes, and I told him he was being stupid. That he should use it for his education or something more valuable than a stupid street gang. He didn't like that and we got into a shoving match. I shoved a bit too hard and he . . ."

He broke down again and I didn't have to finish the rest. A good number of people had killed family members accidently in similar fights. The incidents not only killed one person, it usually destroyed the one who did the killing and the rest of the family.

"So why the burning? Why didn't you just go to the police and tell them what happened? If they charged you, it probably would have been only aggravated assault. Even if you were convicted, they would have given you time served and let you go with probation."

"I don't know, I just panicked," he said, shaking. "I thought if I burnt him, it would look like someone from his gang did it. And for a while it did."

I knew I couldn't judge him for that. I had once taken a dead ex-policeman's body to a farmer's field in the middle of the night, put his own gun to his head and pulled the trigger to hide the fact that I had killed him. And I hadn't killed him by mistake, I had done it on purpose because he had killed Grace Cardinal.

Suddenly there was a heavy metallic crash against the box of the truck, one that rocked us back and forth on the shocks as if some-one was jumping up and off the back.

We both leaped in our seats—Norman shouting, "Jesus!," while my frozen heart jumpstarted and beat in a flurry of rhythms—and turned in the direction of the noise to see a large rock teetering against the right rear fender inside the box of the truck.

And then we heard the sound of engines that I first thought was another truck, but the pitch of the engine was too high, a whine instead of a growl. And there were two of them, the sound echoing from opposite sides of the truck, rather than from the access road in front.

I turned to the right and saw the beams of two small headlights bouncing through the trees toward the truck.

The lights turned away, showing me a darkened vision of someone riding an ATV, and when it reached the clearing it was joined by another from the other direction, their bouncing lights settling as they reached smoother ground. They drove around the area for a few seconds, digging up the ground, voices hooting and hollering.

"Sonsabitches!" Norman shouted, forgetting that he had just confessed to killing his nephew, and dashed out of the door. He strode to the back of the truck, screaming obscenities and waving his arms like a madman. At the same time, the two ATVs made a run toward us, coming from the right in a semicircular path that brought them five meters from the truck.

They roared past, and a second later a hail of rocks rained down on the truck, striking the box and bouncing off the side, smashing into the top of the cab, punching small dents into the metal. I threw myself into my seat, covering my head with my arms, hoping that none of the rocks broke through the glass.

I heard the engines rev up for another pass, and at the peak of it I cringed, gritting my teeth, waiting for another onslaught. There was another volley of rocks, this time one of them hitting the glass, raining shards against my back. There was also a buzzing noise, followed by a loud bang that rattled the truck.

It was stupid, I knew, because if it was a shot another one could be coming, but at the sound I instinctively jumped up, searching for the bullet hole and the origin of the noise. I looked around, seeing nothing except the lights of the ATVs bouncing through the trees, moving away from us.

A second later, I realized I couldn't see Norman. I perked up, shouted, "Norman!," and tried to peer over the back of the truck, my eyes frantically scanning the area to see where he had gone. I couldn't spot him.

I jumped out of the truck. "Norman!" I shouted again, my voice cracking with fear. I ran around the back, almost slipping on the wet ground, catching myself by grabbing the side tailgate, and then I saw Norman lying on his back, his mouth open to the falling flakes.

He's been shot. The thought exploded in my brain.

42

I slid to my knees, running my hand over his body, trying to find the wound, trying to determine if he was still alive. My heart caught in my throat, my lungs frozen. "Norman! Norman! Norman!" I was sputtering, spit flying out of my mouth with my words, striking him in the face.

Norman jerked, his arms flailing at me, knocking me on my ass. "Jesus Christ, Jesus Christ, Leo! I'm okay, leave me the fuck alone. Jesus."

He sat up, rubbing his back like an old man, and relief surged through my body. My heart leaped, battering my breastbone, and my lungs sucked in gasps of air.

"Thank God you're alive. I thought they shot you," I stammered.

"That wasn't a shot," he said, his voice full of annoyance. "It was a firecracker. Those sonsabitches were just trying to scare us, and by your reaction, I think they did a good job of it."

"I thought they shot you. That's what I thought when I heard the bang, and then you weren't there, and then you were lying on the ground. I thought you got shot."

"Relax, Leo. Nobody got shot," he said, raising his hand to the top of his head, wincing when he touched it. He pulled his hand away and his fingertips were dabbed with blood. "Rock got me in the head and knocked me down, that's all. A little bit of blood and

I'll probably need a few stitches, but I'll be fine. Nothing to worry about, they were just trying to scare . . ."

Norman finished his sentence, but his voice was drowned out by another engine roar, this one heavy and deep, gunning with acceleration up the access road. We turned, and in that instant the high beams of a pickup truck flashed on, stabbing our retinas into blindness. But there was enough time to see that the truck was racing toward us with no intention of slowing.

Or at least, that was what I thought. I jumped to my feet, turning toward the lights to determine its intended path, to decide which direction to flee.

There was another loud bang, a deafening blast that seem to burst from my soul, and then something kicked into my stomach, a punch like Dad used to give, like he gave that day I shot an eighty-five and beat him for the first time in golf. Hard and painful, but heartening.

There was a crack of breaking glass, a scream, and the harsh scrape of wheels coming to a quick stop on gravel. I heard another scream and then there was a wailing. The sound reached into my chest and squeezed my heart.

"Jesus fucking Christ!" someone else shouted from the truck, and after a quick pause, there was a spray of gravel striking metal as the pickup backed away as fast as it had approached. The tires squealed when they hit the main road, and the engine roared away toward the reserve.

When the silence returned, I realized that I was still holding the rifle that I had just used to get Norman to confess to killing Marvin. In the melee of the quads, my fear of the falling rocks, the bang of the firecracker, and my thought that Norman had been shot, I had jumped out of the truck carrying the gun. A puff of smoke drifted from the barrel, and my wrists ached from the kickback of the shot.

Norman stared at me, eyes wide in a mix of surprise and fear. "What the hell did you do, Leo?"

"It was an accident. I didn't mean to."

"What the hell did you do, Leo?" His voice grew in volume, almost a shout.

"I—I thought you were shot. I thought they shot you. I—I . . . I didn't mean it. I didn't want to shoot anyone. I was only trying to scare them."

My head was spinning. *I shot someone. I did. Someone. Shot them.*

My brain whirled with images: Brad the foreman, sitting in the passenger seat of the truck, talking on his cell phone, angry but his face tight as he held in his emotions. A bullet-sized hole popped through the windshield in front of him and he reached across with his right hand to clutch his chest as if he was having a heart attack. But as his fingers tightened their grip, streams of blood surged through his knuckles. His face was shocked, surprised, annoyed, his emotions able to break free at that moment.

And then he fell over, disappearing behind the dashboard.

Or else it was the native driver, smiling like a used car salesman with just his mouth and teeth, the eyes watchful and wary, cocking his finger and thumb like a gun, the way he did a few days ago.

"Gotcha." That's what he said. "Gotcha." And then a puff of smoke drifted in front of him, obscuring his face, and when it cleared, his eyes were empty and his mouth slack, a trickle of blood dripping from a perfectly round circle in the center of the forehead. His neck was loose and his head dropped back against the headrest, just taking a nap, nothing serious.

The images ran over and over in my head, the explosion of the shot bouncing off the walls of my skull. I knew I never really saw those images, never saw who got shot, but I was lost in terror, lost in my uncontrollable mind, the world around me meaningless because, because . . . *I shot someone. I killed them. But the gun, the gun . . . Fuck the gun, it makes no difference now, it wasn't really a prop, it was loaded and you shot someone. . . . You shot Brad, you shot whats-his-name, the driver, you killed him. No, I did it. I killed him. But I didn't mean it, it was an accident. . . . Makes no difference, accident or not, I killed them.*

I felt someone wrench the gun from my hands, and a bit later, heard the sound of something falling in the distant brush.

"Leo," a voice called out to me. "Leo." It was quiet, yet strong, and jerked me out of my thoughts. Hands gripped my biceps and squeezed my arms against my sides. The deep pressure, the sensory stimulation pressing against me, settled my brain and gave me enough presence to focus my vision. Eyes stared at mine, warm and welcoming eyes, familiar ones.

"Leo," Norman said. "Come back, Leo."

"I shot someone."

"No. You didn't. Nobody got shot."

"No. I did shoot someone. I killed them."

"No. You didn't. Nobody got shot. Nobody got killed, you got that? The gun went off accidently, but you didn't shoot anybody, you didn't kill anyone. Everybody's fine, all right?"

"Really? I thought I—"

"Forget about that, Leo. Forget about the gun. You didn't kill anyone. Nobody got shot."

"Really? Nobody got shot?"

"Nobody got shot."

For a second, I believed him; I understood his words as the truth and a wave of relief flooded over me and my legs gave out. Norman hung on, and though we both slumped, he kept me on my feet, his soothing voice centering me in the moment.

"Leo. Stay with me, okay? You gotta pay attention. Okay? Pay attention."

I regained control of my legs and snapped upright. "Right. Right."

"You with me, Leo?"

"I'm here. What's up?"

"You have to go, you understand me? You have to leave now, got that? Take the truck and go. Right now."

"Take the truck? But it's your truck."

"Don't worry about me. The main thing you have to worry about is you, and you have to go. You can't stay here anymore."

"Why not?"

"Because . . . because you can't be here. You don't belong here and you have to leave."

"But I—"

"Shut up, Leo. This isn't the place for a fucked-up white man like you. Even a fucked-up Indian like you. Especially now. You have to go."

"I have to go?"

"Yes, you have to go. Take my truck and head back to the city."

"What about you? If I take the truck, you can't go home."

Norman smiled and slapped me on the left shoulder. "Don't worry about me. Just take the truck. I have my phone and I can call someone to give me a ride."

"You'll get a ride from someone else?"

"Yeah, I'll get a ride. But you," he said, steering me toward the truck, "have to go. Drive back to the city."

I climbed into the truck and Norman reached around me, pulling the seat belt over and clicking it into place.

"But what about your truck? How will I get your truck back to you?"

"Just park it somewhere downtown and I'll find it later."

"Downtown's a big place."

"Jesus, Leo, just get the fuck out of here." He reached across and turned the key in the ignition, the engine jumping to life. "There's not a lot of time. Just park the fucking truck downtown and forget about it. I'll find it when I need to find it."

"You sure? I don't want to—"

Norman slammed the door, cutting me off. He waved his hand toward the access road. "Get the fuck out of here, Leo. Just go! Now!"

I looked at the road, trying to remember how to drive. Something told me to grab the gearshift, and once I did that, body memory came into play. My foot stepped on the brake, I pulled the lever toward D, and my other hand tightened its grip on the steering wheel. I felt the short jerk as the transmission slipped into gear, and was about to release the brake, but I held off for a second. I turned toward Norman and pushed the button to roll down the window. Despite Norman's assurances that everything was okay, I knew things weren't good.

"You'll take care of the gun, won't you, Norman?"

He nodded, but waved me on. "Forget about the gun, Leo. You never had a gun. Just get the fuck out of here and go back to the city."

I nodded. He was right. It was time to go back to the city where we fucked-up white men and Indians belonged. I traded the brake for the gas and pulled out along the access road.

When I got to the hardtop a few seconds later, I turned right, away from the reserve. I pushed the gas pedal down, accelerating to a hundred kilometers per hour, letting the cold wind blow in so I could clear my head and find the focus I needed to make the trip into the city. I was lost, and not just directionally. After a few minutes, I pulled onto the shoulder, shoved the gear out of drive, and just managed to open the door before I puked my guts out.

Everything came out, the half-digested bits of a sandwich the Redd Alert gave me, bitter stomach acid and bile. And when everything was gone, I dry heaved, my stomach wrenching until I almost passed out from the pain and effort. Finally it stopped. And a second later, the grief of killing again burst out of me. I wailed like a mother who had just lost her child, the metallic pinging of Norman's door-ajar alert keeping time with my sobs, and echoing through the killing winter air.

43

As I drove back to the city, unsure of what would happen next, the images of Brad and his driver getting shot started to play again, but I was able to keep them in the back part of my brain while the front part drove the truck. It was a sensation that I had to get used to, because although the scenes were imaginary I knew they would never leave.

Despite the accidental nature of the night's events, the guilt would cling to me forever, adding to my already heavy baggage and my other crimes, the most heinous of the lot being my leaving Peter and Eileen without saying good-bye, leaving them to grow up with the whispers of the town to drift about them, leaving them to wonder if Dad really loved them—*If he really did love us, then why did he leave?*—leaving them to wonder if they were responsible for my departure, and leaving Joan to deal with the whole mess all by herself.

And that brought up the question: Which was the worse crime? Taking the life of someone, removing them from the confines of the earth to the fates of whatever afterlife was waiting for them, or leaving the lives of your children in pieces they'd be picking up for the rest of their lives?

Chances were I would never find the answer to that question and the guilt would manifest itself in a perpetual reliving of each crime, in an eternal and futile effort to gauge which crime was the most serious of all.

I finally closed the window and in the distance I saw the glow of the city, a beacon stretching across the horizon. I kept it in my sights, and at the next major intersection I made my turn, not sure which highway I was on or whether I was moving north, south, east, or west, but knowing I was heading in the right direction, back to the light, back to the city. There was no other place for me to go.

A couple hours later, I parked the pickup in the lot near the bus station. I made a quick search of the truck, looking for any incriminating evidence or remnants of my presence. In the ashtray, I found a mound of change and I pocketed it. I slipped four quarters into a machine and it spat out a card saying I had two hours to park. I brought the card back to the truck, tossed it faceup on the dash, and headed toward the bus depot. I would leave the truck behind, not worrying about leaving a clue.

In the bus station, I ignored all the activity and the signs offering tickets and boarding passes to Toronto, Calgary, Fort St. John, and Jasper. I went into the public washroom. The two urinals were occupied, so I leaned against the counter until one of them was free.

The first guy to finish looked a little like I did, not exactly, but in the way we dressed, storm rider over a flannel shirt, jeans over work boots, and face and hands scarred and weathered by labor. He turned from the urinal and moved to a sink to wash his hands. We stepped around each other, making brief eye contact and nodding once, as men do in such situations.

I stepped up to the urinal and began my business. The pee flowed fast and free, an uninhibited stream as my body did its best to remove all the toxins that had collected over the last several hours.

Physically, I could feel a great weight lift off me, but that only made the emotional and mental weights seem heavier. I concentrated on the wall of tiles directly in front of me, ignoring the man next to me, but there was an unusual sound coming from the urinal. Pee splattering against porcelain has a distinctive ping, but my pee sounded heavier, almost fleshy. I looked down.

There was a green apple at the bottom of the urinal, a bright green, perfectly formed Granny Smith apple, the skin glistening and spotted with drops of urine. I looked over at the guy next to me to see if he had seen the same vision, but he was finishing, his shoulders rising as he zipped up.

He gave me a noncommittal smile, a quick nod, and left the washroom without washing up. I turned to see if the other guy had also seen this vision while he peed, but he was no longer in the room. I turned back and stared at the apple, this perfect piece of fruit in the most incongruous of locations.

Apples of this pedigree are found at roadside stops in the Okanagan, not on one of the main highways but on a side road, a road to nowhere and everywhere. Places where the fog of the semimoist Pacific air, light after dumping part of its rain before climbing over the coastal mountains, kisses the sides of the round hills of the valley; where the people offering the apples for sale are the same ones who picked the apples that very morning; where families have been growing and picking apples since people discovered that they could grow apples in that climate.

Apples of this pedigree are found in the still life paintings of master Impressionist painters, where the colors and shapes of the fruit blend into each other like droplets of rain on a window.

Apples of this pedigree are not found at the bottom of urinals in the men's washroom of the Edmonton Greyhound bus depot.

Someone stepped into the urinal next to me, and even though I was finished, I stood there and stared at the apple. A second or two later, I heard someone say, "Hey, buddy, you finished?" It took a moment to realize that the voice was speaking to me, so I quickly zipped up and stepped away, mumbling an apology.

276 ⊛ WAYNE ARTHURSON

The guy pushed past me, but I didn't complain. He would understand as soon as he saw the apple. I watched his urine strike the apple, but he made no comment, made no sign if he saw the vision of produce below him.

Reluctantly, I turned away from the apple. I chose a sink at the far end of the counter, and removed my jacket and shirt, draping them over the door of one of the stalls behind me.

I started a combination of cold and hot water and stabbed the base of my right palm against the soap dispenser, gathering as much soap as I could in my hand. I lathered and spread it over my face, my arms, my underarms, and my torso. I reached behind, and as best as I could, I washed my back.

I wasn't worried about the response of my fellow patrons; they might give me strange looks, but the sight of someone taking a sink-side shower in a bus depot washroom wasn't all that unique. No one would call security to complain. I grabbed a succession of paper towel wads and did my best to dry myself. I tossed the towels into the garbage and waited a moment or two for the air to dry the rest.

But it was getting cold in the washroom; pinpricks of goose bumps formed on my skin and a shiver rolled through, so I turned and grabbed my shirt from the top of the stall door. My arms slipped into the sleeves and I started to button up when I saw that the apple was still there, gleaming like a green diamond in the rain.

With my eyes still staring at the apple, I pulled my storm rider down and slid it on. The weight of the layers faded the cold away. Even though I knew I was still laden with weight, I felt clean and refreshed. And before anybody came in, I stepped to the urinal, bent down and picked up the apple. It was warm and wet, yet at the same time it was cool and dry. I shook off the excess urine droplets into the urinal and took the apple to the sink.

I turned on the same combination of hot and cold water that I had used on myself, and spent the next five minutes rinsing the apple. I rubbed the skin with my hands and turned the apple over and over, making sure the tap water reached every inch.

I left the bus depot and stepped back into the city. I looked at the parking lot, trying to find where I had left Norman's truck, but thankfully it was lost in the pack of vehicles. Behind the lot, I could see the large neon sign of the casino across the street and to the north. I stared at it for a while, I don't know how long, but I knew that the doors had probably just opened.

There was still a crispness in the air outside, but there was also something else. Maybe it was the sun, hanging higher and longer in the sky. Maybe it was the smell of the new growth that was waiting to come forth. Maybe it was the way the fog of my breath dissipated just a second or two faster than before.

Maybe it was all the other signs that we register only instinctively, subconsciously, but know they are there, know we are feeling them, even if we can't describe them.

How can one describe love, fear, hate, or joy? It was the same. It would still be a month, maybe two, there would still be several more dumps of snow, a week of dangerous cold and wind, but there was no doubt that the end of a long, cold winter was near.

I had only to wait.

I reached into my pocket and pulled out the apple. The green had diminished slightly, but with the grayish-brown snow surrounding me on the street, the sidewalk, everywhere, it glowed with freshness. I took a large bite, my teeth breaking through its skin and crunching through the white flesh of the fruit. And headed toward the paper.

I had a story to write. Not the story I had hoped to write; I wouldn't write anything about who killed Marvin. Instead, I had a shooting at an oilfield blockade near a reserve. Someone might be dead. I knew there was a weight in that death, but I also knew my story would lift that weight. Writing the stories always did and I would do my best to keep writing stories for as long as I could.

I didn't know how long I would last. A couple of years, maybe more. Maybe I would fall apart when Mandy imploded as the city editor and we could fall apart together, I didn't know.

But I would keep writing until I did.

44

Dr. Sen was at the security desk. I waved and gave him a smile. I tossed the apple core into the garbage. I said hello and asked him how his day was going, but he said nothing. His face was blank but he gave a small shake of his head. It was weird because of how he always said something to me, even when he was busy or I had to rush up to meet a deadline.

I didn't think much about it because I had been writing and rewriting the story of the shooting at the blockade over and over again in my mind. It was all I could do to keep from falling apart, from falling into the abyss that I escaped from eighteen months ago. I knew there was a time when I would plunge into that hole again, be it accidentally or on purpose, but today wasn't that day. Even with all that had happened—Marvin's body, the blockade, the bit with the cheese grater, the shooting—I wasn't going to fail today. I wasn't going to let anyone down, not Marvin, not Larry, not Mandy, not Peter. Not myself.

I kept the story in my mind as I rode the elevator up to Editorial. I didn't think about anything else because I couldn't finish the story if I thought too much about who pulled the trigger. Even though it was an accident I would dream about that moment forever. But the nightmare would have to wait until tomorrow.

I had a deadline to meet and a story to write.

I stepped out of the elevator and made my way down the hallway into the newsroom. It was packed with reporters but no one was working. The room was silent. I had experienced such silence in the newsroom before but only when it was empty. It was full, but no one was saying or doing a thing. Except watching me make my way to the desk. Mandy was standing by my desk and I smiled at her.

The look on her face told me there was bad news. But I would turn that news into something good. Brent had his back to me but turned when Mandy jerked her chin in my direction. His face was dark; the only time I had seen him look like that was when he got the phone call from his wife telling him that his daughter had broken her arm at school.

I knew there was a weight in the room, that everyone was expecting me to be fired. And I knew my story would lift that weight. Death on a reserve, even violent death, wouldn't rate much coverage. But since oil was involved, it was big news. Front-page news. I knew the RCMP detachment in the area would be surprised to hear from a big-city journalist, especially this early in the story, but I wouldn't need much from them. Maybe confirmation about who got shot and their condition, but the rest would come from eyewitness accounts.

Me being the eyewitness. I wouldn't tell Larry that, unless he forced me to tell him. And I knew he would forgive my trespasses when I showed up with this story.

And it wouldn't stop with just the story I would write today. This kind of story had legs. It not only had the criminal aspect of the shooting, it had political and economic repercussions. Fingers would point and the specter of aboriginal land claims and the denial of protection of traditional lands would rise again. Lloyd Robertson might lead with this story on the national news in a day or so, but only after I broke the story.

And before the week was out I would probably need to get

quotes from the provincial minster of energy, someone from Native Affairs, the grand chief of the Assembly of First Nations, probably the premier and maybe even the PM.

I was almost to my desk when Larry came out of his office. I expected anger, a shout of "Leo!" across the newsroom. But he was silent. His expression was a mix of disappointment, sadness, and shock. He looked like someone who has just received the news that a beloved relative had died.

A second later, a uniformed cop followed him. Out of the corner of my eye, there was movement. I turned my head and two uniformed constables were coming from behind the reception area. In my determination to get to my desk and pound out my story, I hadn't noticed them when I came in. They moved toward me.

The banks, I thought. *They finally figured out that I was the one robbing all the banks.*

But when Detective Al Whitford came out of the office a half second later, a look of hardness on his face, a look that I had never seen before, I knew it was something else.

All he had said about the Gardiner case being dead and me no longer being a suspect were lies. All these months he had been fooling me, making me feel I was safe, making me feel that I had gotten away with killing that crazy killer.

But then again, maybe that wasn't why they were here. Maybe Norman had lied to me about covering up the shooting at the blockade site. Maybe to cover up that I knew he killed Marvin, he had decided to turn me in.

I had my money on the Gardiner murder, but whatever it was, I was on the losing side. I had made some high-stakes bets in the past several months, some of the biggest bets of my life. And even though I had gotten ahead for a while, I had kept making more bets. And now, it was time to lose. All gamblers know that the time to lose always comes. The smart ones try to get out before, or at the very least, minimize those losses. But gamblers like me don't operate that way; we just keep laying down the bets until it's too late.

We all converged at my desk. Brent Anderson remained in his seat, watching the situation with horror.

"Leo Desroches?" Whitford said in an officious tone, as one of the constables placed a hand on my shoulder.

"Hey, Al, what's up?" I said, trying to be as light as possible.

And then it all happened so quickly. The constable that had come out of Larry's office put his hand on my shoulder, spun me around, pressed me forward against my desk, and swept my right hand behind my back, all in one quick, fluid motion. There was a click as one half of the handcuffs snapped onto my wrist. The metal was cold and hard, biting into my skin.

Whitford read the charge, but since my head was pressed against the desk, I could barely hear it. The constable seamlessly pulled my other arm around my back and snapped on the other cuff. He leaned his weight into me, pressing me against the desk, and I felt his right hand pat me down.

Detective Whitford continued to read my rights under the Canadian Charter of Rights and Freedoms, but I had stopped listening by then. A feeling of sadness came over me, but it had nothing to do with being arrested. I knew I should have been upset that I might be going to prison and that I would probably never see my friends or family again.

But it was not being able to write the story that bothered me the most. That great story that I had in my head would never be written. Some other media outlet would break the news about the shooting at the reserve. Some other reporter would follow the story, maybe get to ask the PM about the situation.

Brent might get the initial crime story and all the immediate fallout. But as the story progressed into something more political, it would go to the government side of the newsroom. With the cutbacks in the system, it would probably be handed to some national reporter and we would run it like a wire piece.

I looked at Brent. The look of horror deepened on his face. But I smiled at him. Not that I found what was happening funny, but because even though one of his closest colleagues was being arrested, cuffed, and searched right in front of him, he didn't move. He watched and heard it all.

More importantly, he took notes.

That made me smile.

-30-

ABOUT THE AUTHOR

Wayne Arthurson, a native of Edmonton, Alberta, is, like Leo Desroches, the son of Cree and French-Canadian parents. He is a freelance journalist and former rock musician. *A Killing Winter* is his second Leo Desroches mystery. The first, *Fall from Grace,* was published in 2011. He lives in Edmonton, Alberta. Visit his Web site at www.bigtimewriteryeahright.blogspot.com.